DEAD MEN'S MONEY

DEAD MEN'S MONEY

JOSEPH SMITH FLETCHER

ISBN: 978-93-5336-497-7

First Published: 1920

LECTOR HOUSE LLP
E-MAIL: lectorpublishing@gmail.com

DEAD MEN'S MONEY

BY

J.S. FLETCHER

1920

CONTENTS

CHAPTER I

THE ONE-EYED MAN

The very beginning of this affair, which involved me, before I was aware of it, in as much villainy and wickedness as ever man heard of, was, of course, that spring evening, now ten years ago, whereon I looked out of my mother's front parlour window in the main street of Berwick-upon-Tweed and saw, standing right before the house, a man who had a black patch over his left eye, an old plaid thrown loosely round his shoulders, and in his right hand a stout stick and an old-fashioned carpet-bag. He caught sight of me as I caught sight of him, and he stirred, and made at once for our door. If I had possessed the power of seeing more than the obvious, I should have seen robbery, and murder, and the very devil himself coming in close attendance upon him as he crossed the pavement. But as it was, I saw nothing but a stranger, and I threw open the window and asked the man what he might be wanting.

"Lodgings!" he answered, jerking a thickly made thumb at a paper which my mother had that day set in the transom above the door. "Lodgings! You've lodgings to let for a single gentleman. I'm a single gentleman, and I want lodgings. For a month—maybe more. Money no object. Thorough respectability—on my part. Few needs and modest requirements. Not likely to give trouble. Open the door!"

I went into the passage and opened the door to him. He strode in without as much as a word, and, not waiting for my invitation, lurched heavily—he was a big, heavy-moving fellow—into the parlour, where he set down his bag, his plaid, and his stick, and dropping into an easy chair, gave a sort of groan as he looked at me.

"And what's your name?" he demanded, as if he had all the right in the world to walk into folks' houses and ask his questions. "Whatever it is, you're a likely-looking youngster!"

"My name's Hugh Moneylaws," I answered, thinking it no harm to humour him. "If you want to know about lodgings you must wait till my mother comes in. Just now she's away up the street—she'll be back presently."

"No hurry, my lad," he replied. "None whatever. This is a comfortable anchorage. Quiet. Your mother'll be a widow woman, now?"

"Yes," said I shortly.

"Any more of you—brothers and sisters?" he asked. "Any—aye, of course!— any young children in the house? Because young children is what I cannot abide— except at a distance."

"There's nobody but me and my mother, and a servant lass," I said. "This is a quiet enough house, if that's what you mean."

"Quiet is the word," said he. "Nice, quiet, respectable lodgings. In this town of Berwick. For a month. If not more. As I say, a comfortable anchorage. And time, too!—when you've seen as many queer places as I have in my day, young fellow, you'll know that peace and quiet is meat and drink to an ageing man."

It struck me as I looked at him that he was just the sort of man that you would expect to hear of as having been in queer places—a sort of gnarled and stubbly man, with a wealth of seams and wrinkles about his face and what could be seen of his neck, and much grizzled hair, and an eye—only one being visible—that looked as if it had been on the watch ever since he was born. He was a fellow of evident great strength and stout muscle, and his hands, which he had clasped in front of him as he sat talking to me, were big enough to go round another man's throat, or to fell a bullock. And as for the rest of his appearance, he had gold rings in his ears, and he wore a great, heavy gold chain across his waistcoat, and was dressed in a new suit of blue serge, somewhat large for him, that he had evidently purchased at a ready-made-clothing shop, not so long before.

My mother came quietly in upon us before I could reply to the stranger's last remark, and I saw at once that he was a man of some politeness and manners, for he got himself up out of his chair and made her a sort of bow, in an old-fashioned way. And without waiting for me, he let his tongue loose on her.

"Servant, ma'am," said he. "You'll be the lady of the house—Mrs. Moneylaws. I'm seeking lodgings, Mrs. Moneylaws, and seeing your paper at the door-light, and your son's face at the window, I came in. Nice, quiet lodgings for a few weeks is what I'm wanting—a bit of plain cooking—no fal-lals. And as for money—no object! Charge me what you like, and I'll pay beforehand, any hand, whatever's convenient."

My mother, a shrewd little woman, who had had a good deal to do since my father died, smiled at the corners of her mouth as she looked the would-be lodger up and down.

"Why, sir," said she. "I like to know who I'm taking in. You're a stranger in the place, I'm thinking."

"Fifty years since I last clapped eyes on it, ma'am," he answered. "And I was then a youngster of no more than twelve years or so. But as to who and what I am—name of James Gilverthwaite. Late master of as good a ship as ever a man sailed. A quiet, respectable man. No swearer. No drinker—saving in reason and sobriety. And as I say—money no object, and cash down whenever it's wanted. Look here!"

He plunged one of the big hands into a trousers' pocket, and pulled it out again running over with gold. And opening his fingers he extended the gold-laden palm towards us. We were poor folk at that time, and it was a strange sight to us, all that money lying in the man's hand, and he apparently thinking no more of it than if it had been a heap of six-penny pieces.

"Help yourself to whatever'll pay you for a month," he exclaimed. "And don't be afraid—there's a lot more where that came from."

But my mother laughed, and motioned him to put up his money.

"Nay, nay, sir!" said she. "There's no need. And all I'm asking at you is just to know who it is I'm taking in. You'll be having business in the town for a while?"

"Not business in the ordinary sense, ma'am," he answered. "But there's kin of mine lying in more than one graveyard just by, and it's a fancy of my own to take a look at their resting-places, d'ye see, and to wander round the old quarters where they lived. And while I'm doing that, it's a quiet, and respectable, and comfortable lodging I'm wanting."

I could see that the sentiment in his speech touched my mother, who was fond of visiting graveyards herself, and she turned to Mr. James Gilverthwaite with a nod of acquiescence.

"Well, now, what might you be wanting in the way of accommodation?" she asked, and she began to tell him that he could have that parlour in which they were talking, and the bedchamber immediately above it. I left them arranging their affairs, and went into another room to attend to some of my own, and after a while my mother came there to me. "I've let him the rooms, Hugh," she said, with a note of satisfaction in her voice which told me that the big man was going to pay well for them. "He's a great bear of a man to look at," she went on, "but he seems quiet and civil-spoken. And here's a ticket for a chest of his that he's left up at the railway station, and as he's tired, maybe you'll get somebody yourself to fetch it down for him?"

I went out to a man who lived close by and had a light cart, and sent him up to the station with the ticket for the chest; he was back with it before long, and I had to help him carry it up to Mr. Gilverthwaite's room. And never had I felt or seen a chest like that before, nor had the man who had fetched it, either. It was made of some very hard and dark wood, and clamped at all the corners with brass, and underneath it there were a couple of bars of iron, and though it was no more than two and a half feet square, it took us all our time to lift it. And when, under Mr. Gilverthwaite's orders, we set it down on a stout stand at the side of his bed, there it remained until—but to say until when would be anticipating.

Now that he was established in our house, the new lodger proved himself all that he had said. He was a quiet, respectable, sober sort of man, giving no trouble and paying down his money without question or murmur every Saturday morning at his breakfast-time. All his days were passed in pretty much the same fashion. After breakfast he would go out—you might see him on the pier, or on the old town walls, or taking a walk across the Border Bridge; now and then we heard of his longer excursions into the country, one side or other of the Tweed. He took his dinner in the evenings, having made a special arrangement with my mother to that effect, and a very hearty eater he was, and fond of good things, which he provided generously for himself; and when that episode of the day's events was over, he would spend an hour or two over the newspapers, of which he was a great reader, in company with his cigar and his glass. And I'll say for him that from first to last he never put anything out, and was always civil and polite, and there was never a Saturday that he did not give the servant-maid a half-crown to buy herself a present.

All the same—we said it to ourselves afterwards, though not at the time—there was an atmosphere of mystery about Mr. Gilverthwaite. He made no acquaintance in the town. He was never seen in even brief conversation with any of the men that hung about the pier, on the walls, or by the shipping. He never visited the inns, nor brought anybody in to drink and smoke with him. And until the last days of his lodging with us he never received a letter.

A letter and the end of things came all at once. His stay had lengthened beyond the month he had first spoken of. It was in the seventh week of his coming that he came home to his dinner one June evening, complaining to my mother of having got a great wetting in a sudden storm that had come on that afternoon while he was away out in the country, and next morning he was in bed with a bad pain in his chest, and not over well able to talk. My mother kept him in his bed and began to doctor him; that day, about noon, came for him the first and only letter he ever had while he was with us—a letter that came in a registered envelope. The servant-maid took it up to him when it was delivered, and she said later that he started a bit when he saw it. But he said nothing about it to my mother during that afternoon, nor indeed to me, specifically, when, later on, he sent for me to go up to his room. All the same, having heard of what he had got, I felt sure that it was because of it that, when I went in to him, he beckoned me first to close the door on us and then to come close to his side as he lay propped on his pillow.

"Private, my lad!" he whispered hoarsely. "There's a word I have for you in private!"

CHAPTER II

THE MIDNIGHT MISSION

Before he said a word more, I knew that Mr. Gilverthwaite was very ill—much worse, I fancied, than my mother had any notion of. It was evidently hard work for him to get his breath, and the veins in his temples and forehead swelled out, big and black, with the effort of talking. He motioned to me to hand him a bottle of some stuff which he had sent for from the chemist, and he took a swig of its contents from the bottle neck before he spoke again. Then he pointed to a chair at the bed-head, close to his pillow.

"My lungs!" he said, a bit more easily. "Mortal bad! Queer thing, a great man like me, but I was always delicate in that way, ever since I was a nipper—strong as a bull in all else. But this word is private. Look here, you're a lawyer's clerk?"

He had known that, of course, for some time—known that I was clerk to a solicitor of the town, and hoping to get my articles, and in due course become a solicitor myself. So there was no need for me to do more than nod in silence.

"And being so," he went on, "you'll be a good hand at keeping a secret very well. Can you keep one for me, now?"

He had put out one of his big hands as he spoke, and had gripped my wrist with it—ill as he was, the grip of his fingers was like steel, and yet I could see that he had no idea that he was doing more than laying his hand on me with the appeal of a sick man.

"It depends what it is, Mr. Gilverthwaite," I answered. "I should like to do anything I can for you."

"You wouldn't do it for nothing," he put in sharply. "I'll make it well worth your while. See here!"

He took his hand away from my wrist, put it under his pillow, and drew out a bank-note, which he unfolded before me.

"Ten pound!" he said. "It's yours, if you'll do a bit of a job for me—in private. Ten pound'll be useful to you. What do you say, now?"

"That it depends on what it is," said I. "I'd be as glad of ten pounds as any-body, but I must know first what I'm expected to do for it."

"It's an easy enough thing to do," he replied. "Only it's got to be done this very night, and I'm laid here, and can't do it. You can do it, without danger, and at little trouble—only—it must be done private."

"You want me to do something that nobody's to know about?" I asked.

"Precisely!" said he. "Nobody! Not even your mother—for even the best of women have tongues."

I hesitated a little—something warned me that there was more in all this than I saw or understood at the moment.

"I'll promise this, Mr. Gilverthwaite," I said presently. "If you'll tell me now what it is you want, I'll keep that a dead secret from anybody for ever. Whether I'll do it or not'll depend on the nature of your communication."

"Well spoken, lad!" he answered, with a feeble laugh. "You've the makings of a good lawyer, anyway. Well, now, it's this—do you know this neighbourhood well?"

"I've never known any other," said I.

"Do you know where Till meets Tweed?" he asked.

"As well as I know my own mother's door!" I answered.

"You know where that old—what do they call it?—chapel, cell, something of that nature, is?" he asked again.

"Aye!—well enough, Mr. Gilverthwaite," I answered him. "Ever since I was in breeches!"

"Well," said he, "if I was my own man, I ought to meet another man near there this very night. And—here I am!"

"You want me to meet this other man?" I asked.

"I'm offering you ten pound if you will," he answered, with a quick look. "Aye, that is what I'm wanting!"

"To do—what?" I inquired.

"Simple enough," he said. "Nothing to do but to meet him, to give him a word that'll establish what they term your bony fides, and a message from me that I'll have you learn by heart before you go. No more!"

"There's no danger in it?" I asked.

"Not a spice of danger!" he asserted. "Not half as much as you'd find in serving a writ."

"You seem inclined to pay very handsomely for it, all the same," I remarked, still feeling a bit suspicious.

"And for a simple reason," he retorted. "I must have some one to do the job—aye, if it costs twenty pound! Somebody must meet this friend o' mine, and to-night—and why shouldn't you have ten pound as well as another?"

"There's nothing to do but what you say?" I asked.

"Nothing—not a thing!" he affirmed.

"And the time?" I said. "And the word—for surety?"

"Eleven o'clock is the time," he answered. "Eleven—an hour before midnight. And as for the word—get you to the place and wait about a bit, and if you see nobody there, say out loud, 'From James Gilverthwaite as is sick and can't come himself'; and when the man appears, as he will, say—aye!—say 'Panama,' my lad, and he'll understand in a jiffy!"

"Eleven o'clock—Panama," said I. "And—the message?"

"Aye!" he answered, "the message. Just this, then: 'James Gilverthwaite is laid by for a day or two, and you'll bide quiet in the place you know of till you hear from him.' That's all. And—how will you get out there, now?—it's a goodish way."

"I have a bicycle," I answered, and at his question a thought struck me. "How did you intend to get out there yourself, Mr. Gilverthwaite?" I asked. "That far— and at that time of night?"

"Aye!" he said. "Just so—but I'd ha' done it easy enough, my lad—if I hadn't been laid here. I'd ha' gone out by the last train to the nighest station, and it being summer I'd ha' shifted for myself somehow during the rest of the night—I'm used to night work. But—that's neither here nor there. You'll go? And—private?"

"I'll go—and privately," I answered him. "Make yourself easy."

"And not a word to your mother?" he asked anxiously.

"Just so," I replied. "Leave it to me."

He looked vastly relieved at that, and after assuring him that I had the message by heart I left his chamber and went downstairs. After all, it was no great task that he had put on me. I had often stayed until very late at the office, where I had the privilege of reading law-books at nights, and it was an easy business to mention to my mother that I wouldn't be in that night so very early. That part of my contract with the sick man upstairs I could keep well enough, in letter and spirit—all the same, I was not going out along Tweed-side at that hour of the night without some safeguard, and though I would tell no one of what my business for Mr. Gilverthwaite precisely amounted to, I would tell one person where it would take me, in case anything untoward happened and I had to be looked for. That person was the proper one for a lad to go to under the circumstances—my sweet-heart, Maisie Dunlop.

And here I'll take you into confidence and say that at that time Maisie and I had been sweethearting a good two years, and were as certain of each other as if the two had been twelve. I doubt if there was such another old-fashioned couple as we were anywhere else in the British Islands, for already we were as much bound up in each other as if we had been married half a lifetime, and there was not an affair of mine that I did not tell her of, nor had she a secret that she did not share with me. But then, to be sure, we had been neighbours all our lives, for her father, Andrew Dunlop, kept a grocer's shop not fifty yards from our house, and she and I had been playmates ever since our school-days, and had fallen to sober and serious love as soon as we arrived at what we at any rate called years of discretion—which means that I was nineteen, and she seventeen, when we first spoke definitely about getting married. And two years had gone by since then, and one reason why I had no objection to earning Mr. Gilverthwaite's ten pounds was that Maisie and I meant to wed as soon as my salary was lifted to three pounds a week, as it soon was to be, and we were saving money for our furnishing—and ten pounds, of course, would be a nice help.

So presently I went along the street to Dunlop's and called Maisie out, and we went down to the walls by the river mouth, which was a regular evening performance of ours. And in a quiet corner, where there was a seat on which we often sat whispering together of our future, I told her that I had to do a piece of business for our lodger that night and that the precise nature of it was a secret which I must not let out even to her.

"But here's this much in it, Maisie," I went on, taking care that there was no one near us that could catch a word of what I was saying; "I can tell you where the spot is that I'm to do the business at, for a fine lonely spot it is to be in at the time of night I'm to be there—an hour before midnight, and the place is that old ruin that's close by where Till meets Tweed—you know it well enough yourself."

I felt her shiver a bit at that, and I knew what it was that was in her mind, for Maisie was a girl of imagination, and the mention of a lonely place like that, to be visited at such an hour, set it working.

"Yon's a queer man, that lodger of your mother's, Hughie," she said. "And it's a strange time and place you're talking of. I hope nothing'll come to you in the way of mischance."

"Oh, it's nothing, nothing at all!" I hastened to say. "If you knew it all, you'd see it's a very ordinary business that this man can't do himself, being kept to his bed. But all the same, there's naught like taking precautions beforehand, and so I'll tell you what we'll do. I should be back in town soon after twelve, and I'll give a tap at your window as I pass it, and then you'll know all's right."

That would be an easy enough thing to manage, for Maisie's room, where she slept with a younger sister, was on the ground floor of her father's house in a wing that butted on to the street, and I could knock at the pane as I passed by. Yet still she seemed uneasy, and I hastened to say what—not even then knowing her quite as well as I did later—I thought would comfort her in any fears she had. "It's a very easy job, Maisie," I said; "and the ten pounds'll go a long way in buying that furniture we're always talking about."

She started worse than before when I said that and gripped the hand that I had round her waist.

"Hughie!" she exclaimed. "He'll not be giving you ten pounds for a bit of a ride like that! Oh, now I'm sure there's danger in it! What would a man be paying ten pounds for to anybody just to take a message? Don't go, Hughie! What do you know of yon man except that he's a stranger that never speaks to a soul in the place, and wanders about like he was spying things? And I would liefer go without chair or table, pot or pan, than that you should be running risks in a lonesome place like that, and at that time, with nobody near if you should be needing help. Don't go!"

"You're misunderstanding," said I. "It's a plain and easy thing—I've nothing to do but ride there and back. And as for the ten pounds, it's just this way: yon Mr. Gilverthwaite has more money than he knows what to do with. He carries sovereigns in his pockets like they were sixpenny pieces! Ten pounds is no more to him that ten pennies to us. And we've had the man in our house seven weeks now, and there's nobody could say an ill word of him."

"It's not so much him," she answered. "It's what you may meet—there! For you've got to meet—somebody. You're going, then?"

"I've given my word, Maisie," I said. "And you'll see there'll be no harm, and I'll give you a tap at the window as I pass your house coming back. And we'll do grand things with that ten pounds, too."

"I'll never close my eyes till I hear you, then," she replied. "And I'll not be satisfied with any tap, neither. If you give one, I'll draw the blind an inch, and make sure it's yourself, Hughie."

We settled it at that, with a kiss that was meant on my part to be one of reassurance, and presently we parted, and I went off to get my bicycle in readiness for the ride.

CHAPTER III

THE RED STAIN

It was just half-past nine by the town clocks when I rode out across the old Border Bridge and turned up the first climb of the road that runs alongside the railway in the direction of Tillmouth Park, which was, of course, my first objective. A hot, close night it was—there had been thunder hanging about all day, and folk had expected it to break at any minute, but up to this it had not come, and the air was thick and oppressive. I was running with sweat before I had ridden two miles along the road, and my head ached with the heaviness of the air, that seemed to press on me till I was like to be stifled. Under ordinary circumstances nothing would have taken me out on such a night. But the circumstances were not ordinary, for it was the first time I had ever had the chance of earning ten pounds by doing what appeared to be a very simple errand; and though I was well enough inclined to be neighbourly to Mr. Gilverthwaite, it was certainly his money that was my chief inducement in going on his business at a time when all decent folk should be in their beds. And for this first part of my journey my thoughts ran on that money, and on what Maisie and I would do with it when it was safely in my pocket. We had already bought the beginnings of our furnishing, and had them stored in an unused warehouse at the back of her father's premises; with Mr. Gilverthwaite's bank-note, lying there snugly in waiting for me, we should be able to make considerable additions to our stock, and the wedding-day would come nearer.

But from these anticipations I presently began to think about the undertaking on which I was now fairly engaged. When I came to consider it, it seemed a queer affair. As I understood it, it amounted to this:—Here was Mr. Gilverthwaite, a man that was a stranger in Berwick, and who appeared to have plenty of money and no business, suddenly getting a letter which asked him to meet a man, near midnight, and in about as lonely a spot as you could select out of the whole district. Why at such a place, and at such an hour? And why was this meeting of so much importance that Mr. Gilverthwaite, being unable to keep the appointment himself, must pay as much as ten pounds to another person to keep it for him? What I had said to Maisie about Mr. Gilverthwaite having so much money that ten pounds was no more to him than ten pence to me was, of course, all nonsense, said just to quieten her fears and suspicions—I knew well enough, having seen a bit of the world in a solicitor's office for the past six years, that even millionaires don't throw their money about as if pounds were empty peascods. No! Mr. Gilverthwaite was giving me that money because he thought that I, as a lawyer's clerk, would see the thing in its right light as a secret and an important business, and hold my tongue about it. And see it as a secret business I did—for what else could it be that would make two men meet near an old ruin at midnight, when in a town where, at any rate, one of them was a stranger, and the other probably just as much so, they could have met by broad day at a more convenient trysting-place without anybody having the least concern in their doings? There was strange and subtle mystery in all this, and the thinking and pondering it over led me before long to wondering about its first natural consequence—who and what was the man I was now on my way to meet, and where on earth could he be coming from to keep a tryst at a place like that, and at that hour?

However, before I had covered three parts of that outward journey, I was to meet another man who, all unknown to me, was to come into this truly extraordinary series of events in which I, with no will of my own, was just beginning—all unawares—to be mixed up. Taking it roughly, and as the crow flies, it is a distance of some nine or ten miles from Berwick town to Twizel Bridge on the Till, whereat I was to turn off from the main road and take another, a by-lane, that would lead me down by the old ruin, close by which Till and Tweed meet. Hot as the night was, and unpleasant for riding, I had plenty and to spare of time in hand, and when I came to the cross-ways between Norham and Grindon, I got off my machine and sat down on the bank at the roadside to rest a bit before going further. It was a quiet and a very lonely spot that; for three miles or more I had not met a soul along the road, and there being next to nothing in the way of village or farmstead between me and Cornhill, I did not expect to meet one in the next stages of my journey. But as I sat there on the bank, under a thick hedge, my bicycle lying at my side, I heard steps coming along the road in the gloom—swift, sure steps, as of a man who walks fast, and puts his feet firmly down as with determination to get somewhere as soon as he may. And hearing that—and to this day I have often wondered what made me do it—I off with my cap, and laid it over the bicycle-lamp, and myself sat as still as any of the wee creatures that were doubtless lying behind me in the hedge.

The steps came from the direction in which I was bound. There was a bit of a dip in the road just there: they came steadily, strongly, up it. And presently—for this was the height of June, when the nights are never really dark—the figure of a man came over the ridge of the dip, and showed itself plain against a piece of grey sky that was framed by the fingers of the pines and firs on either side of the way. A strongly-built figure it was, and, as I said before, the man put his feet, evidently well shod, firmly and swiftly down, and with this alternate sound came the steady and equally swift tapping of an iron-shod stick. Whoever this night-traveller was, it was certain he was making his way somewhere without losing any time in the business.

The man came close by me and my cover, seeing nothing, and at a few yards' distance stopped dead. I knew why. He had come to the cross-roads, and it was evident from his movements that he was puzzled and uncertain. He went to the corners of each way: it seemed to me that he was seeking for a guide-post. But, as I knew very well, there was no guide-post at any corner, and presently he came to the middle of the roads again and stood, looking this way and that, as if still in a dubious mood. And then I heard a crackling and rustling as of stiff paper—he was never more than a dozen yards from me all the time,—and in another minute there was a spurt up of bluish flame, and I saw that the man had turned on the light of an electric pocket-torch and was shining it on a map which he had unfolded and shaken out, and was holding in his right hand.

At this point I profited by a lesson which had been dinned into my ears a good many times since boyhood. Andrew Dunlop, Maisie's father, was one of those men who are uncommonly fond of lecturing young folk in season and out of season. He would get a lot of us, boys and girls, together in his parlour at such times as he was not behind the counter and give us admonitions on what he called the practical things of life. And one of his favourite precepts—especially addressed to us boys—was "Cultivate your powers of observation." This advice fitted in very well with the affairs of the career I had mapped out for myself—a solicitor should naturally be an observant man, and I had made steady effort to do as Andrew Dunlop counselled. Therefore it was with a keenly observant eye that I, all unseen, watched the man with his electric torch and his map, and it did not escape my notice that the hand which held the map was short of the two middle fingers. But of the rest of him, except that he was a tallish, well-made man, dressed in—as far as I could see things—a gentlemanlike fashion in grey tweeds, I could see nothing. I never caught one glimpse of his face, for all the time that he stood there it was in shadow.

He did not stay there long either. The light of the electric torch was suddenly switched off; I heard the crackling of the map again as he folded it up and pocketed it. And just as suddenly he was once more on the move, taking the by-way up to the north, which, as I knew well, led to Norham, and—if he was going far—over the Tweed to Ladykirk. He went away at the same quick pace; but the surface in that by-way was not as hard and ringing as that of the main road, and before long the sound of his steps died away into silence, and the hot, oppressive night became as still as ever.

I presently mounted my bicycle again and rode forward on my last stage, and having crossed Twizel Bridge, turned down the lane to the old ruin close by where Till runs into Tweed. It was now as dark as ever it would be that night, and the thunderclouds which hung all over the valley deepened the gloom. Gloomy and dark the spot indeed was where I was to meet the man of whom Mr. Gilverthwaite had spoken. By the light of my bicycle lamp I saw that it was just turned eleven when I reached the spot; but so far as I could judge there was no man there to meet anybody. And remembering what I had been bidden to do, I spoke out loud.

"From James Gilverthwaite, who is sick, and can't come himself," I repeated. And then, getting no immediate response, I spoke the password in just as loud a voice. But there was no response to that either, and for the instant I thought how ridiculous it was to stand there and say Panama to nobody.

I made it out that the man had not yet come, and I was wheeling my bicycle to the side of the lane, there to place it against the hedge and to sit down myself, when the glancing light of the lamp fell on a great red stain that had spread itself, and was still spreading, over the sandy ground in front of me. And I knew on the instant that this was the stain of blood, and I do not think I was surprised when, advancing a step or two further, I saw, lying in the roadside grass at my feet, the still figure and white face of a man who, I knew with a sure and certain instinct, was not only dead but had been cruelly murdered.

CHAPTER IV

THE MURDERED MAN

There may be folk in the world to whom the finding of a dead man, lying grim and stark by the roadside, with the blood freshly run from it and making ugly patches of crimson on the grass and the gravel, would be an ordinary thing; but to me that had never seen blood let in violence, except in such matters as a bout of fisticuffs at school, it was the biggest thing that had ever happened, and I stood staring down at the white face as if I should never look at anything else as long as I lived. I remember all about that scene and that moment as freshly now as if the affair had happened last night. The dead man lying in the crushed grass—his arms thrown out helplessly on either side of him—the gloom of the trees all around—the murmuring of the waters, where Till was pouring its sluggish flood into the more active swirl and rush of the Tweed—the hot, oppressive air of the night—and the blood on the dry road—all that was what, at Mr. Gilverthwaite's bidding, I had ridden out from Berwick to find in that lonely spot.

But I knew, of course, that James Gilverthwaite himself had not foreseen this affair, nor thought that I should find a murdered man. And as I at last drew breath, and lifted myself up a little from staring at the corpse, a great many thoughts rushed into my head, and began to tumble about over each other. Was this the man Mr. Gilverthwaite meant me to meet? Would Mr. Gilverthwaite have been murdered, too, if he had come there in person? And had the man been murdered for the sake of robbery? But I answered that last question as soon as I asked it, and in the negative, for the light of my lamp showed a fine, heavy gold watch-chain festooned across the man's waistcoat—if murderously inclined thieves had been at him, they were not like to have left that. Then I wondered if I had disturbed the murderers—it was fixed in me from the beginning that there must have been more than one in at this dreadful game—and if they were still lurking about and watching me from the brushwood; and I made an effort, and bent down and touched one of the nerveless hands. It was stiffened already, and I knew then that the man had been dead some time.

And I knew another thing in that moment: poor Maisie, lying awake to listen for the tap at her window, so that she might get up and peep round the corner of her blind to assure herself that her Hughie was alive and safe, would have to lie quaking and speculating through the dark hours of that night, for here was work that was going to keep me busied till day broke. I set to it there and then, leaving the man just as I had found him, and hastening back in the direction of the main road. As luck would have it, I heard voices of men on Twizel Bridge, and ran right on the local police-sergeant and a constable, who had met there in the course of their night rounds. I knew them both, the sergeant being one Chisholm, and the constable a man named Turndale, and they knew me well enough from having seen me in the court at Berwick; and it was with open-mouthed surprise that they listened to what I had to tell them. Presently we were all three round the dead man, and this time there was the light of three lamps on his face and on the gouts of blood that were all about him, and Chisholm clicked his tongue sharply at what he saw.

"Here's a sore sight for honest folk!" he said in a low voice, as he bent down and touched one of the hands. "Aye, and he's been dead a good hour, I should say, by the feel of him! You heard nothing as you came down yon lane, Mr. Hugh?"

"Not a sound!" I answered.

"And saw nothing?" he questioned.

"Nothing and nobody!" I said.

"Well," said he, "we'll have to get him away from this. You'll have to get help," he went on, turning to the constable. "Fetch some men to help us carry him. He'll have to be taken to the nearest inn for the inquest—that's how the law is. I wasn't going to ask it while yon man was about, Mr. Hugh," he continued, when Turndale had gone hurrying towards the village; "but you'll not mind me asking it now—what were you doing here yourself, at this hour?"

"You've a good right, Chisholm," said I; "and I'll tell you, for by all I can see, there'll be no way of keeping it back, and it's no concern of mine to keep it back, and I don't care who knows all about it—not me! The truth is, we've a lodger at our house, one Mr. James Gilverthwaite, that's a mysterious sort of man, and he's at present in his bed with a chill or something that's like to keep him there; and tonight he got me to ride out here to meet a man whom he ought to have met himself—and that's why I'm here and all that I have to do with it."

"You don't mean to say that—that!" he exclaimed, jerking his thumb at the dead man; "that—that's the man you were to meet?"

"Who else?" said I. "Can you think of any other that it would be? And I'm wondering if whoever killed this fellow, whoever he may be, wouldn't have killed Mr. Gilverthwaite, too, if he'd come? This is no by-chance murder, Chisholm, as you'll be finding out."

"Well, well, I never knew its like!" he remarked, staring from me to the body, and from it to me. "You saw nobody about close by—nor in the neighbourhood— no strangers on the road?"

I was ready for that question. Ever since finding the body, I had been wondering what I should say when authority, either in the shape of a coroner or a policeman, asked me about my own adventures that night. To be sure, I had seen a stranger, and I had observed that he had lost a couple of fingers, the first and second, of his right hand; and it was certainly a queer thing that he should be in that immediate neighbourhood about the time when this unfortunate man met his death. But it had been borne in on my mind pretty strongly that the man I had seen looking at his map was some gentleman-tourist who was walking the district, and had as like as not been tramping it over Plodden Field and that historic corner of the country, and had become benighted ere he could reach wherever his head-quarters were. And I was not going to bring suspicion on what was in all probabil-ity an innocent stranger, so I answered Chisholm's question as I meant to answer any similar one—unless, indeed, I had reason to alter my mind.

"I saw nobody and heard nothing—about here," said I. "It's not likely there'd be strangers in this spot at midnight."

"For that matter, the poor fellow is a stranger himself," said he, once more turning his lamp on the dead face. "Anyway, he's not known to me, and I've been in these parts twenty years. And altogether it's a fine mystery you've hit on, Mr. Hugh, and there'll be strange doings before we're at the bottom of it, I'm thinking."

That there was mystery in this affair was surer than ever when, having got the man to the nearest inn, and brought more help, including a doctor, they began to examine him and his clothing. And now that I saw him in a stronger light, I found that he was a strongly built, well-made man of about Mr. Gilverthwaite's age—say, just over sixty years or so,—dressed in a gentlemanlike fashion, and wearing good boots and linen and a tweed suit of the sort affected by tourists. There was a good deal of money in his pockets—bank-notes, gold, and silver—and an expen-sive watch and chain, and other such things that a gentleman would carry; and it seemed very evident that robbery had not been the motive of the murderers. But of papers that could identify the man there was nothing—in the shape of paper or its like there was not one scrap in all the clothing, except the return half of a railway ticket between Peebles and Coldstream, and a bit of a torn bill-head giving the name and address of a tradesman in Dundee.

"There's something to go on, anyway," remarked Chisholm, as he carefully put these things aside after pointing out to us that the ticket was dated on what was now the previous day (for it was already well past midnight, and the time was creeping on to morning), and that the dead man must accordingly have come to Coldstream not many hours before his death; "and we'll likely find something about him from either Dundee or Peebles. But I'm inclined to think, Mr. Hugh," he continued, drawing me aside, "that even though they didn't rob the man of his money and valuables, they took something else from him that may have been of much more value than either."

"What?" I asked.

"Papers!" said he. "Look at the general appearance of the man! He's no com-mon or ordinary sort. Is it likely, now, such a man would be without letters and that sort of thing in his pockets? Like as not he'd carry his pocket-book, and it may have been this pocket-book with what was in it they were after, and not troubling about his purse at all."

"They made sure of him, anyway," said I, and went out of the room where they had laid the body, not caring to stay longer. For I had heard what the doctor said—that the man had been killed on the spot by a single blow from a knife or dagger which had been thrust into his heart from behind with tremendous force, and the thought of it was sickening me. "What are you going to do now?" I asked of Chisholm, who had followed me. "And do you want me any more, sergeant?—for, if not, I'm anxious to get back to Berwick."

"That's just where I'm coming with you," he answered. "I've my bicycle close by, and we'll ride into the town together at once. For, do you see, Mr. Hugh, there's just one man hereabouts that can give us some light on this affair straightaway—if he will—and that the lodger you were telling me of. And I must get in and see the superintendent, and we must get speech with this Mr. Gilverthwaite of yours—for, if he knows no more, he'll know who yon man is!"

I made no answer to that. I had no certain answer to make. I was already wondering about a lot of conjectures. Would Mr. Gilverthwaite know who the man was? Was he the man I ought to have met? Or had that man been there, witnessed the murder, and gone away, frightened to stop where the murder had been done? Or—yet again—was this some man who had come upon Mr. Gilverthwaite's correspondent, and, for some reason, been murdered by him? It was, however, all beyond me just then, and presently the sergeant and I were on our machines and making for Berwick. But we had not been set out half an hour, and were only just where we could see the town's lights before us in the night, when two folk came riding bicycles through the mist that lay thick in a dip of the road, and, calling to me, let me know that they were Maisie Dunlop and her brother Tom that she had made to come with her, and in another minute Maisie and I were whispering together.

"It's all right now that I know you're safe, Hugh," she said breathlessly. "But you must get back with me quickly. Yon lodger of yours is dead, and your mother in a fine way, wondering where you are!"

CHAPTER V

THE BRASS-BOUND CHEST

The police-sergeant had got off his bicycle at the same time that I jumped from mine, and he was close behind me when Maisie and I met, and I heard him give a sharp whistle at her news. And as for me, I was dumbfounded, for though I had seen well enough that Mr. Gilverthwaite was very ill when I left him, I was certainly a long way from thinking him like to die. Indeed, I was so astonished that all I could do was to stand staring at Maisie in the grey light which was just coming between the midnight and the morning. But the sergeant found his tongue more readily.

"I suppose he died in his bed, miss?" he asked softly. "Mr. Hugh here said he was ill; it would be a turn for the worse, no doubt, after Mr. Hugh left him?"

"He died suddenly just after eleven o'clock," answered Maisie; "and your mother sought you at Mr. Lindsey's office, Hugh, and when she found you weren't there, she came down to our house, and I had to tell her that you'd come out this way on an errand for Mr. Gilverthwaite. And I told her, too, what I wasn't so sure of myself, that there'd no harm come to you of it, and that you'd be back soon after twelve, and I went down to your house and waited with her; and when you didn't come, and didn't come, why, I got Tom here to get our bicycles out and we came to seek you. And let's be getting back, for your mother's anxious about you, and the man's death has upset her—he went all at once, she said, while she was with him."

We all got on our bicycles again and set off homewards, and Chisholm wheeled alongside me and we dropped behind a little.

"This is a strange affair," said he, in a low voice; "and it's like to be made stranger by this man's sudden death. I'd been looking to him to get news of this other man. What do you know of Mr. Gilverthwaite, now?"

"Nothing!" said I.

"But he's lodged with you seven weeks?" said he.

"If you'd known him, sergeant," I answered, "you'd know that he was this sort of man—you'd know no more of him at the end of seven months than you would at the end of seven weeks, and no more at the end of seven years than at the end of seven months. We knew nothing, my mother and I, except that he was a decent, well-spoken man, free with his money and having plenty of it, and that his name was what he called it, and that he said he'd been a master mariner. But who he was, or where he came from, I know no more than you do."

"Well, he'll have papers, letters, something or other that'll throw some light on matters, no doubt?" he suggested. "Can you say as to that?"

"I can tell you that he's got a chest in his chamber that's nigh as heavy as if it were made of solid lead," I answered. "And doubtless he'll have a key on him or about him that'll unlock it. But what might be in it, I can't say, never having seen him open it at any time."

"Well," he said, "I'll have to bring the superintendent down, and we must trouble your mother to let us take a look at this Mr. Gilverthwaite's effects. Had he a doctor to him since he was taken ill?"

"Dr. Watson—this—I mean yesterday—afternoon," I answered.

"Then there'll be no inquest in his case," said the sergeant, "for the doctor'll be able to certify. But there'll be a searching inquiry in this murder affair, and as Gilverthwaite sent you to meet the man that's been murdered—"

"Wait a bit!" said I. "You don't know, and I don't, that the man who's been murdered is the man I was sent to meet. The man I was to meet may have been the murderer; you don't know who the murdered man is. So you'd better put it this way: since Gilverthwaite sent me to meet some man at the place where this murder's been committed—well?"

"That'll be one of your lawyer's quibbles," said he calmly. "My meaning's plain enough—we'll want to find out, if we can, who it was that Gilverthwaite sent you to meet. And—for what reason? And—where it was that the man was to wait for him? And I'll get the superintendent to come down presently."

"Make it in, say, half an hour," said I. "This is a queer business altogether, sergeant, and I'm so much in it that I'm not going to do things on my own responsibility. I'll call Mr. Lindsey up from his bed, and get him to come down to talk over what's to be done."

"Aye, you're in the right of it there," he said. "Mr. Lindsey'll know all the law on such matters. Half an hour or so, then."

He made off to the county police-station, and Maisie and Tom and I went on to our house, and were presently inside. My mother was so relieved at the sight of me that she forbore to scold me at that time for going off on such an errand without telling her of my business; but she grew white as her cap when I told her of what I had chanced on, and she glanced at the stair and shook her head.

"And indeed I wish that poor man had never come here, if it's this sort of dreadfulness follows him!" she said. "And though I was slow to say it, Hugh, I always had a feeling of mystery about him. However, he's gone now—and died that suddenly and quietly!—and we've laid him out in his bed; and—and—what's to be done now?" she exclaimed. "We don't know who he is!"

"Don't trouble yourself, mother," said I. "You've done your duty by him. And now that you've seen I'm safe, I'm away to bring Mr. Lindsey down and he'll tell us all that should be done."

I left Maisie and Tom Dunlop keeping my mother company and made haste to Mr. Lindsey's house, and after a little trouble roused him out of his bed and got him down to me. It was nearly daylight by that time, and the grey morning was breaking over the sea and the river as he and I walked back through the empty streets—I telling him of all the events of the night, and he listening with an occasional word of surprise. He was not a native of our parts, but a Yorkshireman that had bought a practice in the town some years before, and had gained a great character for shrewdness and ability, and I knew that he was the very man to turn to in an affair of this sort.

"There's a lot more in this than's on the surface, Hugh, my lad," he remarked when I had made an end of my tale. "And it'll be a nice job to find out all the meaning of it, and if the man that's been murdered was the man Gilverthwaite sent you to meet, or if he's some other that got there before you, and was got rid of for some extraordinary reason that we know nothing about. But one thing's certain: we've got to get some light on your late lodger. That's step number one—and a most important one."

The superintendent of police, Mr. Murray, a big, bustling man, was outside our house with Chisholm when we got there, and after a word or two between us, we went in, and were presently upstairs in Gilverthwaite's room. He lay there in his bed, the sheet drawn about him and a napkin over his face; and though the police took a look at him, I kept away, being too much upset by the doings of the night to stand any more just then. What I was anxious about was to get some inkling of what all this meant, and I waited impatiently to see what Mr. Lindsey would do. He was looking about the room, and when the others turned away from the dead man he pointed to Gilverthwaite's clothes, that were laid tidily folded on a chair.

"The first thing to do is to search for his papers and his keys," he said. "Go carefully through his pockets, sergeant, and let's see what there is."

But there was as little in the way of papers there, as there had been in the case of the murdered man. There were no letters. There was a map of the district, and under the names of several of the villages and places on either side of the Tweed, between Berwick and Kelso, heavy marks in blue pencil had been made. I, who knew something of Gilverthwaite's habits, took it that these were the places he had visited during his seven weeks' stay with us. And folded in the map were scraps of newspaper cuttings, every one of them about some antiquity or other in the neighbourhood, as if such things had an interest for him. And in another pocket was a guide-book, much thumbed, and between two of the leaves, slipped as if to mark a place, was a registered envelope.

"That'll be what he got yesterday afternoon!" I exclaimed. "I'm certain it was whatever there was in it that made him send me out last night, and maybe the letter in it'll tell us something."

However, there was no letter in the envelope—there was nothing. But on the envelope itself was a postmark, at which Chisholm instantly pointed.

"Peebles!" said he. "Yon man that you found murdered—his half-ticket's for Peebles. There's something of a clue, anyway."

They went on searching the clothing, only to find money—plenty of it, notes in an old pocket-book, and gold in a wash-leather bag—and the man's watch and chain, and his pocket-knife and the like, and a bunch of keys. And with the keys in his hand Mr. Lindsey turned to the chest.

"If we're going to find anything that'll throw any light on the question of this man's identity, it'll be in this box," he said. "I'll take the responsibility of opening it, in Mrs. Moneylaws' interest, anyway. Lift it on to that table, and let's see if one of these keys'll fit the lock."

There was no difficulty about finding the key—there were but a few on the bunch, and he hit on the right one straightaway, and we all crowded round him as he threw back the heavy lid. There was a curious aromatic smell came from within, a sort of mingling of cedar and camphor and spices—a smell that made you think of foreign parts and queer, far-off places. And it was indeed a strange collection of things and objects that Mr. Lindsey took out of the chest and set down on the table. There was an old cigar-box, tied about with twine, full to the brim with money— over two thousand pounds in bank-notes and gold, as we found on counting it up later on,—and there were others filled with cigars, and yet others in which the man had packed all manner of curiosities such as three of us at any rate had never seen in our lives before. But Mr. Lindsey, who was something of a curiosity collector himself, nodded his head at the sight of some of them.

"Wherever else this man may have been in his roving life," he said, "here's one thing certain—he's spent a lot of time in Mexico and Central America. And—what was the name he told you to use as a password once you met his man, Hugh— wasn't it Panama?"

"Panama!" I answered. "Just that—Panama."

"Well, and he's picked up lots of these things in those parts—Panama, Nicaragua, Mexico," he said. "And very interesting matters they are. But—you see, superintendent?—there's not a paper nor anything in this chest to tell us who this man is, nor where he came from when he came here, nor where his relations are to be found, if he has any. There's literally nothing whatever of that sort."

The police officials nodded in silence.

"And so—there's where things are," concluded Mr. Lindsey. "You've two dead men on your hands, and you know nothing whatever about either of them!"

CHAPTER VI

MR. JOHN PHILLIPS

He began to put back the various boxes and parcels into the chest as he spoke, and we all looked at each other as men might look who, taking a way unknown to them, come up against a blank wall. But Chisholm, who was a sharp fellow, with a good headpiece on him, suddenly spoke.

"There's the fact that the murdered man sent that letter from Peebles," said he, "and that he himself appears to have travelled from Peebles but yesterday. We might be hearing something of him at Peebles, and from what we might hear, there or elsewhere, we might get some connection between the two of them."

"You're right in all that, sergeant," said Mr. Lindsey, "and it's to Peebles some of you'll have to go. For the thing's plain—that man has been murdered by somebody, and the first way to get at the somebody is to find out who the murdered man is, and why he came into these parts. As for him," he continued, pointing significantly to the bed, "his secret—whatever it is—has gone with him. And our question now is, Can we get at it in any other way?"

We had more talk downstairs, and it was settled that Chisholm and I should go on to Peebles by the first train that morning, find out what we could there, and work back to the Cornhill station, where, according to the half-ticket which had been found on him, the murdered man appeared to have come on the evening of his death. Meanwhile, Murray would have the scene of the murder thoroughly and strictly searched—the daylight might reveal things which we had not been able to discover by the light of the lamps.

"And there's another thing you can do," suggested Lindsey. "That scrap of a bill-head with a name and address in Dundee on it, that you found on him, you might wire there and see if anything is known of the man. Any bit of information you can get in that way—"

"You're forgetting, Mr. Lindsey, that we don't know any name by which we can call the man," objected Chisholm. "We'll have to find a name for him before we can wire to Dundee or anywhere else. But if we can trace a name to him in Peebles—"

"Aye, that'll be the way of it," said Murray. "Let's be getting all the information we can during the day, and I'll settle with the coroner's officer for the inquest at yon inn where you've taken him—it can't be held before tomorrow morning. Mr. Lindsey," he went on, "what are you going to do as regards this man that's lying dead upstairs? Mrs. Moneylaws says the doctor had been twice with him, and'll be able to give a certificate, so there'll be no inquest about him; but what's to be done about his friends and relations? It's likely there'll be somebody, somewhere. And—all that money on him and in his chest?"

Mr. Lindsey shook his head and smiled.

"If you think all this'll be done in hole-and-corner fashion, superintendent," he said, "you're not the wise man I take you for. Lord bless you, man, the news'll be all over the country within forty-eight hours! If this Gilverthwaite has folk of his own, they'll be here fast as crows hurry to a new-sown field! Let the news of it once out, and you'll wish that such men as newspaper reporters had never been born. You can't keep these things quiet; and if we're going to get to the bottom of all this, then publicity's the very thing that's needed."

All this was said in the presence of my mother, who, being by nature as quiet a body as ever lived, was by no means pleased to know that her house was, as it were, to be made a centre of attraction. And when Mr. Lindsey and the police had gone away, and she began getting some breakfast ready for me before my going to meet Chisholm at the station, she set on to bewail our misfortune in ever taking Gilverthwaite into the house, and so getting mixed up with such awful things as murder. She should have had references with the man, she said, before taking him in, and so have known who she was dealing with. And nothing that either I or Maisie—who was still there, staying to be of help, Tom Dunlop having gone home to tell his father the great news—could say would drive out of her head the idea that Gilverthwaite, somehow or other, had something to do with the killing of the strange man. And, womanlike, and not being over-amenable to reason, she saw no cause for a great fuss about the affair in her own house, at any rate. The man was dead, she said, and let them get him put decently away, and hold his money till somebody came forward to claim it—all quietly and without the pieces in the paper that Mr. Lindsey talked about.

"And how are we to let people know anything about him if there isn't news in the papers?" I asked. "It's only that way that we can let his relatives know he's dead, mother. You're forgetting that we don't even know where the man's from!"

"Maybe I've a better idea of where he was from, when he came here, than any lawyer-folk or police-folk either, my man!" she retorted, giving me and Maisie a sharp look. "I've eyes in my head, anyway, and it doesn't take me long to see a thing that's put plain before them."

"Well?" said I, seeing quick enough that she'd some notion in her mind. "You've found something out?"

Without answering the question in words she went out of the kitchen and up the stairs, and presently came back to us, carrying in one hand a man's collar and in the other Gilverthwaite's blue serge jacket. And she turned the inside of the collar to us, pointing her finger to some words stamped in black on the linen.

"Take heed of that!" she said. "He'd a dozen of those collars, brand-new, when he came, and this, you see, is where he bought them; and where he bought them, there, too, he bought his ready-made suit of clothes—that was brand-new as well,—here's the name on a tab inside the coat: Brown Brothers, Gentlemen's Outfitters, Exchange Street, Liverpool. What does all that prove but that it was from Liverpool he came?"

"Aye!" I said. "And it proves, too, that he was wanting an outfit when he came to Liverpool from—where? A long way further afield, I'm thinking! But it's something to know as much as that, and you've no doubt hit on a clue that might be useful, mother. And if we can find out that the other man came from Liverpool, too, why then—"

But I stopped short there, having a sudden vision of a very wide world of which Liverpool was but an outlet. Where had Gilverthwaite last come from when he struck Liverpool, and set himself up with new clothes and linen? And had this mysterious man who had met such a terrible fate come also from some far-off part, to join him in whatever it was that had brought Gilverthwaite to Berwick? And—a far more important thing,—mysterious as these two men were, what about the equally mysterious man that was somewhere in the background—the murderer?

Chisholm and I had no great difficulty—indeed, we had nothing that you might call a difficulty—in finding out something about the murdered man at Peebles. We had the half-ticket with us, and we soon got hold of the booking-clerk who had issued it on the previous afternoon. He remembered the looks of the man to whom he had sold it, and described him to us well enough. Moreover, he found us a ticket-collector who remembered that same man arriving in Peebles two days before, and giving up a ticket from Glasgow. He had a reason for remembering him, for the man had asked him to recommend him to a good hotel, and had given him a two-shilling piece for his trouble. So far, then, we had plain sailing, and it continued plain and easy during the short time we stayed in Peebles. And it came to this: the man we were asking about came to the town early in the afternoon of the day before the murder; he put himself up at the best hotel in the place; he was in and out of it all the afternoon and evening; he stayed there until the middle of the afternoon of the next day, when he paid his bill and left. And there was the name he had written in the register book—Mr. John Phillips, Glasgow.

Chisholm drew me out of the hotel where we had heard all this and pulled the scrap of bill-head from his pocket-book.

"Now that we've got the name to go on," said he, "we'll send a wire to this address in Dundee asking if anything's known there of Mr. John Phillips. And we'll have the reply sent to Berwick—it'll be waiting us when we get back this morning."

The name and address in Dundee was of one Gavin Smeaton, Agent, 131A Bank Street. And the question which Chisholm sent him over the wire was plain and direct enough: Could he give the Berwick police any information about a man named John Phillips, found dead, on whose body Mr. Smeaton's name and address had been discovered?

"We may get something out of that," said Chisholm, as we left the post-office, "and we may get nothing. And now that we do know that this man left here for

Coldstream, let's get back there, and go on with our tracing of his movements last night."

But when we had got back to our own district we were quickly at a dead loss. The folk at Cornhill station remembered the man well enough. He had arrived there about half-past eight the previous evening. He had been seen to go down the road to the bridge which leads over the Tweed to Coldstream. We could not find out that he had asked the way of anybody—he appeared to have just walked that way as if he were well acquainted with the place. But we got news of him at an inn just across the bridge. Such a man—a gentleman, the inn folk called him—had walked in there, asked for a glass of whisky, lingered for a few minutes while he drank it, and had gone out again. And from that point we lost all trace of him. We were now, of course, within a few miles of the place where the man had been murdered, and the people on both sides of the river were all in a high state of excitement about it; but we could learn nothing more. From the moment of the man's leaving the inn on the Coldstream side of the bridge, nobody seemed to have seen him until I myself found his body.

There was another back-set for us when we reached Berwick—in the reply from Dundee. It was brief and decisive enough. "Have no knowledge whatever of any person named John Phillips—Gavin Smeaton." So, for the moment, there was nothing to be gained from that quarter.

Mr. Lindsey and I were at the inn where the body had been taken, and where the inquest was to be held, early next morning, in company with the police, and amidst a crowd that had gathered from all parts of the country. As we hung about, waiting the coroner's arrival, a gentleman rode up on a fine bay horse—a good-looking elderly man, whose coming attracted much attention. He dismounted and came towards the inn door, and as he drew the glove off his right hand I saw that the first and second fingers of that hand were missing. Here, without doubt, was the man whom I had seen at the cross-roads just before my discovery of the murder!

CHAPTER VII
THE INQUEST ON JOHN PHILLIPS

Several of the notabilities of the neighbourhood had ridden or driven to the inn, attracted, of course, by curiosity, and the man with the maimed hand immediately joined them as they stood talking apart from the rest of us. Now, I knew all such people of our parts well enough by sight, but I did not know this man, who certainly belonged to their class, and I turned to Mr. Lindsey, asking him who was this gentleman that had just ridden up. He glanced at me with evident surprise at my question.

"What?" said he. "You don't know him? That's the man there's been so much talk about lately—Sir Gilbert Carstairs of Hathercleugh House, the new successor to the old baronetcy."

I knew at once what he meant. Between Norham and Berwick, overlooking the Tweed, and on the English side of the river, stood an ancient, picturesque, romantic old place, half-mansion, half-castle, set in its own grounds, and shut off from the rest of the world by high walls and groves of pine and fir, which had belonged for many a generation to the old family of Carstairs. Its last proprietor, Sir Alexander Carstairs, sixth baronet, had been a good deal of a recluse, and I never remember seeing him but once, when I caught sight of him driving in the town—a very, very old man who looked like what he really was, a hermit. He had been a widower for many long years, and though he had three children, it was little company that he seemed to have ever got out of them, for his elder son, Mr. Michael Carstairs, had long since gone away to foreign parts, and had died there; his younger son, Mr. Gilbert, was, it was understood, a doctor in London, and never came near the old place; and his one daughter, Mrs. Ralston, though she lived within ten miles of her father, was not on good terms with him. It was said that the old gentleman was queer and eccentric, and hard to please or manage; however that may be, it is certain that he lived a lonely life till he was well over eighty years of age. And he had died suddenly, not so very long before James Gilverthwaite came to lodge with us; and Mr. Michael being dead, unmarried, and therefore without family, the title and estate had passed to Mr. Gilbert, who had recently come down to Hathercleugh House and taken possession, bringing with him—though he himself was getting on in years, being certainly over fifty—a beautiful young wife whom, they said, he had recently married, and was, according to various accounts which had crept out, a very wealthy woman in her own right.

So here was Sir Gilbert Carstairs, seventh baronet, before me, chatting away to some of the other gentlemen of the neighbourhood, and there was not a doubt in my mind that he was the man whom I had seen on the road the night of the murder. I was close enough to him now to look more particularly at his hand, and I saw that the two first fingers had completely disappeared, and that the rest of it was no more than a claw. It was not likely there could be two men in our neighbourhood thus disfigured. Moreover, the general build of the man, the tweed suit of grey that he was wearing, the attitude in which he stood, all convinced me that this was the person I had seen at the cross-roads, holding his electric torch to the face of his map. And I made up my mind there and then to say nothing in my evidence about that meeting, for I had no reason to connect such a great gentleman as Sir Gilbert Carstairs with the murder, and it seemed to me that his presence at those cross-roads was easily enough explained. He was a big, athletic man and was likely fond of a walk, and had been taking one that evening, and, not as yet being over-familiar with the neighbourhood—having lived so long away from it,—had got somewhat out of his way in returning home. No, I would say nothing. I had been brought up to have a firm belief in the old proverb which tells you that the least said is soonest mended. We were all packed pretty tightly in the big room of the inn when the coroner opened his inquiry. And at the very onset of the proceedings he made a remark which was expected by all of us that knew how these things are done and are likely to go. We could not do much that day; there would have to be an adjournment, after taking what he might call the surface evidence. He understood, he remarked, with a significant glance at the police officials and at one or two solicitors that were there, that there was some extraordinary mystery at the back of this matter, and that a good many things would have to be brought to light before the jury could get even an idea as to who it was that had killed the man whose body had been found, and as to the reason for his murder. And all they could do that day, he went on, was to hear such evidence—not much—as had already been collected, and then to adjourn.

Mr. Lindsey had said to me as we drove along to the inn that I should find myself the principal witness, and that Gilverthwaite would come into the matter more prominently than anybody fancied. And this, of course, was soon made evident. What there was to tell of the dead man, up to that time, was little. There was the medical evidence that he had been stabbed to death by a blow from a very formidable knife or dagger, which had been driven into his heart from behind. There was the evidence which Chisholm and I had collected in Peebles and at Cornhill station, and at the inn across the Coldstream Bridge. There was the telegram which had been sent by Mr. Gavin Smeaton—whoever he might be—from Dundee. And that was about all, and it came to this: that here was a man who, in registering at a Peebles hotel, called himself John Phillips and wrote down that he came from Glasgow, where, up to that moment, the police had failed to trace anything relating to such a person; and this man had travelled to Cornhill station from Peebles, been seen in an adjacent inn, had then disappeared, and had been found, about two hours later, murdered in a lonely place.

"And the question comes to this," observed the coroner, "what was this man doing at that place, and who was he likely to meet there? We have some evidence on that point, and," he added, with one shrewd glance at the legal folk in front of him and another at the jurymen at his side, "I think you'll find, gentlemen of the jury, that it's just enough to whet your appetite for more."

They had kept my evidence to the last, and if there had been a good deal of suppressed excitement in the crowded room while Chisholm and the doctor and the landlord of the inn on the other side of Coldstream Bridge gave their testimonies, there was much more when I got up to tell my tale, and to answer any questions that anybody liked to put to me. Mine, of course, was a straight enough story, told in a few sentences, and I did not see what great amount of questioning could arise out of it. But whether it was that he fancied I was keeping something back, or that he wanted, even at that initial stage of the proceedings, to make matters as plain as possible, a solicitor that was representing the county police began to ask me questions.

"There was no one else with you in the room when this man Gilverthwaite gave you his orders?" he asked.

"No one," I answered.

"And you've told me everything that he said to you?"

"As near as I can recollect it, every word."

"He didn't describe the man you were to meet?"

"He didn't—in any way."

"Nor tell you his name?"

"Nor tell me his name."

"So that you'd no idea whatever as to who it was that you were to meet, nor for what purpose he was coming to meet Gilverthwaite, if Gilverthwaite had been able to meet him?"

"I'd no idea," said I. "I knew nothing but that I was to meet a man and give him a message."

He seemed to consider matters a little, keeping silence, and then he went off on another tack.

"What do you know of the movements of this man Gilverthwaite while he was lodging with your mother?" he asked.

"Next to nothing," I replied.

"But how much?" he inquired. "You'd know something."

"Of my own knowledge, next to nothing," I repeated. "I've seen him in the streets, and on the pier, and taking his walks on the walls and over the Border Bridge; and I've heard him say that he'd been out in the country. And that's all."

"Was he always alone?" he asked.

"I never saw him with anybody, never heard of his talking to anybody, nor of his going to see a soul in the place," I answered; "and first and last, he never brought any one into our house, nor had anybody asked at the door for him."

"And with the exception of that registered letter we've heard of, he never had a letter delivered to him all the time he lodged with you?" he said.

"Not one," said I. "From first to last, not one."

He was silent again for a time, and all the folk staring at him and me; and for the life of me I could not think what other questions he could get out of his brain to throw at me. But he found one, and put it with a sharp cast of his eye.

"Now, did this man ever give you, while he was in your house, any reason at all for his coming to Berwick?" he asked.

"Yes," I answered; "he did that when he came asking for lodgings. He said he had folk of his own buried in the neighbourhood, and he was minded to take a look at their graves and at the old places where they'd lived."

"Giving you, in fact, an impression that he was either a native of these parts, or had lived here at some time, or had kindred that had?" he asked.

"Just that," I replied.

"Did he tell you the names of such folk, or where they were buried, or anything of that sort?" he suggested.

"No—never," said I. "He never mentioned the matter again."

"And you don't know that he ever went to any particular place to look at any particular grave or house?" he inquired.

"No," I replied; "but we knew that he took his walks into the country on both sides Tweed."

He hesitated a bit, looked at me and back at his papers, and then, with a glance at the coroner, sat down. And the coroner, nodding at him as if there was some understanding between them, turned to the jury.

"It may seem without the scope of this inquiry, gentlemen," he said, "but the presence of this man Gilverthwaite in the neighbourhood has evidently so much to do with the death of the other man, whom we know as John Phillips, that we must not neglect any pertinent evidence. There is a gentleman present that can tell us something. Call the Reverend Septimus Ridley."

CHAPTER VIII

THE PARISH REGISTERS

I had noticed the Reverend Mr. Ridley sitting in the room with some other gentlemen of the neighbourhood, and had wondered what had brought him, a clergyman, there. I knew him well enough by sight. He was a vicar of a lonely parish away up in the hills—a tall, thin, student-looking man that you might occasionally see in the Berwick streets, walking very fast with his eyes on the ground, as if, as the youngsters say, he was seeking sixpences; and I should not have thought him likely to be attracted to an affair of that sort by mere curiosity. And, whatever he might be in his pulpit, he looked very nervous and shy as he stood up between the coroner and the jury to give his evidence.

"Whatever are we going to hear now?" whispered Mr. Lindsey in my ear. "Didn't I tell you there'd be revelations about Gilverthwaite, Hugh, my lad? Well, there's something coming out! But what can this parson know?"

As it soon appeared, Mr. Ridley knew a good deal. After a bit of preliminary questioning, making things right in the proper legal fashion as to who he was, and so on, the coroner put a plain inquiry to him. "Mr. Ridley, you have had some recent dealings with this man James Gilverthwaite, who has just been mentioned in connection with this inquiry?" he asked.

"Some dealings recently—yes," answered the clergyman.

"Just tell us, in your own way, what they were," said the coroner. "And, of course, when they took place."

"Gilverthwaite," said Mr. Ridley, "came to me, at my vicarage, about a month or five weeks ago. I had previously seen him about the church and churchyard. He told me he was interested in parish registers, and in antiquities generally, and asked if he could see our registers, offering to pay whatever fee was charged. I allowed him to look at the registers, but I soon discovered that his interest was confined to a particular period. The fact was, he wished to examine the various entries made between 1870 and 1880. That became very plain; but as he did not express his wish in so many words, I humoured him. Still, as I was with him during the whole of the time he was looking at the books, I saw what it was that he examined."

Here Mr. Ridley paused, glancing at the coroner.

"That is really about all that I can tell," he said. "He only came to me on that one occasion."

"Perhaps I can get a little more out of you, Mr. Ridley," remarked the coroner with a smile. "A question or two, now. What particular registers did this man examine? Births, deaths, marriages—which?"

"All three, between the dates I have mentioned—1870 to 1880," replied Mr. Ridley.

"Did you think that he was searching for some particular entry?"

"I certainly did think so."

"Did he seem to find it?" asked the coroner, with a shrewd glance.

"If he did find such an entry," replied Mr. Ridley slowly, "he gave no sign of it; he did not copy or make a note of it, and he did not ask any copy of it from me. My impression—whatever it is worth—is that he did not find what he wanted in our registers. I am all the more convinced of that because—"

Here Mr. Ridley paused, as if uncertain whether to proceed or not; but at an encouraging nod from the coroner he went on.

"I was merely going to say—and I don't suppose it is evidence—" he added, "that I understand this man visited several of my brother clergymen in the neighbourhood on the same errand. It was talked of at the last meeting of our rural deanery."

"Ah!" remarked the coroner significantly. "He appears, then, to have been going round examining the parish registers—we must get more evidence of that later, for I'm convinced it has a bearing on the subject of this present inquiry. But a question or two more, Mr. Ridley. There are stipulated fees for searching the registers, I believe. Did Gilverthwaite pay them in your case?"

Mr. Ridley smiled.

"He not only paid the fees," he answered, "but he forced me to accept something for the poor box. He struck me as being a man who was inclined to be free with his money."

The coroner looked at the solicitor who was representing the police.

"I don't know if you want to ask this witness any questions?" he inquired.

"Yes," said the solicitor. He turned to Mr. Ridley. "You heard what the witness Hugh Moneylaws said?—that Gilverthwaite mentioned on his coming to Berwick that he had kinsfolk buried in the neighbourhood? You did? Well, Mr. Ridley, do you know if there are people of that name buried in your churchyard?"

"There are not," replied Mr. Ridley promptly. "What is more, the name Gilverthwaite does not occur in our parish registers. I have a complete index of the registers from 1580, when they began to be kept, and there is no such name in it. I can also tell you this," he added, "I am, I think I may say, something of an authority on the parish registers of this district—I have prepared and edited several of them for publication, and I am familiar with most of them. I do not think that name, Gilverthwaite, occurs in any of them."

"What do you deduce from that, now?" asked the solicitor.

"That whatever it was that the man was searching for—and I am sure he was searching—it was not for particulars of his father's family," answered Mr. Ridley. "That is, of course, if his name really was what he gave it out to be—Gilverthwaite."

"Precisely!" said the coroner. "It may have been an assumed name."

"The man may have been searching for particulars of his mother's family," remarked the solicitor.

"That line of thought would carry us too far afield just now," said the coroner. He turned to the jury. "I've allowed this evidence about the man Gilverthwaite, gentlemen," he said, "because it's very evident that Gilverthwaite came to this neighbourhood for some special purpose and wanted to get some particular information; and it's more than probable that the man into the circumstances of whose death we're inquiring was concerned with him in his purpose. But we cannot go any further today," he concluded, "and I shall adjourn the inquiry for a fortnight, when, no doubt, there'll be more evidence to put before you."

I think that the folk who had crowded into that room, all agog to hear whatever could be told, went out of it more puzzled than when they came in. They split up into groups outside the inn, and began to discuss matters amongst themselves. And presently two sharp-looking young fellows, whom I had seen taking notes at the end of the big table whereat the coroner and the officials sat, came up to me, and telling me that they were reporters, specially sent over, one from Edinburgh, the other from Newcastle, begged me to give them a faithful and detailed account of my doings and experiences on the night of the murder—there was already vast interest in this affair all over the country, they affirmed, and whatever I could or would tell them would make splendid reading and be printed in big type in their journals. But Mr. Lindsey, who was close by, seized my arm and steered me away from these persistent seekers after copy.

"Not just now, my lads!" said he good-humouredly. "You've got plenty enough to go on with—you've heard plenty in there this morning to keep your readers going for a bit. Not a word, Hugh! And as for you, gentlemen, if you want to do something towards clearing up this mystery, and assisting justice, there's something you can do—and nobody can do it better."

"What's that?" asked one of them eagerly.

"Ask through your columns for the relations, friends, acquaintances, anybody who knows them or aught about them, of these two men, James Gilverthwaite and John Phillips," replied Mr. Lindsey. "Noise it abroad as much as you like and can! If they've folk belonging to them, let them come forward. For," he went on, giving them a knowing look, "there's a bigger mystery in this affair than any one of us has any conception of, and the more we can find out the sooner it'll be solved. And I'll say this to you young fellows: the press can do more than the police. There's a hint for you!"

Then he led me off, and we got into the trap in which he and I had driven out from Berwick, and as soon as we had started homeward he fell into a brown study and continued in it until we were in sight of the town.

"Hugh, my lad!" he suddenly exclaimed, at last starting out of his reverie. "I'd give a good deal if I could see daylight in this affair! I've had two-and-twenty years' experience of the law, and I've known some queer matters, and some dark matters, and some ugly matters in my time; but hang me if I ever knew one that promises to be as ugly and as dark and as queer as this does—that's a fact!"

"You're thinking it's all that, Mr. Lindsey?" I asked, knowing him as I did to be an uncommonly sharp man.

"I'm thinking there's more than meets the eye," he answered. "Bloody murder we know there is—maybe there'll be more, or maybe there has been more already. What was that deep old fish Gilverthwaite after? What took place between Phillips's walking out of that inn at Coldstream Bridge and your finding of his body? Who met Phillips? Who did him to his death? And what were the two of 'em after in this corner of the country? Black mystery, my lad, on all hands!"

I made no answer just then. I was thinking, wondering if I should tell him about my meeting with Sir Gilbert Carstairs at the cross-roads. Mr. Lindsey was just the man you could and would tell anything to, and it would maybe have been best if I had told him of that matter there and then. But there's a curious run of caution and reserve in our family. I got it from both father and mother, and deepened it on my own account, and I could not bring myself to be incriminating and suspicioning a man whose presence so near the place of the murder might be innocent enough. So I held my tongue.

"I wonder will all the stuff in the newspapers bring any one forward?" he said, presently. "It ought to!—if there is anybody."

Nothing, however, was heard by the police or by ourselves for the next three or four days; and then—I think it was the fourth day after the inquest—I looked up from my desk in Mr. Lindsey's outer office one afternoon to see Maisie Dunlop coming in at the door, followed by an elderly woman, poorly but respectably dressed, a stranger.

"Hugh," said Maisie, coming up to my side, "your mother asked me to bring this woman up to see Mr. Lindsey. She's just come in from the south, and she says she's yon James Gilverthwaite's sister."

CHAPTER IX
THE MARINE-STORE DEALER

Mr. Lindsey was standing just within his own room when Maisie and the strange woman came into the office, and hearing what was said, he called us all three to go into him. And, like myself, he looked at the woman with a good deal of curiosity, wanting—as I did—to see some likeness to the dead man. But there was no likeness to be seen, for whereas Gilverthwaite was a big and stalwart fellow, this was a small and spare woman, whose rusty black clothes made her look thinner and more meagre than she really was. All the same, when she spoke I knew there was a likeness between them, for her speech was like his, different altogether from ours of the Border.

"So you believe you're the sister of this man James Gilverthwaite, ma'am?" began Mr. Lindsey, motioning the visitor to sit down, and beckoning Maisie to stop with us. "What might your name be, now?"

"I believe this man that's talked about in the newspapers is my brother, sir," answered the woman. "Else I shouldn't have taken the trouble to come all this way. My name's Hanson—Mrs. Hanson. I come from Garston, near Liverpool."

"Aye—just so—a Lancashire woman," said Mr. Lindsey, nodding. "Your name would be Gilverthwaite, then, before you were married?"

"To be sure, sir—same as James's," she replied. "Him and me was the only two there was. I've brought papers with me that'll prove what I say. I went to a lawyer before ever I came, and he told me to come at once, and to bring my marriage lines, and a copy of James's birth certificate, and one or two other things of that sort. There's no doubt that this man we've read about in the newspapers was my brother, and of course I would like to put in my claim to what he's left—if he's left it to nobody else."

"Just so," agreed Mr. Lindsey. "Aye—and how long is it since you last saw your brother, now?"

The woman shook her head as if this question presented difficulties.

"I couldn't rightly say to a year or two, no, not even to a few years," she answered. "And to the best of my belief, sir, it'll be a good thirty years, at the least. It was just after I was married to Hanson, and that was when I was about three-and-twenty, and I was fifty-six last birthday. James came—once—to see me and Hanson soon after we was settled down, and I've never set eyes on him from that day to this. But—I should know him now."

"He was buried yesterday," remarked Mr. Lindsey. "It's a pity you didn't telegraph to some of us."

"The lawyer I went to, sir, said, 'Go yourself!'" replied Mrs. Hanson. "So I set off—first thing this morning."

"Let me have a look at those papers," said Mr. Lindsey.

He motioned me to his side, and together we looked through two or three documents which the woman produced.

The most important was a certified copy of James Gilverthwaite's birth certificate, which went to prove that this man had been born in Liverpool about sixty-two years previously; that, as Mr. Lindsey was quick to point out, fitted in with what Gilverthwaite had told my mother and myself about his age.

"Well," he said, turning to Mrs. Hanson, "you can answer some questions, no doubt, about your brother, and about matters in relation to him. First of all, do you know if any of your folks hailed from this part?"

"Not that I ever heard of, sir," she replied. "No, I'm sure they wouldn't. They were all Lancashire folks, on both sides. I know all about them as far back as my great-grandfather's and great-grandmother's."

"Do you know if your brother ever came to Berwick as a lad?" asked Mr. Lindsey, with a glance at me.

"He might ha' done that, sir," said Mrs. Hanson. "He was a great, masterful, strong lad, and he'd run off to sea by the time he was ten years old—there'd been no doing aught with him for a couple of years before that. I knew that when he was about twelve or thirteen he was on a coasting steamer that used to go in and out of Sunderland and Newcastle, and he might have put in here."

"To be sure," said Mr. Lindsey. "But what's more important is to get on to his later history. You say you've never seen him for thirty years, or more? But have you never heard of him?"

She nodded her head with decision at that question.

"Yes," she replied, "I have heard of him—just once. There was a man, a neighbour of ours, came home from Central America, maybe five years ago, and he told us he'd seen our James out there, and that he was working as a sub-contractor, or something of that sort, on that Panama Canal there was so much talk about in them days."

Mr. Lindsey and I looked at each other. Panama!—that was the password which James Gilverthwaite had given me. So—here, at any rate, was something, however little, that had the makings of a clue in it.

"Aye!" he said, "Panama, now? He was there? And that's the last you ever heard?"

"That's the very last we ever heard, sir," she answered. "Till, of course, we saw these pieces in the papers this last day or two."

Mr. Lindsey twisted round on her with a sharp look.

"Do you know aught of that man, John Phillips, whose name's in the papers too?" he asked.

"No, sir, nothing!" she replied promptly. "Never heard tell of him!"

"And you've never heard of your brother's having been seen in Liverpool of late?" he went on. "Never heard that he called to see any old friends at all? For we know, as you have seen in the papers, Mrs. Hanson, that he was certainly in Liverpool, and bought clothes and linen there, within this last three months."

"He never came near me, sir," she said. "And I never heard word of his being there from anybody."

There was a bit of a silence then, and at last the woman put the question which, it was evident, she was anxious to have answered definitely.

"Do you think there's a will, mister?" she asked. "For, if not, the lawyer I went to said what there was would come to me—and I could do with it."

"We've seen nothing of any will," answered Mr. Lindsey. "And I should say there is none, and on satisfactory proof of your being next-of-kin, you'll get all he left. I've no doubt you're his sister, and I'll take the responsibility of going through his effects with you. You'll be stopping in the town a day or two? Maybe your mother, Hugh, can find Mrs. Hanson a lodging?"

I answered that my mother would no doubt do what she could to look after Mrs. Hanson; and presently the woman went away with Maisie, leaving her papers with Mr. Lindsey. He turned to me when we were alone.

"Some folks would think that was a bit of help to me in solving the mystery, Hugh," said he; "but hang me if I don't think it makes the whole thing more mysterious than ever! And do you know, my lad, where, in my opinion, the very beginning of it may have to be sought for?"

"I can't put a word to that, Mr. Lindsey," I answered. "Where, sir?"

"Panama!" he exclaimed, with a jerk of his head. "Panama! just that! It began a long way off—Panama, as far as I see it. And what did begin, and what was going on? The two men that knew, and could have told, are dead as door-nails—and both buried, for that matter."

So, in spite of Mrs. Hanson's coming and her revelations as to some, at any rate, of James Gilverthwaite's history, we were just as wise as ever at the end of the first week after the murder of John Phillips. And it was just the eighth night after my finding of the body that I got into the hands of Abel Crone.

Abel Crone was a man that had come to Berwick about three years before this, from heaven only knows where, and had set himself up in business as a marine-store dealer, in a back street which ran down to the shore of the Tweed. He was a little red-haired, pale-eyed rat of a man, with ferrety eyes and a goatee beard, quiet and peaceable in his ways and inoffensive enough, but a rare hand at gossiping about the beach and the walls—you might find him at all odd hours either in these public places or in the door of his shop, talking away with any idler like himself. And how I came to get into talk with him on that particular night was here: Tom Dunlop, Maisie's young brother, was for keeping tame rabbits just then, and I was helping him to build hutches for the beasts in his father's back-yard, and we were wanting some bits of stuff, iron and wire and the like, and knowing I would pick it up for a few pence at Crone's shop, I went round there alone. Before I knew how it came about, Crone was deep into the murder business.

"They'll not have found much out by this time, yon police fellows, no doubt, Mr. Moneylaws?" he said, eyeing me inquisitively in the light of the one naphtha lamp that was spurting and jumping in his untidy shop. "They're a slow unoriginal lot, the police—there's no imagination in their brains and no ingenuity in their minds. What's wanted in an affair like this is one of those geniuses you read about in the storybooks—the men that can trace a murder from the way a man turns out his toes, or by the fashion he's bitten into a bit of bread that he's left on his plate, or the like of that—something more than by ordinary, you'll understand me to mean, Mr. Moneylaws?"

"Maybe you'll be for taking a hand in this game yourself, Mr. Crone?" said I, thinking to joke with him. "You seem to have the right instinct for it, anyway."

"Aye, well," he answered, "and I might be doing as well as anybody else, and no worse. You haven't thought of following anything up yourself, Mr. Moneylaws, I suppose?"

"Me!" I exclaimed. "What should I be following up, man? I know no more than the mere surface facts of the affair."

He gave a sharp glance at his open door when I thus answered him, and the next instant he was close to me in the gloom and looking sharply in my face.

"Are you so sure of that, now?" he whispered cunningly. "Come now, I'll put a question to yourself, Mr. Moneylaws. What for did you not let on in your evidence that you saw Sir Gilbert Carstairs at yon cross-roads just before you found the dead man? Come!"

You could have knocked me down with a feather, as the saying is, when he said that. And before I could recover from the surprise of it, he had a hand on my arm.

"Come this way," he said. "I'll have a word with you in private."

CHAPTER X
THE OTHER WITNESS

It was with a thumping heart and nerves all a-tingle that I followed Abel Crone out of his front shop into a sort of office that he had at the back of it—a little, dirty hole of a place, in which there was a ramshackle table, a chair or two, a stand-up desk, a cupboard, and a variety of odds and ends that he had picked up in his trade. The man's sudden revelation of knowledge had knocked all the confidence out of me. It had never crossed my mind that any living soul had a notion of my secret—for secret, of course, it was, and one that I would not have trusted to Crone, of all men in the world, knowing him as I did to be such a one for gossip. And he had let this challenge out on me so sharply, catching me unawares that I was alone with him, and, as it were, at his mercy, before I could pull my wits together. Everything in me was confused. I was thinking several things all at a time. How did he come to know? Had I been watched? Had some person followed me out of Berwick that night? Was this part of the general mystery? And what was going to come of it, now that Abel Crone was aware that I knew something which, up to then, I had kept back?

I stood helplessly staring at him as he turned up the wick of an oil lamp that stood on a mantelpiece littered with a mess of small things, and he caught a sight of my face when there was more light, and as he shut the door on us he laughed— laughed as if he knew that he had me in a trap. And before he spoke again he went over to the cupboard and took out a bottle and glasses.

"Will you taste?" he asked, leering at me. "A wee drop, now? It'll do you good."

"No!" said I.

"Then I'll drink for the two of us," he responded, and poured out a half-tumblerful of whisky, to which he added precious little water. "Here's to you, my lad; and may you have grace to take advantage of your chances!"

He winked over the rim of his glass as he took a big pull at its contents, and there was something so villainous in the look of him that it did me good in the way of steeling my nerves again. For I now saw that here was an uncommonly bad man to deal with, and that I had best be on my guard.

"Mr. Crone," said I, gazing straight at him, "what's this you have to say to me?"

"Sit you down," he answered, pointing at a chair that was shoved under one side of the little table. "Pull that out and sit you down. What we shall have to say to each other'll not be said in five minutes. Let's confer in the proper and comfortable fashion."

I did what he asked, and he took another chair himself and sat down opposite me, propping his elbow on the table and leaning across it, so that, the table being but narrow, his sharp eyes and questioning lips were closer to mine than I cared for. And while he leaned forward in his chair I sat back in mine, keeping as far from him as I could, and just staring at him—perhaps as if I had been some trapped animal that couldn't get itself away from the eyes of another that meant presently to kill it. Once again I asked him what he wanted.

"You didn't answer my question," he said. "I'll put it again, and you needn't be afraid that anybody'll overhear us in this place, it's safe! I say once more, what for did you not tell in your evidence at that inquest that you saw Sir Gilbert Carstairs at the cross-roads on the night of the murder! Um?"

"That's my business!" said I

"Just so," said he. "And I'll agree with you in that. It is your business. But if by that you mean that it's yours alone, and nobody else's, then I don't agree. Neither would the police."

We stared at each other across the table for a minute of silence, and then I put the question directly to him that I had been wanting to put ever since he had first spoken. And I put it crudely enough.

"How did you know?" I asked.

He laughed at that—sneeringly, of course.

"Aye, that's plain enough," said he. "No fencing about that! How did I know? Because when you saw Sir Gilbert I wasn't five feet away from you, and what you saw, I saw. I saw you both!"

"You were there?" I exclaimed.

"Snug behind the hedge in front of which you planted yourself," he answered. "And if you want to know what I was doing there, I'll tell you. I was doing—or had been doing—a bit of poaching. And, as I say, what you saw, I saw!"

"Then I'll ask you a question, Mr. Crone," I said. "Why haven't you told, yourself?"

"Aye!" he said. "You may well ask me that. But I wasn't called as a witness at yon inquest."

"You could have come forward," I suggested.

"I didn't choose," he retorted.

We both looked at each other again, and while we looked he swigged off his drink and helped himself, just as generously, to more. And, as I was getting bolder by that time, I set to work at questioning him.

"You'll be attaching some importance to what you saw?" said I.

"Well," he replied slowly, "it's not a pleasant thing—for a man's safety—to be as near as what he was to a place where another man's just been done to his death."

"You and I were near enough, anyway," I remarked.

"We know what we were there for," he flung back at me. "We don't know what he was there for."

"Put your tongue to it, Mr. Crone," I said boldly. "The fact is, you suspicion him?"

"I suspicion a good deal, maybe," he admitted. "After all, even a man of that degree's only a man, when all's said and done, and there might be reasons that you and me knows nothing about. Let me ask you a question," he went on, edging nearer at me across the table. "Have you mentioned it to a soul?"

I made a mistake at that, but he was on me so sharp, and his manner was so insistent, that I had the word out of my lips before I thought.

"No!" I replied. "I haven't."

"Nor me," he said. "Nor me. So—you and me are the only two folk that know."

"Well?" I asked.

He took another pull at his liquor and for a moment or two sat silent, tapping his finger-nails against the rim of the glass.

"It's a queer business, Moneylaws," he said at last. "Look at it anyway you like, it's a queer business! Here's one man, yon lodger of your mother's, comes into the town and goes round the neighbourhood reading the old parish registers and asking questions at the parson's—aye, and he was at it both sides of the Tweed—I've found that much out for myself! For what purpose? Is there money at the back of it—property—something of that sort, dependent on this Gilverthwaite unearthing some facts or other out of those old books? And then comes another man, a stranger, that's as mysterious in his movements as Gilverthwaite was, and he's to meet Gilverthwaite at a certain lonely spot, and at a very strange hour, and Gilverthwaite can't go, and he gets you to go, and you find the man—murdered! And—close by—you've seen this other man, who, between you and me—though it's no secret—is as much a stranger to the neighbourhood as ever Gilverthwaite was or Phillips was!"

"I don't follow you at that," I said.

"No?" said he. "Then I'll make it plainer to you. Do you know that until yon Sir Gilbert Carstairs came here, not so long since, to take up his title and his house and the estate, he'd never set foot in the place, never been near the place, this thirty year? Man! his own father, old Sir Alec, and his own sister, Mrs. Ralston of Craig, had never clapped eyes on him since he went away from Hathercleugh a youngster of one-and-twenty!"

"Do you tell me that, Mr. Crone?" I exclaimed, much surprised at his words. "I didn't know so much. Where had he been, then?"

"God knows!" said he. "And himself. It was said he was a doctor in London, and in foreign parts. Him and his brother—elder brother, you're aware, Mr. Michael—they both quarrelled with the old baronet when they were little more than lads, and out they cleared, going their own ways. And news of Michael's death, and the proofs of it, came home not so long before old Sir Alec died, and as Michael had never married, of course the younger brother succeeded when his father came to his end last winter. And, as I say, who knows anything about his past doings when he was away more than thirty years, nor what company he kept, nor what secrets he has? Do you follow me?"

"Aye, I'm following you, Mr. Crone," I answered. "It comes to this—you suspect Sir Gilbert?"

"What I say," he answered, "is this: he may have had something to do with the affair. You cannot tell. But you and me knows he was near the place—coming from its direction—at the time the murder would be in the doing. And—there is nobody knows but you—and me!"

"What are you going to do about it?" I asked.

He had another period of reflection before he replied, and when he spoke it was to the accompaniment of a warning look.

"It's an ill-advised thing to talk about rich men," said he. "Yon man not only has money of his own, in what you might call considerable quantity, but his wife he brought with him is a woman of vast wealth, they tell me. It would be no very wise action on your part to set rumours going, Moneylaws, unless you could substantiate them."

"What about yourself?" I asked. "You know as much as I do."

"Aye, and there's one word that sums all up," said he. "And it's a short one. Wait! There'll be more coming out. Keep your counsel a bit. And when the moment comes, and if the moment comes—why, you know there's me behind you to corroborate. And—that's all!"

He got up then, with a nod, as if to show that the interview was over, and I was that glad to get away from him that I walked off without another word.

CHAPTER XI

SIGNATURES TO THE WILL

I was so knocked out of the usual run of things by this conversation with Crone that I went away forgetting the bits of stuff I had bought for Tom Dunlop's rabbit-hutches and Tom himself, and, for that matter, Maisie as well; and, instead of going back to Dunlop's, I turned down the riverside, thinking. It was beyond me at that moment to get a clear understanding of the new situation. I could not make out what Crone was at. Clearly, he had strong suspicions that Sir Gilbert Carstairs had something to do with, or some knowledge of, the murder of Phillips, and he knew now that there were two of us to bear out each other's testimony that Sir Gilbert was near the scene of the murder at the time it was committed. Why, then, should he counsel waiting? Why should not the two of us go to the police and tell what we knew? What was it that Crone advised we should wait for? Was something going on, some inquiry being made in the background of things, of which he knew and would not tell me? And—this, I think, was what was chiefly in my thoughts—was Crone playing some game of his own and designing to use me as a puppet in it? For there was a general atmosphere of subtlety and slyness about the man that forced itself upon me, young as I was; and the way he kept eyeing me as we talked made me feel that I had to do with one that would be hard to circumvent if it came to a matter of craftiness. And at last, after a lot of thinking, as I walked about in the dusk, it struck me that Crone might be for taking a hand in the game of which I had heard, but had never seen played—blackmail.

The more I thought over that idea, the more I felt certain of it. His hints about Sir Gilbert's money and his wealthy wife, his advice to wait until we knew more, all seemed to point to this—that evidence might come out which would but require our joint testimony, Crone's and mine, to make it complete. If that were so, then, of course, Crone or I, or—as he probably designed—the two of us, would be in a position to go to Sir Gilbert Carstairs and tell him what we knew, and ask him how much he would give us to hold our tongues. I saw all the theory of it at last, clear enough, and it was just what I would have expected of Abel Crone, knowing him even as little as I did. Wait until we were sure—and then strike! That was his game. And I was not going to have anything to do with it.

I went home to my bed resolved on that. I had heard of blackmailing, and had a good notion of its wickedness—and of its danger—and I was not taking shares with Crone in any venture of that sort. But there Crone was, an actual, concrete fact that I had got to deal with, and to come to some terms with, simply because he knew that I was in possession of knowledge which, to be sure, I ought to have communicated to the police at once. And I was awake much during the night, thinking matters over, and by the time I rose in the morning I had come to a decision. I would see Crone at once, and give him a sort of an ultimatum. Let him come, there and then, with me to Mr. Murray, and let the two of us tell what we knew and be done with it: if not, then I myself would go straight to Mr. Lindsey and tell him.

I set out for the office earlier than usual that morning, and went round by way of the back street at the bottom of which Crone's store stood facing the river. I sometimes walked round that way of a morning, and I knew that Crone was as a rule at his place very early, amongst his old rubbish, or at his favourite game of gossiping with the fishermen that had their boats drawn up there. But when I reached it, the shop was still shut, and though I waited as long as I could, Crone did not come. I knew where he lived, at the top end of the town, and I thought to meet him as I walked up to Mr. Lindsey's; but I had seen nothing of him by the time I reached our office door, so I laid the matter aside until noon, meaning to get a word with him when I went home to my dinner. And though I could have done so there and then, I determined not to say anything to Mr. Lindsey until I had given Crone the chance of saying it with me—to him, or to the police. I expected, of course, that Crone would fly into a rage at my suggestion—if so, then I would tell him, straight out, that I would just take my own way, and take it at once.

But before noon there was another development in this affair. In the course of the morning Mr. Lindsey bade me go with him down to my mother's house, where Mrs. Hanson had been lodged for the night—we would go through Gilverthwaite's effects with her, he said, with a view to doing what we could to put her in possession. It might—probably would—be a lengthy and a difficult business that, he remarked, seeing that there was so much that was dark about her brother's recent movements; and as the woman was obviously poor, we had best be stirring on her behalf. So down we went, and in my mother's front parlour, the same that Gilverthwaite had taken as his sitting-room, Mr. Lindsey opened the heavy box for the second time, in Mrs. Hanson's presence, and I began to make a list of its contents. At the sight of the money it contained, the woman began to tremble.

"Eh, mister!" she exclaimed, almost tearfully, "but that's a sight of money to be lying there, doing naught! I hope there'll be some way of bringing it to me and mine—we could do with it, I promise you!"

"We'll do our best, ma'am," said Mr. Lindsey. "As you're next of kin there oughtn't to be much difficulty, and I'll hurry matters up for you as quickly as possible. What I want this morning is for you to see all there is in this chest; he seems to have had no other belongings than this and his clothes—here at Mrs. Moneylaws', at any rate. And as you see, beyond the money, there's little else in the chest but cigars, and box after box of curiosities that he's evidently picked up in his travels—coins, shells, ornaments, all sorts of queer things—some of 'em no doubt of value. But no papers—no letters—no documents of any sort."

A notion suddenly occurred to me.

"Mr. Lindsey," said I, "you never turned out the contents of any of these smaller boxes the other night. There might be papers in one or other of them."

"Good notion, Hugh, my lad!" he exclaimed. "True—there might. Here goes, then—we'll look through them systematically."

In addition to the half-dozen boxes full of prime Havana cigars, which lay at the top of the chest, there were quite a dozen of similar boxes, emptied of cigars and literally packed full of the curiosities of which Mr. Lindsey had just spoken. He had turned out, and carefully replaced, the contents of three or four of these, when, at the bottom of one, filled with old coins, which, he said, were Mexican and Peruvian, and probably of great interest to collectors, he came across a paper, folded and endorsed in bold letters. And he let out an exclamation as he took this paper out and pointed us to the endorsement.

"Do you see that?" said he. "It's the man's will!"

The endorsement was plain enough—My will: *James Gilverthwaite*. And beneath it was a date, 27-8-1904.

There was a dead silence amongst the four of us—my mother had been with us all the time—as Mr. Lindsey unfolded the paper—a thick, half-sheet of foolscap, and read what was written on it.

"This is the last will and testament of me, James Gilverthwaite, a British subject, born at Liverpool, and formerly of Garston, in Lancashire, England, now residing temporarily at Colon, in the Republic of Panama. I devise and bequeath all my estate and effects, real and personal, which I may be possessed of or entitled to, unto my sister, Sarah Ellen Hanson, the wife of Matthew Hanson, of 37 Preston Street, Garston, Lancashire, England, absolutely, and failing her to any children she may have had by her marriage with Matthew Hanson, in equal shares. And I appoint the said Sarah Ellen Hanson, or in the case of her death, her eldest child, the executor of this my will; and I revoke all former wills. Dated this twenty-seventh day of August, 1904. *James Gilverthwaite*. Signed by the testator in the presence of us—"

Mr. Lindsey suddenly broke off. And I, looking at him, saw his eyes screw themselves up with sheer wonder at something he saw. Without another word he folded up the paper, put it in his pocket, and turning to Mrs. Hanson, clapped her on the shoulder.

"That's all right, ma'am!" he said heartily. "That's a good will, duly signed and attested, and there'll be no difficulty about getting it admitted to probate; leave it to me, and I'll see to it, and get it through for you as soon as ever I can. And we must do what's possible to find out if this brother of yours has left any other property; and meanwhile we'll just lock everything up again that we've taken out of this chest."

It was close on my dinner hour when we had finished, but Mr. Lindsey, at his going, motioned me out into the street with him. In a quiet corner, he turned to me and pulled the will from his pocket.

"Hugh!" he said. "Do you know who's one of the witnesses to this will? Aye, who are the two witnesses? Man!—you could have knocked me down with a feather when I saw the names! Look for yourself!"

He handed me the paper and pointed to the attestation clause with which it ended. And I saw the two names at once—John Phillips, Michael Carstairs—and I let out a cry of astonishment.

"Aye, you may well exclaim!" said he, taking the will back. "John Phillips!— that's the man was murdered the other night! Michael Carstairs—that's the elder brother of Sir Gilbert yonder at Hathercleugh, the man that would have succeeded to the title and estates if he hadn't predeceased old Sir Alexander. What would he be doing now, a friend of Gilverthwaite's?"

"I've heard that this Mr. Michael Carstairs went abroad as a young man, Mr. Lindsey, and never came home again," I remarked. "Likely he foregathered with Gilverthwaite out yonder."

"Just that," he agreed. "That would be the way of it, no doubt. To be sure! He's set down in this attestation clause as Michael Carstairs, engineer, American Quarter, Colon; and John Phillips is described as sub-contractor, of the same address. The three of 'em'll have been working in connection with the Panama Canal. But—God bless us!—there's some queer facts coming out, my lad! Michael Carstairs knows Gilverthwaite and Phillips in yon corner of the world—Phillips and Gilverthwaite, when Michael Carstairs is dead, come home to the corner of the world that Michael Carstairs sprang from. And Phillips is murdered as soon as he gets here—and Gilverthwaite dies that suddenly that he can't tell us a word of what it's all about! What is it all about—and who's going to piece it all together? Man!—there's more than murder at the bottom of all this!"

It's a wonder that I didn't let out everything that I knew at that minute. And it may have been on the tip of my tongue, but just then he gave me a push towards our door.

"I heard your mother say your dinner was waiting you," he said. "Go in, now; we'll talk more this afternoon."

He strode off up the street, and I turned back and made haste with my dinner. I wanted to drop in at Crone's before I went again to the office: what had just happened, had made me resolved that Crone and I should speak out; and if he wouldn't, then I would. And presently I was hurrying away to his place, and as I turned into the back lane that led to it I ran up against Sergeant Chisholm.

"Here's another fine to-do, Mr. Moneylaws!" said he. "You'll know yon Abel Crone, the marine-store dealer? Aye, well, he's been found drowned, not an hour ago, and by this and that, there's queer marks, that looks like violence, on him!"

CHAPTER XII

THE SALMON GAFF

I gave such a jump on hearing this that Chisholm himself started, and he stared at me with a question in his eyes. But I was quick enough to let him know that he was giving me news that I hadn't heard until he opened his lips.

"You don't tell me that!" I exclaimed. "What!—more of it?"

"Aye!" he said. "You'll be thinking that this is all of a piece with the other affair. And to be sure, they found Crone's body close by where you found yon other man—Phillips."

"Where, then?" I asked. "And when?"

"I tell you, not an hour ago," he replied. "The news just came in. I was going down here to see if any of the neighbours at the shop saw Crone in any strange company last night."

I hesitated for a second or two, and then spoke out.

"I saw him myself last night," said I. "I went to his shop—maybe it was nine o'clock—to buy some bits of stuff to make Tom Dunlop a door to his rabbit-hutch, and I was there talking to him ten minutes or so. He was all right then—and I saw nobody else with him."

"Aye, well, he never went home to his house last night," observed Chisholm. "I called in there on my way down—he lived, you know, in a cottage by the police-station, and I dropped in and asked the woman that keeps house for him had she seen him this morning, and she said he never came home last night at all. And no wonder—as things are!"

"But you were saying where it happened," I said.

"Where he was found?" said he. "Well, and it was where Till runs into Tweed—leastways, a bit up the Till. Do you know John McIlwraith's lad—yon youngster that they've had such a bother with about the school—always running away to his play, and stopping out at nights, and the like—there was the question of sending him to a reformatory, you'll remember? Aye, well, it turns out the young waster was out last night in those woods below Twizel, and early this morning—though he didn't let on at it till some time after—he saw the body of a man lying in one of them deep pools in Till. And when he himself was caught by Turndale, who was on the look out for him, he told of what he'd seen, and Turndale and some other men went there, and they found—Crone!"

"You were saying there were marks of violence," said I.

"I haven't seen them myself," he answered. "But by Turndale's account—it was him brought in the news—there is queer marks on the body. Like as if—as near as Turndale could describe it—as if the man had been struck down before he was drowned. Bruises, you understand."

"Where is he?" I asked.

"He's where they took Phillips," replied Chisholm. "Dod!—that's two of 'em that's been taken there within—aye, nearly within the week!"

"What are you going to do, now?" I inquired.

"I was just going, as I said, to ask a question or two down here—did anybody hear Crone say anything last night about going out that way?" he answered. "But, there, I don't see the good of it. Between you and me, Crone was a bit of a night-bird—I've suspected him of poaching, time and again. Well, he'll do no more of that! You'll be on your way to the office, likely?"

"Straight there," said I. "I'll tell Mr. Lindsey of this."

But when I reached the office, Mr. Lindsey, who had been out to get his lunch, knew all about it. He was standing outside the door, talking to Mr. Murray, and as I went up the superintendent turned away to the police station, and Mr. Lindsey took a step or two towards me.

"Have you heard this about that man Crone?" he asked.

"I've heard just now," I answered. "Chisholm told me."

He looked at me, and I at him; there were questions in the eyes of both of us. But between parting from the police-sergeant and meeting Mr. Lindsey, I had made up my mind, by a bit of sharp thinking and reflection, on what my own plan of action was going to be about all this, once and for all, and I spoke before he could ask anything.

"Chisholm," said I, "was down that way, wondering could he hear word of Crone's being seen with anybody last night. I saw Crone last night. I went to his shop, buying some bits of old stuff. He was all right then—I saw nothing. Chisholm—he says Crone was a poacher. That would account, likely, for his being out there."

"Aye!" said Mr. Lindsey. "But—they say there's marks of violence on the body. And—the long and short of it is, my lad!" he went on, first interrupting himself, and then giving me an odd look; "the long and short of it is, it's a queer thing that Crone should have come by his death close to the spot where you found yon man Phillips! There may be nothing but coincidence in it—but there's no denying it's a queer thing. Go and order a conveyance, and we'll drive out yonder."

In pursuance of the determination I had come to, I said no more about Crone to Mr. Lindsey. I had made up my mind on a certain course, and until it was taken I could not let out a word of what was by that time nobody's secret but mine to him, nor to any one—not even to Maisie Dunlop, to whom, purposely, I had not as yet said anything about my seeing Sir Gilbert Carstairs on the night of Phillips's murder. And all the way out to the inn there was silence between Mr. Lindsey and me, and the event of the morning, about Gilverthwaite's will, and the odd circumstance of its attestation by Michael Carstairs, was not once mentioned. We kept silence, indeed, until we were in the place to which they had carried Crone's dead body. Mr. Murray and Sergeant Chisholm had got there before us, and with them was a doctor—the same that had been fetched to Phillips—and they were all talking together quietly when we went in. The superintendent came up to Mr. Lindsey.

"According to what the doctor here says," he whispered, jerking his head at the body, which lay on a table with a sheet thrown over it, "there's a question as to whether the man met his death by drowning. Look here!"

He led us up to the table, drew back the sheet from the head and face, and motioning the doctor to come up, pointed to a mark that was just between the left temple and the top of the ear, where the hair was wearing thin.

"D'ye see that, now?" he murmured. "You'll notice there's some sort of a weapon penetrated there—penetrated! But the doctor can say more than I can on that point."

"The man was struck—felled—by some sort of a weapon," said the doctor. "It's penetrated, I should say from mere superficial examination, to the brain. You'll observe there's a bruise outwardly—aye, but this has been a sharp weapon as well, something with a point, and there's the puncture—how far it may extend I can't tell yet. But on the surface of things, Mr. Lindsey, I should incline to the opinion that the poor fellow was dead, or dying, when he was thrown into yon pool. Anyway, after a blow like that, he'd be unconscious. But I'm thinking he was dead before the water closed on him."

Mr. Lindsey looked closer at the mark, and at the hole in the centre of it.

"Has it struck any of you how that could be caused?" he asked suddenly. "It hasn't? Then I'll suggest something to you. There's an implement in pretty constant use hereabouts that would do just that—a salmon gaff!"

The two police officials started—the doctor nodded his head.

"Aye, and that's a sensible remark," said he. "A salmon gaff would just do it." He turned to Chisholm with a sharp look. "You were saying this man was suspected of poaching?" he asked. "Likely it'll have been some poaching affair he was after last night—him and others. And they may have quarrelled and come to blows—and there you are!"

"Were there any signs of an affray close by—or near, on the bank?" asked Mr. Lindsey.

"We're going down there now ourselves to have a look round," answered Mr. Murray. "But according to Turndale, the body was lying in a deep pool in the Till, under the trees on the bank—it might have lain there for many a month if it hadn't been for yon young McIlwraith that has a turn for prying into dark and out-of-the-way corners. Well, here's more matter for the coroner."

Mr. Lindsey and I went back to Berwick after that. And, once more, he said little on the journey, except that it would be well if it came out that this was but a poaching affair in which Crone had got across with some companion of his; and for the rest of the afternoon he made no further remark to me about the matter, nor about the discovery of the morning. But as I was leaving the office at night, he gave me a word.

"Say nothing about that will, to anybody," said he. "I'll think that matter over to-night, and see what'll come of my thinking. It's as I said before, Hugh—to get at the bottom of all this, we'll have to go back—maybe a far way."

I said nothing and went home. For now I had work of my own—I was going to what I had resolved on after Chisholm told me the news about Crone. I would not tell my secret to Mr. Lindsey, nor to the police, nor even to Maisie. I would go straight and tell it to the one man whom it concerned—Sir Gilbert Carstairs. I would speak plainly to him, and be done with it. And as soon as I had eaten my supper, I mounted my bicycle, and, as the dusk was coming on, rode off to Hathercleugh House.

CHAPTER XIII

SIR GILBERT CARSTAIRS

It was probably with a notion of justifying my present course of procedure to myself that during that ride I went over the reasons which had kept my tongue quiet up to that time, and now led me to go to Sir Gilbert Carstairs. Why I had not told the police nor Mr. Lindsey of what I had seen, I have already explained—my own natural caution and reserve made me afraid of saying anything that might cast suspicion on an innocent man; and also I wanted to await developments. I was not concerned much with that feature of the matter. But I had undergone some qualms because I had not told Maisie Dunlop, for ever since the time at which she and I had come to a serious and sober understanding, it had been a settled thing between us that we would never have any secrets from each other. Why, then, had I not told her of this? That took a lot of explaining afterwards, when things so turned out that it would have been the best thing ever I did in my life if I only had confided in her; but this explanation was, after all, to my credit—I did not tell Maisie because I knew that, taking all the circumstances into consideration, she would fill herself with doubts and fears for me, and would for ever be living in an atmosphere of dread lest I, like Phillips, should be found with a knife-thrust in me. So much for that—it was in Maisie's own interest. And why, after keeping silence to everybody, did I decide to break it to Sir Gilbert Carstairs? There, Andrew Dunlop came in—of course, unawares to himself. For in those lecturings that he was so fond of giving us young folk, there was a moral precept of his kept cropping up which he seemed to set great store by—"If you've anything against a man, or reason to mistrust him," he would say, "don't keep it to yourself, or hint it to other people behind his back, but go straight to him and tell him to his face, and have it out with him." He was a wise man, Andrew Dunlop, as all his acquaintance knew, and I felt that I could do no better than take a lesson from him in this matter. So I would go straight to Sir Gilbert Carstairs, and tell him what was in my mind—let the consequences be what they might.

It was well after sunset, and the gloaming was over the hills and the river, when I turned into the grounds of Hathercleugh and looked round me at a place which, though I had lived close to it ever since I was born, I had never set foot in before. The house stood on a plateau of ground high above Tweed, with a deep shawl of wood behind it and a fringe of plantations on either side; house and pleasure-grounds were enclosed by a high ivied wall on all sides—you could see little of either until you were within the gates. It looked, in that evening light, a romantic and picturesque old spot and one in which you might well expect to see ghosts, or fairies, or the like. The house itself was something between an eigh-teenth-century mansion and an old Border fortress; its centre part was very high in the roof, and had turrets, with outer stairs to them, at the corners; the parapets were embattled, and in the turrets were arrow-slits. But romantic as the place was, there was nothing gloomy about it, and as I passed to the front, between the grey walls and a sunk balustered garden that lay at the foot of a terrace, I heard through the open windows of one brilliantly lighted room the click of billiard balls and the sound of men's light-hearted laughter, and through another the notes of a piano.

There was a grand butler man met me at the hall door, and looked sourly at me as I leaned my bicycle against one of the pillars and made up to him. He was sourer still when I asked to see his master, and he shook his head at me, looking me up and down as if I were some undesirable.

"You can't see Sir Gilbert at this time of the evening," said he. "What do you want?"

"Will you tell Sir Gilbert that Mr. Moneylaws, clerk to Mr. Lindsey, solicitor, wishes to see him on important business?" I answered, looking him hard in the face. "I think he'll be quick to see me when you give him that message."

He stared and growled at me a second or two before he went off with an ill grace, leaving me on the steps. But, as I had expected, he was back almost at once, and beckoning me to enter and follow him. And follow him I did, past more flun-keys who stared at me as if I had come to steal the silver, and through soft-carpet-ed passages, to a room into which he led me with small politeness.

"You're to sit down and wait," he said gruffly. "Sir Gilbert will attend to you presently."

He closed the door on me, and I sat down and looked around. I was in a small room that was filled with books from floor to ceiling—big books and little, in fine leather bindings, and the gilt of their letterings and labels shining in the rays of a tall lamp that stood on a big desk in the centre. It was a fine room that, with every-thing luxurious in the way of furnishing and appointments; you could have sunk your feet in the warmth of the carpets and rugs, and there were things in it for comfort and convenience that I had never heard tell of. I had never been in a rich man's house before, and the grandeur of it, and the idea that it gave one of wealth, made me feel that there's a vast gulf fixed between them that have and them that have not. And in the middle of these philosophies the door suddenly opened, and in walked Sir Gilbert Carstairs, and I stood up and made my politest bow to him. He nodded affably enough, and he laughed as he nodded.

"Oh!" said he. "Mr. Moneylaws! I've seen you before—at that inquest the oth-er day, I think. Didn't I?"

"That is so, Sir Gilbert," I answered. "I was there, with Mr. Lindsey."

"Why, of course, and you gave evidence," he said. "I remember. Well, and what did you want to see me about, Mr. Moneylaws? Will you smoke a cigar?" he went on, picking up a box from the table and holding it out to me. "Help yourself."

"Thank you, Sir Gilbert," I answered, "but I haven't started that yet."

"Well, then, I will," he laughed, and he picked out a cigar, lighted it, and flinging himself into an easy chair, motioned me to take another exactly opposite to him. "Now, then, fire away!" he said. "Nobody'll interrupt us, and my time's yours. You've some message for me?"

I took a good look at him before I spoke. He was a big, fine, handsome man, some five-and-fifty years of age, I should have said, but uncommonly well preserved—a clean-shaven, powerful-faced man, with quick eyes and a very alert glance; maybe, if there was anything struck me particularly about him, it was the rapidity and watchfulness of his glances, the determination in his square jaw, and the extraordinary strength and whiteness of his teeth. He was quick at smiling, and quick, too, in the use of his hands, which were always moving as he spoke, as if to emphasize whatever he said. And he made a very fine and elegant figure as he sat there in his grand evening clothes, and I was puzzled to know which struck me most—the fact that he was what he was, the seventh baronet and head of an old family, or the familiar, easy, good-natured fashion which he treated me, and talked to me, as if I had been a man of his own rank.

I had determined what to do as I sat waiting him; and now that he had bidden me to speak, I told him the whole story from start to finish, beginning with Gilverthwaite and ending with Crone, and sparing no detail or explanation of my own conduct. He listened in silence, and with more intentness and watchfulness than I had ever seen a man show in my life, and now and then he nodded and sometimes smiled; and when I had made an end he put a sharp question.

"So—beyond Crone—who, I hear, is dead—you've never told a living soul of this?" he asked, eyeing me closely.

"Not one, Sir Gilbert," I assured him. "Not even—"

"Not even—who?" he inquired quickly.

"Not even my own sweetheart," I said. "And it's the first secret ever I kept from her."

He smiled at that, and gave me a quick look as if he were trying to get a fuller idea of me.

"Well," he said, "and you did right. Not that I should care two pins, Mr. Moneylaws, if you'd told all this out at the inquest. But suspicion is easily aroused, and it spreads—aye, like wildfire! And I'm a stranger, as it were, in this country, so far, and there's people might think things that I wouldn't have them think, and—in short, I'm much obliged to you. And I'll tell you frankly, as you've been frank with me, how I came to be at those cross-roads at that particular time and on that particular night. It's a simple explanation, and could be easily corroborated, if need be. I suffer from a disturbing form of insomnia—sleeplessness—it's a custom of mine to go long walks late at night. Since I came here, I've been out that way almost every night, as my servants could assure you. I walk, as a rule, from nine o'clock to twelve—to induce sleep. And on that night I'd been miles and miles out towards Yetholm, and back; and when you saw me with my map and electric torch, I was looking for the nearest turn home—I'm not too well acquainted with the Border yet," he concluded, with a flash of his white teeth, "and I have to carry a map with me. And—that's how it was; and that's all."

I rose out of my chair at that. He spoke so readily and ingenuously that I had no more doubt of the truth of what he was saying than I had of my own existence.

"Then it's all for me, too, Sir Gilbert," said I. "I shan't say a word more of the matter to anybody. It's—as if it never existed. I was thinking all the time there'd be an explanation of it. So I'll be bidding you good-night."

"Sit you down again a minute," said he, pointing to the easy-chair. "No need for hurry. You're a clerk to Mr. Lindsey, the solicitor?"

"I am that," I answered.

"Are you articled to him?" he asked.

"No," said I. "I'm an ordinary clerk—of seven years' standing."

"Plenty of experience of office work and routine?" he inquired.

"Aye!" I replied. "No end of that, Sir Gilbert!"

"Are you good at figures and accounts?" he asked.

"I've kept all Mr. Lindsey's—and a good many trust accounts—for the last five years," I answered, wondering what all this was about.

"In fact, you're thoroughly well up in all clerical matters?" he suggested. "Keeping books, writing letters, all that sort of thing?"

"I can honestly say I'm a past master in everything of that sort," I affirmed.

He gave me a quick glance, as if he were sizing me up altogether.

"Well, I'll tell you what, Mr. Moneylaws," he said. "The fact is, I'm wanting a sort of steward, and it strikes me that you're just the man I'm looking for!"

CHAPTER XIV

DEAD MAN'S MONEY

I was so much amazed by this extraordinary suggestion, that for the moment I could only stand staring at him, and before I could find my tongue he threw a quick question at me.

"Lindsey wouldn't stand in your way, would he?" he asked. "Such jobs don't go begging, you know."

"Mr. Lindsey wouldn't stand in my way, Sir Gilbert," I answered. "But—"

"But what?" said he, seeing me hesitate. "Is it a post you wouldn't care about, then? There's five hundred a year with it—and a permanency."

Strange as it may seem, considering all the circumstances, it never occurred to me for one moment that the man was buying my silence, buying me. There wasn't the ghost of such a thought in my head—I let out what was there in my next words.

"I'd like such a post fine, Sir Gilbert," I said. "What I'm thinking of—could I give satisfaction?"

He laughed at that, as if my answer amused him.

"Well, there's nothing like a spice of modesty, Moneylaws," said he. "If you can do all we've just talked of, you'll satisfy me well enough. I like the looks of you, and I'm sure you're the sort that'll do the thing thoroughly. The post's at your disposal, if you like to take it."

I was still struggling with my amazement. Five hundred pounds a year!—and a permanency! It seemed a fortune to a lad of my age. And I was trying to find the right words in which to say all that I felt, when he spoke again.

"Look here!" he said. "Don't let us arrange this as if we'd done it behind your present employer's back—I wouldn't like Mr. Lindsey to think I'd gone behind him to get you. Let it be done this way: I'll call on Mr. Lindsey myself, and tell him I'm wanting a steward for the property, and that I've heard good reports of his clerk, and that I'll engage you on his recommendation. He's the sort that would give you a strong word by way of reference, eh?"

"Oh, he'll do that, Sir Gilbert!" I exclaimed. "Anything that'll help me on—"

"Then let's leave it at that," said he. "I'll drop in on him at his office—perhaps to-morrow. In the meantime, keep your own counsel. But—you'll take my offer?"

"I'd be proud and glad to, Sir Gilbert," said I. "And if you'll make allowance for a bit of inexperience—"

"You'll do your best, eh?" he laughed. "That's all right, Moneylaws."

He walked out with me to the door, and on to the terrace. And as I wheeled my bicycle away from the porch, he took a step or two alongside me, his hands in his pockets, his lips humming a careless tune. And suddenly he turned on me.

"Have you heard any more about that affair last night?" he asked. "I mean about Crone?"

"Nothing, Sir Gilbert," I answered.

"I hear that the opinion is that the man was struck down by a gaff," he remarked. "And perhaps killed before he was thrown into the Till."

"So the doctor seemed to think," I said. "And the police, too, I believe."

"Aye, well," said he, "I don't know if the police are aware of it, but I'm very sure there's night-poaching of salmon going on hereabouts, Moneylaws. I've fancied it for some time, and I've had thoughts of talking to the police about it. But you see, my land doesn't touch either Till or Tweed, so I haven't cared to interfere. But I'm sure that it is so, and it wouldn't surprise me if both these men, Crone and Phillips, met their deaths at the hands of the gang I'm thinking of. It's a notion that's worth following up, anyway, and I'll have a word with Murray about it when I'm in the town tomorrow."

Then, with a brief good night, he left me and went into the house, and I got outside Hathercleugh and rode home in a whirl of thoughts. And I'll confess readily that those thoughts had little to do with what Sir Gilbert Carstairs had last talked about—they were not so much of Phillips, nor of Crone, nor of his suggestion of a possible gang of night-poachers, as about myself and this sudden chance of a great change in my fortunes. For, when all is said and done, we must needs look after ourselves, and when a young man of the age I was then arrived at is asked if he would like to exchange a clerkship of a hundred and twenty a year for a stewardship at more than four times as much—as a permanency—you must agree that his mind will fix itself on what such an exchange means to him, to the exclusion of all other affairs. Five hundred a year to me meant all sorts of fine things—independence, and a house of my own, and, not least by a long way, marriage with Maisie Dunlop. And it was a wonder that I managed to keep cool, and to hold my tongue when I got home—but hold it I did, and to some purpose, and more than once. During the half hour which I managed to get with Maisie last thing that night, she asked me why I was so silent, and, hard though it was to keep from doing so, I let nothing out.

The truth was, Sir Gilbert Carstairs had fascinated me, not only with his grand offer, but with his pleasant, off-hand, companionable manners. He had put me at my ease at once; he had spoken so frankly and with such evident sincerity about his doings on that eventful night, that I accepted every word he said. And—in the little that I had thought of it—I was very ready to accept his theory as to how those two men had come by their deaths—and it was one that was certainly feasible, and worth following up. Some years before, I remembered, something of the same sort had gone on, and had resulted in an affray between salmon-poachers and river-watchers—why should it not have cropped up again? The more I thought of it, the more I felt Sir Gilbert's suggestion to have reason in it. And in that case all the mystery would be knocked clean out of these affairs—the murder of Phillips, the death of Crone, might prove to be the outcome of some vulgar encounter between them and desperadoes who had subsequently scuttled to safety and were doubtless quaking near at hand, in fear of their misdeeds coming to light; what appeared to be a perfect tangle might be the simplest matter in the world. So I judged—and next morning there came news that seemed to indicate that matters were going to be explained on the lines which Sir Gilbert had suggested.

Chisholm brought that news to our office, just after Mr. Lindsey had come in. He told it to both of us; and from his manner of telling it, we both saw—I, perhaps, not so clearly as Mr. Lindsey—that the police were already at their favourite trick of going for what seemed to them the obvious line of pursuit.

"I'm thinking we've got on the right clue at last, as regards the murder of yon man Phillips," announced Chisholm, with an air of satisfaction. "And if it is the right clue, as it seems to be, Mr. Lindsey, there'll be no great mystery in the matter, after all. Just a plain case of murder for the sake of robbery—that's it!"

"What's your clue?" asked Mr. Lindsey quietly.

"Well," answered Chisholm, with a sort of sly wink, "you'll understand, Mr. Lindsey, that we haven't been doing nothing these last few days, since yon inquest on Phillips, you know. As a matter of fact, we've been making inquiries wherever there seemed a chance of finding anything out. And we've found something out—through one of the banks yonder at Peebles."

He looked at us as if to see if we were impressed; seeing, at any rate, that we were deeply interested, he went on.

"It appears—I'll tell you the story in order, as it were," he said—"it appears that about eight months ago the agent of the British Linen Bank at Peebles got a letter from one John Phillips, written from a place called Colon, in Panama—that's Central America, as you'll be aware—enclosing a draft for three thousand pounds on the International Banking Corporation of New York. The letter instructed the Peebles agent to collect this sum and to place it in his bank to the writer's credit. Furthermore, it stated that the money was to be there until Phillips came home to Scotland, in a few months' time from the date of writing. This, of course, was all done in due course—there was the three thousand pounds in Phillips's name. There was a bit of correspondence between him at Colon and the bank at Peebles— then, at last, he wrote that he was leaving Panama for Scotland, and would call on the bank soon after his arrival. And on the morning of the day on which he was murdered, Phillips did call at the bank and established his identity, and so on, and he then drew out five hundred pounds of his money—two hundred pounds in gold, and the rest in small notes; and, Mr. Lindsey, he carried that sum away with him in a little handbag that he had with him."

Mr. Lindsey, who had been listening with great attention, nodded.

"Aye!" he said. "Carried five hundred pounds away with him. Go on, then."

"Now," continued Chisholm, evidently very well satisfied with himself for the way he was marshalling his facts, "we—that is, to put it plainly, I myself—have been making more searching inquiries about Cornhill and Coldstream. There's two of the men at Cornhill station will swear that when Phillips got out of the train there, that evening of the murder, he was carrying a little handbag such as the bank cashier remembers—a small, new, brown leather bag. They're certain of it—the ticket-collector remembers him putting it under his arm while he searched his pocket for his ticket. And what's more, the landlord of the inn across the bridge there at Coldstream he remembers the bag, clearly enough, and that Phillips never had his hand off it while he was in his house. And of course, Mr. Lindsey, the probability is that in that bag was the money—just as he had drawn it out of the bank."

"You've more to tell," remarked Mr. Lindsey.

"Just so," replied Chisholm. "And there's two items. First of all—we've found that bag! Empty, you may be sure. In the woods near that old ruin on Till side. Thrown away under a lot of stuff—dead stuff, you'll understand, where it might have lain till Doomsday if I hadn't had a most particular search made. But—that's not all. The second item is here—the railway folk at Cornhill are unanimous in declaring that by that same train which brought Phillips there, two men, strangers, that looked like tourist gentlemen, came as well, whose tickets were from—where d'ye think, then, Mr. Lindsey?"

"Peebles, of course," answered Mr. Lindsey.

"And you've guessed right!" exclaimed Chisholm, triumphantly; "Peebles it was—and now, how do you think this affair looks? There's so many tourists on Tweedside this time of the year that nobody paid any great attention that night to these men, nor where they went. But what could be plainer, d'ye think?—of course, those two had tracked Phillips from the bank, and they followed him till they had him in yon place where he was found, and they murdered him—to rob him!"

CHAPTER XV

FIVE HUNDRED A YEAR

It was very evident that Chisholm was in a state of gleeful assurance about his theory, and I don't think he was very well pleased when Mr. Lindsey, instead of enthusiastically acclaiming it as a promising one, began to ask him questions.

"You found a pretty considerable sum on Phillips as it was when you searched his body, didn't you?" he asked.

"Aye—a good lot!" assented Chisholm. "But it was in a pocket-book in an inner pocket of his coat, and in his purse."

"If it was robbery, why didn't they take everything?" inquired Mr.Lindsey.

"Aye, I knew you'd ask that," replied Chisholm. "But the thing is that they were interrupted. The bag they could carry off—but it's probable that they heard Mr. Moneylaws here coming down the lane before they could search the man's pockets."

"Umph!" said Mr. Lindsey. "And how do you account for two men getting away from the neighbourhood without attracting attention?"

"Easy enough," declared Chisholm. "As I said just now, there's numbers of strangers comes about Tweedside at this time of the year, and who'd think anything of seeing them? What was easier than for these two to separate, to keep close during the rest of the night, and to get away by train from some wayside station or other next morning? They could manage it easily—and we're making inquiries at all the stations in the district on both sides the Tweed, with that idea."

"Well—you'll have a lot of people to follow up, then," remarked Mr. Lindsey drily. "If you're going to follow every tourist that got on a train next morning between Berwick and Wooler, and Berwick and Kelso, and Berwick and Burnmouth, and Berwick and Blyth, you'll have your work set, I'm thinking!"

"All the same," said Chisholm doggedly, "that's how it's been. And the bank at Peebles has the numbers of the notes that Phillips carried off in his little bag—and I'll trace those fellows yet, Mr. Lindsey."

"Good luck to you, sergeant!" answered Mr. Lindsey. He turned to me when Chisholm had gone. "That's the police all over, Hugh," he remarked. "And you might talk till you were black in the face to yon man, and he'd stick to his story."

"You don't believe it, then?" I asked him, somewhat surprised.

"He may be right," he replied. "I'm not saying. Let him attend to his business—and now we'll be seeing to ours."

It was a busy day with us in the office that, being the day before court day, and we had no time to talk of anything but our own affairs. But during the afternoon, at a time when I had left the office for an hour or two on business, Sir Gilbert Carstairs called, and he was closeted with Mr. Lindsey when I returned. And after they had been together some time Mr. Lindsey came out to me and beckoned me into a little waiting-room that we had and shut the door on us, and I saw at once from the expression on his face that he had no idea that Sir Gilbert and I had met the night before, or that I had any notion of what he was going to say to me.

"Hugh, my lad!" said he, clapping me on the shoulder; "you're evidently one of those that are born lucky. What's the old saying—'Some achieve greatness, some have greatness thrust upon them!'—eh? Here's greatness—in a degree—thrusting itself on you!"

"What's this you're talking about, Mr. Lindsey?" I asked. "There's not much greatness about me, I'm thinking!"

"Well, it's not what you're thinking in this case," he answered; "it's what other folks are thinking of you. Here's Sir Gilbert Carstairs in my room yonder. He's wanting a steward—somebody that can keep accounts, and letters, and look after the estate, and he's been looking round for a likely man, and he's heard that Lindsey's clerk, Hugh Moneylaws, is just the sort he wants—and, in short, the job's yours, if you like to take it. And, my lad, it's worth five hundred a year—and a permanency, too! A fine chance for a young fellow of your age!"

"Do you advise me to take it, Mr. Lindsey?" I asked, endeavouring to combine surprise with a proper respect for the value of his counsel. "It's a serious job that for, as you say, a young fellow."

"Not if he's got your headpiece on him," he replied, giving me another clap on the shoulder. "I do advise you to take it. I've given you the strongest recommendations to him. Go into my office now and talk it over with Sir Gilbert by yourself. But when it comes to settling details, call me in—I'll see you're done right to."

I thanked him warmly, and went into his room, where Sir Gilbert was sitting in an easy-chair. He motioned me to shut the door, and, once that was done, he gave a quick, inquiring look.

"You didn't let him know that you and I had talked last night?" he asked at once.

"No," said I.

"That's right—and I didn't either," he went on. "I don't want him to know I spoke to you before speaking to him—it would look as if I were trying to get his clerk away from him. Well, it's settled, then, Moneylaws? You'll take the post?"

"I shall be very glad to, Sir Gilbert," said I. "And I'll serve you to the best of my ability, if you'll have a bit of patience with me at the beginning. There'll be some difference between my present job and this you're giving me, but I'm a quick learner, and—"

"Oh, that's all right, man!" he interrupted carelessly. "You'll do all that I want. I hate accounts, and letter-writing, and all that sort of thing—take all that off my hands, and you'll do. Of course, whenever you're in a fix about anything, come to me—but I can explain all there is to do in an hour's talk with you at the beginning. All right!—ask Mr. Lindsey to step in to me, and we'll put the matter on a business footing."

Mr. Lindsey came in and took over the job of settling matters on my behalf. And the affair was quickly arranged. I was to stay with Mr. Lindsey another month, so as to give him the opportunity of getting a new head clerk, then I was to enter on my new duties at Hathercleugh. I was to have five hundred pounds a year salary, with six months' notice on either side; at the end of five years, if I was still in the situation, the terms were to be revised with a view to an increase—and all this was to be duly set down in black and white. These propositions, of course, were Mr. Lindsey's, and Sir Gilbert assented to all of them readily and promptly. He appeared to be the sort of man who is inclined to accept anything put before him rather than have a lot of talk about it. And presently, remarking that that was all right, and he'd leave Mr. Lindsey to see to it, he rose to go, but at the door paused and came back.

"I'm thinking of dropping in at the police-station and telling Murray my ideas about that Crone affair," he remarked. "It's my opinion, Mr. Lindsey, that there's salmon-poaching going on hereabouts, and if my land adjoined either Tweed or Till I'd have spoken about it before. There are queer characters about along both rivers at nights—I know, because I go out a good deal, very late, walking, to try and cure myself of insomnia; and I know what I've seen. It's my impression that Crone was probably mixed up with some gang, and that his death arose out of an affray between them."

"That's probable," answered Mr. Lindsey. "There was trouble of that sort some years ago, but I haven't heard of it lately. Certainly, it would be a good thing to start the idea in Murray's mind; he might follow it up and find something out."

"That other business—the Phillips murder—might have sprung out of the same cause," suggested Sir Gilbert. "If those chaps caught a stranger in a lonely place—"

"The police have a theory already about Phillips," remarked Mr. Lindsey. "They think he was followed from Peebles, and murdered for the sake of money that he was carrying in a bag he had with him. And my experience," he added with a laugh, "is that if the police once get a theory of their own, it's no use suggesting any other to them—they'll ride theirs, either till it drops or they get home with it."

Sir Gilbert nodded his head, as if he agreed with that, and he suddenly gave Mr. Lindsey an inquiring look.

"What's your own opinion?" he asked.

But Mr. Lindsey was not to be drawn. He laughed and shrugged his shoulders, as if to indicate that the affair was none of his.

"I wouldn't say that I have an opinion, Sir Gilbert," he answered. "It's much too soon to form one, and I haven't the details, and I'm not a detective. But all these matters are very simple—when you get to the bottom of them. The police think this is going to be a very simple affair—mere vulgar murder for the sake of mere vulgar robbery. We shall see!"

Then Sir Gilbert went away, and Mr. Lindsey looked at me, who stood a little apart, and he saw that I was thinking.

"Well, my lad," he said; "a bit dazed by your new opening? It's a fine chance for you, too! Now, I suppose, you'll be wanting to get married. Is it that you're thinking about?"

"Well, I was not, Mr. Lindsey," said I. "I was just wondering—if you must know—how it was that, as he was here, you didn't tell Sir Gilbert about that signature of his brother's that you found on Gilverthwaite's will."

He shared a sharp look between me and the door—but the door was safely shut.

"No!" he said. "Neither to him nor to anybody, yet a while! And don't you mention that, my lad. Keep it dark till I give the word. I'll find out about that in my own way. You understand—on that point, absolute silence."

I replied that, of course, I would not say a word; and presently I went into the office to resume my duties. But I had not been long at that before the door opened, and Chisholm put his face within and looked at me.

"I'm wanting you, Mr. Moneylaws," he said. "You said you were with Crone, buying something, that night before his body was found. You'd be paying him money—and he might be giving you change. Did you happen to see his purse, now?"

"Aye!" answered I. "What for do you ask that?"

"Because," said he, "we've taken a fellow at one of those riverside publics that's been drinking heavily, and, of course, spending money freely. And he has a queer-looking purse on him, and one or two men that's seen it vows and declares it was Abel Crone's."

CHAPTER XVI

THE MAN IN THE CELL

Before I could reply to Chisholm's inquiry, Mr. Lindsey put his head out of his door and seeing the police-sergeant there asked what he was after. And when Chisholm had repeated his inquiry, both looked at me.

"I did see Crone's purse that night," I answered, "an old thing that he kept tied up with a boot-lace. And he'd a lot of money in it, too."

"Come round, then, and see if you can identify this that we found on the man," requested Chisholm. "And," he added, turning to Mr. Lindsey, "there's another thing. The man's sober enough, now that we've got him—it's given him a bit of a pull-together, being arrested. And he's demanding a lawyer. Perhaps you'll come to him, Mr. Lindsey."

"Who is he?" asked Mr. Lindsey. "A Berwick man?"

"He isn't," replied Chisholm. "He's a stranger—a fellow that says he was seeking work, and had been stopping at a common lodging-house in the town. He vows and declares that he'd nothing to do with killing Crone, and he's shouting for a lawyer."

Mr. Lindsey put on his hat, and he and I went off with Chisholm to the police-station. And as we got in sight of it, we became aware that there was a fine to-do in the street before its door. The news of the arrest had spread quickly, and folk had come running to get more particulars. And amongst the women and children and loafers that were crowding around was Crone's housekeeper, a great, heavy, rough-haired Irishwoman called Nance Maguire, and she was waving her big arms and shaking her fists at a couple of policemen, whom she was adjuring to bring out the murderer, so that she might do justice on him then and there—all this being mingled with encomiums on the victim.

"The best man that ever lived!" she was screaming at the top of her voice. "The best and kindest creature ever set foot in your murdering town! And didn't I know he was to be done to death by some of ye? Didn't he tell me himself that there was one would give his two eyes to be seeing his corpse? And if ye've laid hands on him that did it, bring him out to me, so, and I'll—"

Mr. Lindsey laid a quiet hand on the woman's arm and twisted her round in the direction of her cottage.

"Hold your wisht, good wife, and go home!" he whispered to her. "And if you know anything, keep your tongue still till I come to see you. Be away, now, and leave it to me."

I don't know how it was, but Nance Maguire, after a sharp look at Mr. Lindsey, turned away as meekly as a lamb, and went off, tearful enough, but quiet, down the street, followed by half the rabble, while Mr. Lindsey, Chisholm, and myself turned into the police-station. And there we met Mr. Murray, who wagged his head at us as if he were very well satisfied with something.

"Not much doubt about this last affair, anyhow," said he, as he took us into his office. "You might say the man was caught red-handed! All the same, Mr. Lindsey, he's in his rights to ask for a lawyer, and you can see him whenever you like."

"What are the facts?" asked Mr. Lindsey. "Let me know that much first."

Mr. Murray jerked his thumb at Chisholm.

"The sergeant there knows them," he answered. "He took the man."

"It was this way, d'ye see, Mr. Lindsey," said Chisholm, who was becoming an adept at putting statements before people. "You know that bit of a public there is along the river yonder, outside the wall—the Cod and Lobster? Well, James Macfarlane, that keeps it, he came to me, maybe an hour or so ago, and said there was a fellow, a stranger, had been in and out there all day since morning, drinking; and though he wouldn't say the man was what you'd rightly call drunk, still he'd had a skinful, and he was in there again, and they wouldn't serve him, and he was getting quarrelsome and abusive, and in the middle of it had pulled out a purse that another man who was in there vowed and declared, aside, to Macfarlane, was Abel Crone's. So I got a couple of constables and went back with Macfarlane, and there was the man vowing he'd be served, and with a handful of money to prove that he could pay for whatever he called for. And as he began to turn ugly, and show fight, we just clapped the bracelets on him and brought him along, and there he is in the cells—and, of course, it's sobered him down, and he's demanding his rights to see a lawyer."

"Who is he?" asked Mr. Lindsey.

"A stranger to the town," replied Chisholm. "And he'll neither give name nor address but to a lawyer, he declares. But we know he was staying at one of the common lodging-houses—Watson's—three nights ago, and that the last two nights he wasn't in there at all."

"Well—where's that purse?" demanded Mr. Lindsey. "Mr. Moneylaws here says he can identify it, if it's Crone's."

Chisholm opened a drawer and took out what I at once knew to be Abel Crone's purse—which was in reality a sort of old pocket-book or wallet, of some sort of skin, with a good deal of the original hair left on it, and tied about with a bit of old bootlace. There were both gold and silver in it—just as I had seen when Crone pulled it out to find me some change for a five-shilling piece I had given him—and more by token, there was the five-shilling piece itself!

"That's Crone's purse!" I exclaimed. "I've no doubt about that. And that's a crown piece I gave him myself; I've no doubt about that either!"

"Let us see the man," said Mr. Lindsey.

Chisholm led us down a corridor to the cells, and unlocked a door. He stepped within the cell behind it, motioning us to follow. And there, on the one stool which the place contained, sat a big, hulking fellow that looked like a navvy, whose rough clothes bore evidence of his having slept out in them, and whose boots were stained with the mud and clay which they would be likely to collect along the riverside. He was sitting nursing his head in his hands, growling to himself, and he looked up at us as I have seen wild beasts look out through the bars of cages. And somehow, there was that in the man's eyes which made me think, there and then, that he was not reflecting on any murder that he had done, but was sullenly and stupidly angry with himself.

"Now, then, here's a lawyer for you," said Chisholm. "Mr. Lindsey, solicitor."

"Well, my man!" began Mr. Lindsey, taking a careful look at this queer client. "What have you got to say to me?"

The prisoner gave Chisholm a disapproving look.

"Not going to say a word before the likes of him!" he growled. "I know my rights, guv'nor! What I say, I'll say private to you."

"Better leave us, sergeant," said Mr. Lindsey. He waited till Chisholm, a bit unwilling, had left the cell and closed the door, and then he turned to the man. "Now, then," he continued, "you know what they charge you with? You've been drinking hard—are you sober enough to talk sense? Very well, then—what's this you want me for?"

"To defend me, of course!" growled the prisoner. He twisted a hand round to the back of his trousers as if to find something. "I've money of my own—a bit put away in a belt," he said; "I'll pay you."

"Never mind that now," answered Mr. Lindsey. "Who are you?—and what do you want to say?"

"Name of John Carter," replied the man. "General labourer—navvy work— anything of that sort. On tramp—seeking a job. Came here, going north, night before last. And—no more to do with the murder of yon man than you have!"

"They found his purse on you, anyway," remarked Mr. Lindsey bluntly. "What have you got to say to that?"

"What I say is that I'm a damned fool!" answered Carter surlily. "It's all against me, I know, but I'll tell you—you can tell lawyers anything. Who's that young fellow?" he demanded suddenly, glaring at me. "I'm not going to talk be- fore no detectives."

"My clerk," replied Mr. Lindsey. "Now, then—tell your tale. And just remem- ber what a dangerous position you're in."

"Know that as well as you do," muttered the prisoner. "But I'm sober enough, now! It's this way—I stopped here in the town three nights since, and looked about for a job next day, and then I heard of something likely up the river and went after it and didn't get it, so I started back here—late at night it was. And after crossing that bridge at a place called Twizel, I turned down to the river-bank, thinking to take a short cut. And—it was well after dark, then, mind you, guv'nor—in coming along through the woods, just before where the little river runs into the big one, I come across this man's body—stumbled on it. That's the truth!"

"Well!" said Mr. Lindsey.

"He was lying—I could show you the place, easy—between the edge of the wood and the river-bank," continued Carter. "And though he was dead enough when I found him, guv'nor, he hadn't been dead so long. But dead he was—and not from aught of my doing."

"What time was this?" asked Mr. Lindsey.

"It would be past eleven o'clock," replied Carter. "It was ten when I called by Cornhill station. I went the way I did—down through the woods to the river-bank—because I'd noticed a hut there in the morning that I could sleep in—I was making for that when I found the body."

"Well—about the purse?" demanded Mr. Lindsey shortly. "No lies, now!"

The prisoner shook his head at that, and growled—but it was evident he was growling at himself.

"That's right enough," he confessed. "I felt in his pockets, and I did take the purse. But—I didn't put him in the water. True as I'm here, guv'nor. I did no more than take the purse! I left him there—just as he was—and the next day I got drinking, and last night I stopped in that hut again, and today I was drinking, pretty heavy—and I sort of lost my head and pulled the purse out, and—that's the truth, anyway, whether you believe it or not. But I didn't kill yon man, though I'll admit I robbed his body—like the fool I am!"

"Well, you see where it's landed you," remarked Mr. Lindsey. "All right—hold your tongue now, and I'll see what I can do. I'll appear for you when you come before the magistrate tomorrow."

He tapped at the door of the cell, and Chisholm, who had evidently waited in the corridor, let us out. Mr. Lindsey said nothing to him, nor to the superintendent—he led me away into the street. And there he clapped me on the arm.

"I believe every word that man said!" he murmured. "Come on, now—we'll see this Nance Maguire."

CHAPTER XVII

THE IRISH HOUSEKEEPER

I was a good deal surprised that Mr. Lindsey should be—apparently—so anxious to interview Crone's housekeeper, and I said as much. He turned on me sharply, with a knowing look.

"Didn't you hear what the woman was saying when we came across her there outside the police-station?" he exclaimed. "She was saying that Crone had said to her that there was some man who would give his two eyes to be seeing his corpse! Crone's been telling her something. And I'm so convinced that that man in the cells yonder has told us the truth, as regards himself, that I'm going to find out what Crone did tell her. Who is there—who could there be that wanted to see Crone's dead body? Let's try to find that out."

I made no answer—but I was beginning to think; and to wonder, too, in a vague, not very pleasant fashion. Was this—was Crone's death, murder, whatever it was—at all connected with the previous affair of Phillips? Had Crone told me the truth that night I went to buy the stuff for Tom Dunlop's rabbit-hutches? or had he kept something back? And while I was reflecting on these points, Mr. Lindsey began talking again.

"I watched that man closely when he was giving me his account of what happened," he said, "and, as I said just now, I believe he told us the truth. Whoever it was that did Crone to death, he's not in that cell, Hugh, my lad; and, unless I'm much mistaken, all this is of a piece with Phillips's murder. But let's hear what this Irishwoman has to say."

Crone's cottage was a mean, miserable shanty sort of place down a narrow alley in a poor part of the town. When we reached its door there was a group of women and children round it, all agog with excitement. But the door itself was closed, and it was not opened to us until Nance Maguire's face had appeared at the bit of a window, and Nance had assured herself of the identity of her visitors. And when she had let us in, she shut the door once more and slipped a bolt into its socket.

"I an't said a word, your honour," said she, "since your honour told me not to, though them outside is sharp on me to tell 'em this and that. And I wouldn't have said what I did up yonder had I known your honour would be for supporting me. I was feeling there wasn't a soul in the place would see justice done for him that's gone—the poor, good man!"

"If you want justice, my good woman," remarked Mr. Lindsey, "keep your tongue quiet, and don't talk to your neighbours, nor to the police—just keep anything you know till I tell you to let it out. Now, then, what's this you were saying?—that Crone told you there was a man in the place would give his two eyes to see him a corpse?"

"Them very words, your honour; and not once nor twice, but a good many times did he say it," replied the woman. "It was a sort of hint he was giving me, your honour—he had that way of speaking."

"Since when did he give you such hints?" asked Mr. Lindsey. "Was it only lately?"

"It was since that other bloody murder, your honour," said Nance Maguire. "Only since then. He would talk of it as we sat over the fire there at nights. 'There's murder in the air,' says he. 'Bloody murder is all around us!' he says. 'And it's myself will have to pick my steps careful,' he says, 'for there's him about would give his two eyes to see me a stark and staring corpse,' he says. 'Me knowing,' he says, 'more than you'd give me credit for,' says he. And not another word than them could I get out of him, your honour."

"He never told you who the man was that he had his fears of?" inquired Mr. Lindsey.

"He did not, then, your honour," replied Nance. "He was a close man, and you wouldn't be getting more out of him than he liked to tell."

"Now, then, just tell me the truth about a thing or two," said Mr. Lindsey. "Crone used to be out at nights now and then, didn't he?"

"Indeed, then, he did so, your honour," she answered readily. "'Tis true, he would be out at nights, now and again."

"Poaching, as a matter of fact," suggested Mr. Lindsey.

"And that's the truth, your honour," she assented. "He was a clever hand with the rabbits."

"Aye; but did he never bring home a salmon, now?" asked Mr. Lindsey. "Come, out with it."

"I'll not deny that, neither, your honour," admitted the woman. "He was clever at that too."

"Well, now, about that night when he was supposed to be killed," continued Mr. Lindsey; "that's Tuesday last—this being Thursday. Did he ever come home that evening from his shop?"

I had been listening silently all this time, and I listened with redoubled attention for the woman's answer to the last question. It was on the Tuesday evening, about nine o'clock, that I had had my talk with Crone, and I was anxious to know what happened after that. And Nance Maguire replied readily enough—it was evident her memory was clear on these events.

"He did not, then," she said. "He was in here having his tea at six o'clock that evening, and he went away to the shop when he'd had it, and I never put my eyes on him again, alive, your honour. He was never home that night, and he didn't come to his breakfast next morning, and he wasn't at the shop—and I never heard this or that of him till they come and tell me the bad news."

I knew then what must have happened. After I had left him, Crone had gone away up the river towards Tillmouth—he had a crazy old bicycle that he rode about on. And most people, having heard Nance Maguire's admissions, would have said that he had gone poaching. But I was not so sure of that. I was beginning to suspect that Crone had played some game with me, and had not told me anything like the truth during our conversation. There had been more within his knowledge than he had let out—but what was it? And I could not help feeling that his object in setting off in that direction, immediately after I had left him, might have been, not poaching, but somebody to whom he wished to communicate the result of his talk with me. And, in that case, who was the somebody?

But just then I had to leave my own thoughts and speculations alone, and to attend to what was going on between my principal and Nance Maguire. Mr. Lindsey, however, appeared to be satisfied with what he had heard. He gave the woman some further advice about keeping her tongue still, told her what to do as regards Crone's effects, and left the cottage. And when we were out in the main street again on our way back to the office he turned to me with a look of decision.

"I've come to a definite theory about this affair, Hugh," he said. "And I'll lay a fiver to a farthing that it's the right one!"

"Yes, Mr. Lindsey?" said I, keenly interested at hearing that.

"Crone knew who killed Phillips," he said. "And the man who killed Phillips killed Crone, too, because Crone knew! That's been the way of it, my lad! And now, then, who's the man?"

I could make no reply to such a question, and presently he went on—talking as much to himself, I think, as to me.

"I wish I knew certain things!" he muttered. "I wish I knew what Phillips and Gilverthwaite came here for. I wish I knew if Gilverthwaite ever had any secret dealings with Crone. I wish—I do wish!—I knew if there has been—if there is—a third man in this Phillips-Gilverthwaite affair who has managed, and is managing, to keep himself in the background. But—I'll stake my professional reputation on one thing—whoever killed Phillips, killed Abel Crone! It's all of a piece."

Now, of course I know now—have known for many a year—that it was at this exact juncture that I made a fatal, a reprehensible mistake in my share of all this business. It was there, at that exact point, that I ought to have made a clean breast to Mr. Lindsey of everything that I knew. I ought to have told him, there and then, of what I had seen at the cross-roads that night of the murder of Phillips; and of my conversation about that with Abel Crone at his shop; and of my visit to Sir Gilbert Carstairs at Hathercleugh House. Had I done so, matters would have become simplified, and much more horror and trouble avoided, for Mr. Lindsey was just then at the beginning of a straight track and my silence turned him away from it, to get into more twisted and obscure ones. But—I said nothing. And why? The answer is simple, and there's the excuse of human nature in it—I was so much filled with the grand prospects of my stewardship, and of all it would bring me, and was so highly pleased with Sir Gilbert Carstairs for his advancement of my fortunes, that—here's the plain truth—I could not bring myself to think of, or bother with, anything else. Up to then, of course, I had not said a word to my mother or to Maisie Dunlop of the stewardship—I was impatient to tell both. So I held my peace and said nothing to Mr. Lindsey—and presently the office work for the day was over and I was free to race home with my grand news. Is it likely that with such news as that I would be troubling my head any longer about other folks' lives and deaths?

That, I suppose, was the most important evening I had ever spent in my life. To begin with, I felt as if I had suddenly become older, and bigger, and much more important. I became inclined to adopt magisterial airs to my mother and my sweetheart, laying down the law to them as to the future in a fashion which made Maisie poke fun at me for a crowing cockerel. It was only natural that I should suffer a little from swelled head that night—I should not have been human otherwise. But Andrew Dunlop took the conceit out of me with a vengeance when Maisie and I told him the news, and I explained everything to him in his back-parlour. He was at times a man of many words, and at times a man of few words—and when he said little, he meant most.

"Aye!" said he. "Well, that's a fine prospect, Hugh, my man, and I wish you well in it. But there'll be no talk of any wedding for two years—so get that notion out of your heads, both of you! In two years you'll just have got settled to your new job, and you'll be finding out how you suit your master and how he suits you—we'll get the preliminaries over, and see how things promise in that time. And we'll see, too, how much money you've saved out of your salary, my man—so you'll just not hear the wedding-bells calling for a couple of twelvemonths, and'll behave yourselves like good children in the meanwhile. There's a deal of things may happen in two years, I'm thinking."

He might have added that a deal of things may happen in two weeks—and, indeed, he would have had good reason for adding it, could he have looked a few days ahead.

CHAPTER XVIII

THE ICE AX

The police put Carter in the dock before a full bench of magistrates next morning, and the court was so crowded that it was all Mr. Lindsey and I could do to force our way to the solicitors' table. Several minor cases came on before Carter was brought up from the cells, and during this hearing I had leisure to look round the court and see who was there. And almost at once I saw Sir Gilbert Carstairs, who, though not yet a justice of the peace—his commission to that honourable office arrived a few days later, oddly enough,—had been given a seat on the bench, in company with one or two other local dignitaries, one of whom, I observed with some curiosity, was that Reverend Mr. Ridley who had given evidence at the inquest on Phillips. All these folk, it was easy to see, were in a high state of inquisitiveness about Crone's murder; and from certain whispers that I overheard, I gathered that the chief cause of this interest lay in a generally accepted opinion that it was, as Mr. Lindsey had declared to me more than once, all of a piece with the crime of the previous week. And it was very easy to observe that they were not so curious to see Carter as to hear what might be alleged against him.

There appeared to be some general surprise when Mr. Lindsey quietly announced that he was there on behalf of the prisoner. You would have thought from the demeanour of the police that, in their opinion, there was nothing for the bench to do but hear a bit of evidence and commit Carter straight away to the Assizes to take his trial for wilful murder. What evidence they did bring forward was, of course, plain and straightforward enough. Crone had been found lying in a deep pool in the River Till; but the medical testimony showed that he had met his fate by a blow from some sharp instrument, the point of which had penetrated the skull and the frontal part of the brain in such a fashion as to cause instantaneous death. The man in the dock had been apprehended with Crone's purse in his possession—therefore, said the police, he had murdered and robbed Crone. As I say, Mr. Murray and all of them—as you could see—were quite of the opinion that this was sufficient; and I am pretty sure that the magistrates were of the same way of thinking. And the police were not over well pleased, and the rest of the folk in court were, to say the least, a little mystified, when Mr. Lindsey asked a few questions of two witnesses—of whom Chisholm was one, and the doctor who had been fetched to Crone's body the other. And before setting down what questions they were that Mr. Lindsey asked, I will remark here that there was a certain something, a sort of mysterious hinting in his manner of asking them, that suggested a lot more than the mere questions themselves, and made people begin to whisper amongst each other that Lawyer Lindsey knew things that he was not just then minded to let out.

It was to Chisholm that he put his first questions—casually, as if they were very ordinary ones, and yet with an atmosphere of meaning behind them that excited curiosity.

"You made a very exhaustive search of the neighbourhood of the spot where Crone's body was found, didn't you?" he inquired.

"A thorough search," answered Chisholm.

"You found the exact spot where the man had been struck down?"

"Judging by the marks of blood—yes."

"On the river-bank—between the river and a coppice, wasn't it?"

"Just so—between the bank and the coppice."

"How far had the body been dragged before it was thrown into the river?"

"Ten yards," replied Chisholm promptly.

"Did you notice any footprints?" asked Mr. Lindsey.

"It would be difficult to trace any," explained Chisholm. "The grass is very thick in some places, and where it isn't thick it's that close and wiry in texture that a boot wouldn't make any impression."

"One more question," said Mr. Lindsey, leaning forward and looking Chisholm full in the face. "When you charged the man there in the dock with the murder of Abel Crone, didn't he at once—instantly!—show the greatest surprise? Come, now, on your oath—yes or no?"

"Yes!" admitted Chisholm; "he did."

"But he just as readily admitted he was in possession of Crone's purse? Again—yes or no?"

"Yes," said Chisholm. "Yes—that's so."

That was all Mr. Lindsey asked Chisholm. It was not much more that he asked the doctor. But there was more excitement about what he did ask him—arising out of something that he did in asking it.

"There's been talk, doctor, as to what the precise weapon was which caused the fatal injury to this man Crone," he said. "It's been suggested that the wound which occasioned his death might have been—and probably was—caused by a blow from a salmon gaff. What is your opinion?"

"It might have been," said the doctor cautiously.

"It was certainly caused by a pointed weapon—some sort of a spiked weapon?" suggested Mr. Lindsey.

"A sharp, pointed weapon, most certainly," affirmed the doctor.

"There are other things than a salmon gaff that, in your opinion, could have caused it?"

"Oh, of course!" said the doctor.

Mr. Lindsey paused a moment, and looked round the court as if he were thinking over his next question. Then he suddenly plunged his hand under the table at which he was standing, and amidst a dead silence drew out a long, narrow brown-paper parcel which I had seen him bring to the office that morning. Quietly, while the silence grew deeper and the interest stronger, he produced from this an object such as I had never seen before—an implement or weapon about three feet in length, its shaft made of some tough but evidently elastic wood, furnished at one end with a strong iron ferrule, and at the other with a steel head, one extremity of which was shaped like a carpenter's adze, while the other tapered off to a fine point. He balanced this across his open palms for a moment, so that the court might see it—then he passed it over to the witness-box.

"Now, doctor," he said, "look at that—which is one of the latest forms of the ice-ax. Could that wound have been caused by that—or something very similar to it?"

The witness put a forefinger on the sharp point of the head.

"Certainly!" he answered. "It is much more likely to have been caused by such an implement as this than by a salmon gaff."

Mr. Lindsey reached out his hand for the ice-ax, and, repossessing himself of it, passed it and its brown-paper wrapping to me.

"Thank you, doctor," he said; "that's all I wanted to know." He turned to the bench. "I wish to ask your worships, if it is your intention, on the evidence you have heard, to commit the prisoner on the capital charge today?" he asked. "If it is, I shall oppose such a course. What I do ask, knowing what I do, is that you should adjourn this case for a week—when I shall have some evidence to put before you which, I think, will prove that this man did not kill Abel Crone."

There was some discussion. I paid little attention to it, being considerably amazed at the sudden turn which things had taken, and astonished altogether by Mr. Lindsey's production of the ice-ax. But the discussion ended in Mr. Lindsey having his own way, and Carter was remanded in custody, to be brought up again a week later; and presently we were all out in the streets, in groups, everybody talking excitedly about what had just taken place, and speculating on what it was that Lawyer Lindsey was after. Mr. Lindsey himself, however, was more imperturbable and, if anything, cooler than usual. He tapped me on the arm as we went out of court, and at the same time took the parcel containing the ice-ax from me.

"Hugh," he said; "there's nothing more to do today, and I'm going out of town at once, until tomorrow. You can lock up the office now, and you and the other two can take a holiday. I'm going straight home and then to the station."

He turned hurriedly away in the direction of his house, and I went off to the office to carry out his instructions. There was nothing strange in his giving us a holiday—it was a thing he often did in summer, on fine days when we had nothing much to do, and this was a gloriously fine day and the proceedings in court had been so short that it was not yet noon. So I packed off the two junior clerks and the office lad, and locked up, and went away myself—and in the street outside I met Sir Gilbert Carstairs. He was coming along in our direction, evidently deep in thought, and he started a little as he looked up and saw me.

"Hullo, Moneylaws!" he said in his off-hand fashion. "I was just wanting to see you. I say!" he went on, laying a hand on my arm, "you're dead certain that you've never mentioned to a soul but myself anything about that affair of yours and Crone's—you know what I mean?"

"Absolutely certain, Sir Gilbert!" I answered. "There's no living being knows—but yourself."

"That's all right," he said, and I could see he was relieved. "I don't want mixing up with these matters—I should very much dislike it. What's Lindsey trying to get at in his defence of this man Carter?"

"I can't think," I replied. "Unless it is that he's now inclining to the theory of the police that Phillips was murdered by some man or men who followed him from Peebles, and that the same man or men murdered Crone. I think that must be it: there were some men—tourists—about, who haven't been found yet."

He hesitated a moment, and then glanced at our office door.

"Lindsey in?" he asked.

"No, Sir Gilbert," I replied. "He's gone out of town and given us a holiday."

"Oh!" he said, looking at me with a sudden smile. "You've got a holiday, have you, Moneylaws? Look here—I'm going for a run in my bit of a yacht—come with me! How soon can you be ready?"

"As soon as I've taken my dinner, Sir Gilbert," I answered, pleased enough at the invitation. "Would an hour do?"

"You needn't bother about your dinner," he said. "I'm having a lunch basket packed now at the hotel, and I'll step in and tell them to put in enough for two. Go and get a good thick coat, and meet me down at the front in half an hour."

I ran off home, told my mother where I was going, and hurried away to the river-side. The Tweed was like a mirror flashing back the sunlight that day, and out beyond its mouth the open sea was bright and blue as the sky above. How could I foresee that out there, in those far-off dancing waters, there was that awaiting me of which I can only think now, when it is long past, with fear and horror?

CHAPTER XIX

MY TURN

I had known for some time that Sir Gilbert Carstairs had a small yacht lying at one of the boathouses on the riverside; indeed, I had seen her before ever I saw him. She was a trim, graceful thing, with all the appearance of an excellent sea-boat, and though she looked like a craft that could stand a lot of heavy weather, she had the advantage of being so light in draught—something under three feet—that it was possible for her to enter the shallowest harbour. I had heard that Sir Gilbert was constantly sailing her up and down the coast, and sometimes going well out to sea in her. On these occasions he was usually accompanied by a fisher-lad whom he had picked up somehow or other: this lad, Wattie Mason, was down by the yacht when I reached her, and he gave me a glowering look when he found that I was to put his nose out for this time at any rate. He hung around us until we got off, as a hungry dog hangs around a table on the chance of a bone being thrown to him; but he got no recognition from Sir Gilbert, who, though the lad had been useful enough to him before, took no more notice of him that day than of one of the pebbles on the beach. And if I had been more of a student of human nature, I should have gained some idea of my future employer's character from that small circumstance, and have seen that he had no feeling or consideration for anybody unless it happened to be serving and suiting his purpose.

But at that moment I was thinking of nothing but the pleasure of taking a cruise in the yacht, in the company of a man in whom I was naturally interested. I was passionately fond of the sea, and had already learned from the Berwick sea-going folk how to handle small craft, and the management of a three-oar vessel like this was an easy matter to me, as I soon let Sir Gilbert know. Once outside the river mouth, with a nice light breeze blowing off the land, we set squaresail, mainsail, and foresail and stood directly out to sea on as grand a day and under as fair conditions as a yachtsman could desire; and when we were gaily bowling along Sir Gilbert bade me unpack the basket which had been put aboard from the hotel—it was a long time, he said, since his breakfast, and we would eat and drink at the outset of things. If I had not been hungry myself, the sight of the provisions in that basket would have made me so—there was everything in there that a man could desire, from cold salmon and cold chicken to solid roast beef, and there was plenty of claret and whisky to wash it down with. And, considering how readily and healthily Sir Gilbert Carstairs ate and drank, and how he talked and laughed while we lunched side by side under that glorious sky, gliding away over a smooth, innocent-looking sea, I have often wondered since if what was to come before nightfall came of deliberate intention on his part, or from a sudden yielding to temptation when the chance of it arose—and for the life of me I cannot decide! But if the man had murder in his heart, while he sat there at my side, eating his good food and drinking his fine liquor, and sharing both with me and pressing me to help myself to his generous provision—if it was so, I say, then he was of an indescribable cruelty which it makes me cringe to think of, and I would prefer to believe that the impulse to bring about my death came from a sudden temptation springing from a sudden chance. And yet—God knows it is a difficult problem to settle!

For this was what it came to, and before sunset was reddening the western skies behind the Cheviots. We went a long, long way out—far beyond the thirty-fathom line, which is, as all sailors acquainted with those waters know, a good seven miles from shore; indeed, as I afterwards reckoned, we were more than twice that distance from Berwick pier-end when the affair happened—perhaps still further. We had been tacking about all the afternoon, first south, then north, not with any particular purpose, but aimlessly. We scarcely set eyes on another sail, and at a little after seven o'clock in the evening, when there was some talk of going about and catching the wind, which had changed a good deal since noon and was now coming more from the southeast, we were in the midst of a great waste of sea in which I could not make out a sign of any craft but ours—not even a trail of smoke on the horizon. The flat of the land had long since disappeared: the upper slopes of the Cheviots on one side of Tweed and of the Lammermoor Hills on the other, only just showed above the line of the sea. There was, I say, nothing visible on all that level of scarcely stirred water but our own sails, set to catch whatever breeze there was, when that happened which not only brought me to the very gates of death, but, in the mere doing of it, gave me the greatest horror of any that I have ever known.

I was standing up at the moment, one foot on the gunwale, the other on the planking behind me, carelessly balancing myself while I stared across the sea in search of some object which he—this man that I trusted so thoroughly and in whose company I had spent so many pleasant hours that afternoon, and who was standing behind me at the moment—professed to see in the distance, when he suddenly lurched against me, as if he had slipped and lost his footing. That was what I believed in that startling moment—but as I went head first overboard I was aware that his fall was confined to a sprawl into the scuppers. Overboard I went!— but he remained where he was. And my weight—I was weighing a good thirteen stone at that time, being a big and hefty youngster—carried me down and down into the green water, for I had been shot over the side with considerable impetus. And when I came up, a couple of boat's-lengths from the yacht, expecting to find that he was bringing her up so that I could scramble aboard, I saw with amazed and incredulous affright that he was doing nothing of the sort; instead, working at it as hard as he could go, he was letting out a couple of reefs which he had taken up in the mainsail an hour before—in another minute they were out, the yacht moved more swiftly, and, springing to the tiller, he deliberately steered her clear away from me.

I suppose I saw his purpose all at once. Perhaps it drove me wild, mad, frenzied. The yacht was going away from me fast—faster; good swimmer though I was, it was impossible for me to catch up to her—she was making her own length to every stroke I took, and as she drew away he stood there, one hand on the tiller, the other in his pocket (I have often wondered if it was fingering a revolver in there!), his eyes turned steadily on me. And I began first to beg and entreat him to save me, and then to shout out and curse him—and at that, and seeing that we were becoming further and further separated, he deliberately put the yacht still more before the freshening wind, and went swiftly away, and looked at me no more.

So he left me to drown.

We had been talking a lot about swimming during the afternoon, and I had told him that though I had been a swimmer ever since boyhood, I had never done more than a mile at a stretch, and then only in the river. He knew, therefore, that he was leaving me a good fourteen miles from land with not a sail in sight, not a chance of being picked up. Was it likely that I could make land?—was there ever a probability of anything coming along that would sight me? There was small likelihood, anyway; the likelihood was that long before the darkness had come on I should be exhausted, give up, and go down.

You may conceive with what anger, and with what fierce resentment, I watched this man and his yacht going fast away from me—and with what despair too. But even in that moment I was conscious of two facts—I now knew that yonder was the probable murderer of both Phillips and Crone, and that he was leaving me to die because I was the one person living who could throw some light on those matters, and, though I had kept silence up to then, might be tempted, or induced, or obliged to do so—he would silence me while he had so good a chance. And the other was, that although there seemed about as much likelihood of my ever seeing Berwick again as of being made King of England, I must do my utmost to save my strength and my life. I had a wealth of incentives—Maisie, my mother, Mr. Lindsey, youth, the desire to live; and now there was another added to them—the desire to circumvent that cold-hearted, cruel devil, who, I was now sure, had all along been up to some desperate game, and to have my revenge and see justice done on him. I was not going to give in without making a fight for it.

But it was a poor chance that I had—and I was well aware of it. There was small prospect of fishing boats or the like coming out that evening; small likelihood of any coasting steamer sighting a bit of a speck like me. All the same, I was going to keep my chin up as long as possible, and the first thing to do was to take care of my strength. I made shift to divest myself of a heavy pea-jacket that I was wearing and of the unnecessary clothing beneath it; I got rid, too, of my boots. And after resting a bit on my back and considering matters, I decided to make a try for land—I might perhaps meet some boat coming out. I lifted my head well up and took a glance at what I could see—and my heart sank at what I did see! The yacht was a speck in the distance by that time, and far beyond it the Cheviots and the Lammermoors were mere bits of grey outline against the gold and crimson of the sky. One thought instantly filled and depressed me—I was further from land than

I had believed.

At this distance from it I have but confused and vague recollections of that night. Sometimes I dream of it—even now—and wake sweating with fear. In those dreams I am toiling and toiling through a smooth sea—it is always a smooth, oily, slippery sea—towards something to which I make no great headway. Sometimes I give up toiling through sheer and desperate aching of body and limbs, and let myself lie drifting into helplessness and a growing sleep. And then—in my dream—I start to find myself going down into strange cavernous depths of shining green, and I wake—in my dream—to begin fighting and toiling again against my compelling desire to give up.

I do not know how long I made a fight of it in reality; it must have been for hours—alternately swimming, alternately resting myself by floating. I had queer thoughts. It was then about the time that some men were attempting to swim the Channel. I remember laughing grimly, wishing them joy of their job—they were welcome to mine! I remember, too, that at last in the darkness I felt that I must give up, and said my prayers; and it was about that time, when I was beginning to feel a certain numbness of mind as well as weariness of body, that as I struck out in the mechanical and weakening fashion which I kept up from what little determination I had left, I came across my salvation—in the shape of a piece of wreckage that shoved itself against me in the blackness, as if it had been some faithful dog, pushing its nose into my hand to let me know it was there. It was no more than a square of grating, but it was heavy and substantial; and as I clung to and climbed on to it, I knew that it made all the difference to me between life and death.

CHAPTER XX

THE SAMARITAN SKIPPER

I clung to that heaven-sent bit of wreckage, exhausted and weary, until the light began to break in the east. I was numbed and shivering with cold—but I was alive and safe. That square yard of good and solid wood was as much to me as if it had been a floating island. And as the light grew and grew, and the sun at last came up, a ball of fire out of the far horizon, I looked across the sea on all sides, hoping to catch sight of a sail, or of a wisp of smoke—of anything that would tell me of the near presence of human beings. And one fact I realized at once—I was further away from land than when I had begun my battle with death. There was no sign of land in the west. The sky was now clear and bright on all sides, but there was nothing to break the line where it met the sea. Before the fading of the light on the previous evening, I had easily made out the well-known outlines of the Cheviots on one hand and of Says Law on the other—now there was not a vestige of either. I knew from that fact that I had somehow drifted further and further away from the coast. There was accordingly nothing to do but wait the chance of being sighted and picked up, and I set to work, as well as I could on my tiny raft, to chafe my limbs and get some warmth into my body. And never in my life did I bless the sun as I did that morning, for when he sprang out of bed in the northeast skies, it was with his full and hearty vigour of high springtide, and his heat warmed my chilled blood and sent a new glow of hope to my heart. But that heat was not an unmixed blessing—and I was already parched with thirst; and as the sun mounted higher and higher, pouring his rays full upon me, the thirst became almost intolerable, and my tongue felt as if my mouth could no longer contain it.

It was, perhaps, one hour after sunrise, when my agony was becoming almost insupportable, that I first noticed a wisp of smoke on the southern rim of the circle of sea which just then was all my world. I never strained my eyes for anything as I did for that patch of grey against the cloudless blue! It grew bigger and bigger—I knew, of course, that it was some steamer, gradually approaching. But it seemed ages before I could make out her funnels; ages before I saw the first bit of her black bulk show up above the level of the dancing waves. Yet there she was at last—coming bows on, straight in my direction. My nerves must have given out at the sight—I remember the tears rolling down my cheeks; I remember hearing myself make strange sounds, which I suppose were those of relief and thankfulness. And then the horror of being unseen, of being left to endure more tortures of thirst, of the steamer changing her course, fell on me, and long before she was anywhere near me I was trying to balance myself on the grating, so that I could stand erect and attract her attention.

She was a very slow-going craft that—not able to do more than nine or ten knots at best—and another hour passed before she was anywhere near me. But, thank God! she came within a mile of me, and I made shift to stand up on my raft and to wave to her. And thereon she altered her course and lumbered over in my direction. She was one of the ugliest vessels that ever left a shipyard, but I thought I had never seen anything so beautiful in my life as she looked in those moments, and I had certainly never been so thankful for anything as for her solid and dirty deck when willing and kindly hands helped me up on it.

Half an hour after that, with dry clothes on me, and hot coffee and rum inside me, I was closeted with the skipper in his cabin, telling him, under a strict pledge of secrecy, as much of my tale as I felt inclined to share with him. He was a sympathetic and an understanding man, and he swore warmly and plentifully when he heard how treacherously I had been treated, intimating it as the—just then—dearest wish of his heart to have the handling of the man who had played me the trick.

"But you'll be dealing with him yourself!" said he. "Man!—you'll not spare him—promise me you'll not spare him! And you'll send me a newspaper with the full account of all that's done to him when you've set the law to work—dod! I hope they'll quarter him! Them was grand days when there was more licence and liberty in punishing malefactors—oh! I'd like fine to see this man put into boiling oil, or something of that sort, the cold-hearted, murdering villain! You'll be sure to send me the newspaper?"

I laughed—for the first time since—when? It seemed years since I had laughed—and yet it was only a few hours, after all.

"Before I can set the law to work on him, I must get on dry land, captain," I answered. "Where are you going?"

"Dundee," he replied. "Dundee—and we're just between sixty and seventy miles away now, and it's near seven o'clock. We'll be in Dundee early in the afternoon, anyway. And what'll you do there? You'll be for getting the next train to Berwick?"

"I'm not so sure, captain," I answered. "I don't want that man to know I'm alive—yet. It'll be a nice surprise for him—later. But there are those that I must let know as soon as possible—so the first thing I'll do, I'll wire. And in the meantime, let me have a sleep."

The steamer that had picked me up was nothing but a tramp, plodding along with a general cargo from London to Dundee, and its accommodation was as rough as its skipper was homely. But it was a veritable palace of delight and luxury to me after that terrible night, and I was soon hard and fast asleep in the skipper's own bunk—and was still asleep when he laid a hand on me at three o'clock that afternoon.

"We're in the Tay," he said, "and we'll dock in half an hour. And now—you can't go ashore in your underclothing, man! And where's your purse?"

He had rightly sized up the situation. I had got rid of everything but my singlet and drawers in the attempt to keep going; as for my purse, that was where the rest of my possessions were—sunk or floating.

"You and me's about of a build," he remarked. "I'll fit you up with a good suit that I have, and lend you what money you want. But what is it you're going to do?"

"How long are you going to stop here in Dundee, captain?" I asked.

"Four days," he answered. "I'll be discharging tomorrow, and loading the next two days, and then I'll be away again."

"Lend me the clothes and a sovereign," said I. "I'll wire to my principal, the gentleman I told you about, to come here at once with clothes and money, so I'll repay you and hand your suit back first thing tomorrow morning, when I'll bring him to see you."

He immediately pulled a sovereign out of his pocket, and, turning to a locker, produced a new suit of blue serge and some necessary linen.

"Aye?" he remarked, a bit wonderingly. "You'll be for fetching him along here, then? And for what purpose?"

"I want him to take your evidence about picking me up," I answered. "That's one thing—and—there's other reasons that we'll tell you about afterwards. And—don't tell anybody here of what's happened, and pass the word for silence to your crew. It'll be something in their pockets when my friend comes along."

He was a cute man, and he understood that my object was to keep the news of my escape from Sir Gilbert Carstairs, and he promised to do what I asked. And before long—he and I being, as he had observed, very much of a size, and the serge suit fitting me very well—I was in the streets of Dundee, where I had never been before, seeking out a telegraph office, and twiddling the skipper's sovereign between thumb and finger while I worked out a problem that needed some little thought.

I must let my mother and Maisie know of my safety—at once. I must let Mr. Lindsey know, too. I knew what must have happened there at Berwick. That monstrous villain would sneak home and say that a sad accident had happened me. It made me grind my teeth and long to get my hands at his lying tongue when I thought of what Maisie and my mother must have suffered after hearing his tales and excuses. But I did not want him to know I was safe—I did not want the town to know. Should I telephone to Mr. Lindsey's office, it was almost certain one of my fellow-clerks there would answer the ring, and recognize my voice. Then everything would be noised around. And after thinking it all over I sent Mr. Lindsey a telegram in the following words, hoping that he would fully understand:—

"Keep this secret from everybody. Bring suit of clothes, linen, money, mother, and Maisie by next train to Dundee. Give post-office people orders not to let this out, most important. H.M."

I read that over half a dozen times before I finally dispatched it. It seemed all wrong, somehow—and all right in another way. And, however badly put it was, it expressed my meaning. So I handed it in, and my borrowed sovereign with it, and jingling the change which was given back to me, I went out of the telegraph office to stare around me.

It was a queer thing, but I was now as light-hearted as could be—I caught myself laughing from a curious feeling of pleasure. The truth was—if you want to analyse the sources—I was vastly relieved to be able to get in touch with my own people. Within an hour, perhaps sooner, they would have the news, and I knew well that they would lose no time in setting off to me. And finding myself just then in the neighbourhood of the North British Railway Station, I went in and managed to make out that if Mr. Lindsey was at the office when my wire arrived, and acted promptly in accordance with it, he and they could reach Dundee by a late train that evening. That knowledge, of course, made me in a still more light-hearted mood. But there was another source of my satisfaction and complaisance: things were in a grand way now for my revenge on Sir Gilbert Carstairs, and what had been a mystery was one no longer.

I went back to the dock where I had left the tramp-steamer, and told its good-natured skipper what I had done, for he was as much interested in the affair as if he had been my own brother. And that accomplished, I left him again and went sight-seeing, having been wonderfully freshened up and restored by my good sleep of the morning. I wandered up and down and about Dundee till I was leg-weary, and it was nearly six o'clock of the afternoon. And at that time, being in Bank Street, and looking about me for some place where I could get a cup of tea and a bite of food, I chanced by sheer accident to see a name on a brass plate, fixed amongst more of the same sort, on the outer door of a suite of offices. That name was Gavin Smeaton. I recalled it at once—and, moved by a sudden impulse, I went climbing up a lot of steps to Mr. Gavin Smeaton's office.

CHAPTER XXI

MR. GAVIN SMEATON

I walked into a room right at the top of the building, wherein a young man of thirty or thereabouts was sitting at a desk, putting together a quantity of letters which a lad, standing at his side, was evidently about to carry to the post. He was a good-looking, alert, businesslike sort of young man this, of a superior type of countenance, very well dressed, and altogether a noticeable person. What first struck me about him was, that though he gave me a quick glance when, having first tapped at his door and walked inside his office, I stood there confronting him, he finished his immediate concern before giving me any further attention. It was not until he had given all the letters to the lad and bade him hurry off to the post, that he turned to me with another sharp look and one word of interrogation.

"Yes?" he said.

"Mr. Gavin Smeaton?" asked I.

"That's my name," he answered. "What can I do for you?"

Up to that moment I had not the least idea as to the exact reasons which had led me to climb those stairs. The truth was I had acted on impulse. And now that I was actually in the presence of a man who was obviously a very businesslike and matter-of-fact sort of person, I felt awkward and tongue-tied. He was looking me over all the time as if there was a wonder in his mind about me, and when I was slow in answering he stirred a bit impatiently in his chair.

"My business hours are over for the day," he said. "If it's business—"

"It's not business in the ordinary sense, Mr. Smeaton," I made shift to get out. "But it is business for all that. The fact is—you'll remember that the Berwick police sent you a telegram some days ago asking did you know anything about a man named John Phillips?"

He showed a sudden interest at that, and he regarded me with a slight smile.

"You aren't a detective?" he inquired.

"No—I'm a solicitor's clerk," I replied. "From Berwick—my principal, Mr. Lindsey, has to do with that case."

He nodded at a pile of newspapers, which stood, with a heavy book on top of it, on a side table near his desk.

"So I see from these papers," he remarked. "I've read all I could about the affairs of both Phillips and Crone, ever since I heard that my name and address had been found on Phillips. Has any further light been thrown on that? Of course, there was nothing much in my name and address being found on the man, nor would there be if they were found on any man. As you see, I'm a general agent for various sorts of foreign merchandise, and this man had likely been recommended to me—especially if he was from America."

"There's been no further light on that matter, Mr. Smeaton," I answered. He had pointed me to a chair at his desk side by that time, and we were mutually inspecting each other. "Nothing more has been heard on that point."

"Then—have you come purposely to see me about it?" he asked.

"Not at all!" said I. "I was passing along this street below, and I saw your name on the door, and I remembered it—and so I just came up."

"Oh!" he said, looking at me rather blankly. "You're staying in Dundee—taking a holiday?"

"I came to Dundee in a fashion I'd not like to follow on any other occasion!" said I. "If a man hadn't lent me this suit of clothes and a sovereign, I'd have come ashore in my undergarments and without a penny."

He stared at me more blankly than ever when I let this out on him, and suddenly he laughed.

"What riddle's all this?" he asked. "It sounds like a piece out of a story-book— one of those tales of adventure."

"Aye, does it?" said I. "Only, in my case, Mr. Smeaton, fact's been a lot stranger than fiction! You've read all about this Berwick mystery in the newspapers?"

"Every word—seeing that I was mentioned," he answered.

"Then I'll give you the latest chapter," I continued. "You'll know my name when you hear it—Hugh Moneylaws. It was I discovered Phillips's dead body."

I saw that he had been getting more and more interested as we talked—at the mention of my name his interest obviously increased. And suddenly he pulled a box of cigars towards him, took one out, and pushed the box to me.

"Help yourself, Mr. Moneylaws—and go ahead," he said. "I'm willing to hear as many chapters as you like of this story."

I shook my head at the cigars and went on to tell him of all that had happened since the murder of Crone. He was a good listener—he took in every detail, every point, quietly smoking while I talked, and never interrupting me. And when I had made an end, he threw up his head with a significant gesture that implied much.

"That beats all the story-books!" he exclaimed. "I'm glad to see you're safe, anyway, Mr. Moneylaws—and your mother and your young lady'll be glad too."

"They will that, Mr. Smeaton," I said. "I'm much obliged to you."

"You think that man really meant you to drown?" he asked.

"What would you think yourself, Mr. Smeaton?" I replied. "Besides—didn't I see his face as he got himself and his yacht away from me? Yon man is a murder-er!"

"It's a queer, strange business," he remarked, nodding his head. "You'll be thinking now, of course, that it was he murdered both Phillips and Crone—eh?"

"Aye, I do think that!" said I. "What else? And he wanted to silence me because I'm the only living person that could let out about seeing him at the cross-roads that night and could prove that Crone saw him too. My own impression is that Crone went straight to him after his talk with me—and paid the penalty."

"That's likely," he assented. "But what do you think made him turn on you so suddenly, yesterday, when things looked like going smoothly about everything, and he'd given you that stewardship—which was, of course, to stop your mouth?"

"I'll tell you," I said. "It was Mr. Lindsey's fault—he let out too much at the po-lice-court. Carstairs was there—he'd a seat on the bench—and Mr. Lindsey fright-ened him. Maybe it was yon ice-ax. Mr. Lindsey's got some powerful card up his sleeve about that—what it is I don't know. But I'm certain now—now!—that Carstairs took a fear into his head at those proceedings yesterday morning, and he thought he'd settle me once and for all before I could be drawn into it and forced to say things that would be against him."

"I daresay you're right," he agreed. "Well!—it is indeed a strange affair, and there'll be some stranger revelations yet. I'd like to see this Mr. Lindsey—you're sure he'll come to you here?"

"Aye!—unless there's been an earthquake between here and Tweed!" I de-clared. "He'll be here, right enough, Mr. Smeaton, before many hours are over. And he'll like to see you. You can't think, now, of how, or why, yon Phillips man could have got that bit of letter paper of yours on him? It was like that," I added, pointing to a block of memorandum forms that stood in his stationery case at the desk before him. "Just the same!"

"I can't," said he. "But—there's nothing unusual in that; some correspondent of mine might have handed it to him—torn it off one of my letters, do you see? I've correspondents in a great many seaports and mercantile centres—both here and in America."

"These men will appear to have come from Central America," I remarked. "They'd seem to have been employed, one way or another, on that Panama Canal affair that there's been so much in the papers about these last few years. You'd notice that in the accounts, Mr. Smeaton?"

"I did," he replied. "And it interested me, because I'm from those parts my-self—I was born there."

He said that as if this fact was of no significance. But the news made me prick up my ears.

"Do you tell me that!" said I. "Where, now, if it's a fair question?"

"New Orleans—near enough, anyway, to those parts," he answered. "But I was sent across here when I was ten years old, to be educated and brought up, and here I've been ever since."

"But—you're a Scotsman?" I made bold to ask him.

"Aye—on both sides—though I was born out of Scotland," he answered with a laugh. And then he got out of his chair. "It's mighty interesting, all this," he went on. "But I'm a married man, and my wife'll be wanting dinner for me. Now, will you bring Mr. Lindsey to see me in the morning—if he comes?"

"He'll come—and I'll bring him," I answered. "He'll be right glad to see you, too—for it may be, Mr. Smeaton, that there is something to be traced out of that bit of letter paper of yours, yet."

"It may be," he agreed. "And if there's any help I can give, it's at your disposal. But you'll be finding this—you're in a dark lane, with some queer turnings in it, before you come to the plain outcome of all this business!"

We went down into the street together, and after he had asked if there was anything he could do for me that night, and I had assured him there was not, we parted with an agreement that Mr. Lindsey and I should call at his office early next morning. When he had left me, I sought out a place where I could get some supper, and, that over, I idled about the town until it was time for the train from the south to get in. And I was on the platform when it came, and there was my mother and Maisie and Mr. Lindsey, and I saw at a glance that all that was filling each was sheer and infinite surprise. My mother gripped me on the instant.

"Hugh!" she exclaimed. "What are you doing here, and what does all this mean? Such a fright as you've given us! What's the meaning of it?"

I was so taken aback, having been certain that Carstairs would have gone home and told them I was accidentally drowned, that all I could do was to stare from one to the other. As for Maisie, she only looked wonderingly at me; as for Mr. Lindsey, he gazed at me as scrutinizingly as my mother was doing.

"Aye!" said he, "what's the meaning of it, young man? We've done your bidding and more—but—why?"

I found my tongue at that.

"What!" I exclaimed. "Haven't you seen Sir Gilbert Carstairs? Didn't you hear from him that—"

"We know nothing about Sir Gilbert Carstairs," he interrupted. "The fact is, my lad, that until your wire arrived this afternoon, nobody had even heard of you and Sir Gilbert Carstairs since you went off in his yacht yesterday. Neither he nor the yacht have ever returned to Berwick. Where are they?"

CHAPTER XXII
I READ MY OWN OBITUARY

It was my turn to stare again—and stare I did, from one to the other in silence, and being far too much amazed to find ready speech. And before I could get my tongue once more, my mother, who was always remarkably sharp of eye, got her word in.

"What're you doing in that new suit of clothes?" she demanded. "And where's your own good clothes that you went away in yesterday noon? I misdoubt this stewardship's leading you into some strange ways!"

"My own good clothes, mother, are somewhere in the North Sea," retorted I. "Top or bottom, sunk or afloat, it's there you'll find them, if you're more anxious about them than me! Do you tell me that Carstairs has never been home?" I went on, turning to Mr. Lindsey, "Then I don't know where he is, nor his yacht either. All I know is that he left me to drown last night, a good twenty miles from land, and that it's only by a special mercy of Providence that I'm here. Wherever he is, yon man's a murderer—I've settled that, Mr. Lindsey!"

The women began to tremble and to exclaim at this news, and to ask one question after another, and Mr. Lindsey shook his head impatiently.

"We can't stand talking our affairs in the station all night," said he. "Let's get to an hotel, my lad—we're all wanting our suppers. You don't seem as if you were in very bad spirits, yourself."

"I'm all right, Mr. Lindsey," I answered cheerfully. "I've been down to Jericho, it's true, and to worse, but I chanced across a good Samaritan or two. And I've looked out a clean and comfortable hotel for you, and we'll go there now."

I led them away to a good hotel that I had noticed in my walks, and while they took their suppers I sat by and told them all my adventure, to the accompaniment of many exclamations from my mother and Maisie. But Mr. Lindsey made none, and I was quick to notice that what most interested him was that I had been to see Mr. Gavin Smeaton.

"But what for did you not come straight home when you were safely on shore again?" asked my mother, who was thinking of the expense I was putting her to. "What's the reason of fetching us all this way when you're alive and well?"

I looked at Mr. Lindsey—knowingly, I suppose.

"Because, mother," I answered her, "I believed yon Carstairs would go back to Berwick and tell that there'd been a sad accident, and I was dead—drowned—and I wanted to let him go on thinking that I was dead—and so I decided to keep away. And if he is alive, it'll be the best thing to let the man still go on thinking I was drowned—as I'll prove to Mr. Lindsey there. If Carstairs is alive, I say, it's the right policy for me to keep out of his sight and our neighbourhood."

"Aye!" agreed Mr. Lindsey, who was a quick hand at taking up things. "There's something in that, Hugh."

"Well, it's beyond me, all this," observed my mother, "and it all comes of me taking yon Gilverthwaite into the house! But me and Maisie'll away to our beds, and maybe you and Mr. Lindsey'll get more light out of the matter than I can, and glad I'll be when all this mystery's cleared up and we'll be able to live as honest folk should, without all this flying about the country and spending good money."

I contrived to get a few minutes with Maisie, however, before she and my mother retired, and I found then that, had I known it, I need not have been so anxious and disturbed. For they had attached no particular importance to the fact that I had not returned the night before; they had thought that Sir Gilbert had sailed his yacht in elsewhere, and that I would be turning up later, and there had been no great to-do after me until my own telegram had arrived, when, of course, there was consternation and alarm, and nothing but hurry to catch the next train north. But Mr. Lindsey had contrived to find out that nothing had been seen of Sir Gilbert Carstairs and his yacht at Berwick; and to that point he and I at once turned when the women had gone to bed and I went with him into the smoking-room while he had his pipe and his drop of whisky. By that time I had told him of the secret about the meeting at the cross-roads, and about my interview with Crone at his shop, and Sir Gilbert Carstairs at Hathercleugh, when he offered me the stewardship; and I was greatly relieved when Mr. Lindsey let me down lightly and said no more than that if I'd told him these things, at first, there might have been a great difference.

"But we're on the beginning of something," he concluded. "That Sir Gilbert Carstairs has some connection with these murders, I'm now convinced—but what it is, I'm not yet certain. What I am certain about is that he took fright yesterday morning in our court, when I produced that ice-ax and asked the doctor those questions about it."

"And I'm sure of that, too, Mr. Lindsey," said I. "And I've been wondering what there was about yon ice-ax that frightened him. You'll know that yourself, of course?"

"Aye, but I'm not going to tell you!" he answered. "You'll have to await developments on that point, my man. And now we'll be getting to bed, and in the morning we'll see this Mr. Gavin Smeaton. It would be a queer thing now, wouldn't it, if we got some clue to all this through him? But I'm keenly interested in hearing that he comes from the other side of the Atlantic, Hugh, for I've been of opinion that it's across there that the secret of the whole thing will be found."

They had brought me a supply of clothes and money with them, and first thing in the morning I went off to the docks and found my Samaritan skipper, and gave him back his sovereign and his blue serge suit, with my heartiest thanks and a promise to keep him fully posted up in the development of what he called the case. And then I went back to breakfast with the rest of them, and at once there was the question of what was to be done. My mother was all for going homeward as quickly as possible, and it ended up in our seeing her and Maisie away by the next train; Mr. Lindsey having made both swear solemnly that they would not divulge one word of what had happened, nor reveal the fact that I was alive, to any living soul but Andrew Dunlop, who, of course, could be trusted. And my mother agreed, though the proposal was anything but pleasant or proper to her.

"You're putting on me more than any woman ought to be asked to bear, Mr. Lindsey," said she, as we saw them into the train. "You're asking me to go home and behave as if we didn't know whether the lad was alive or dead. I'm not good at the playacting, and I'm far from sure that it's either truthful or honest to be professing things that isn't so. And I'll be much obliged to you if you'll get all this cleared up, and let Hugh there settle down to his work in the proper way, instead of wandering about on business that's no concern of his."

We shook our heads at each other as the train went off, Maisie waving goodbye to us, and my mother sitting very stiff and stern and disapproving in her corner of the compartment.

"No concern of yours, d'ye hear, my lad?" laughed Mr. Lindsey. "Aye, but your mother forgets that in affairs of this sort a lot of people are drawn in where they aren't concerned! It's like being on the edge of a whirlpool—you're dragged into it before you're aware. And now we'll go and see this Mr. Smeaton; but first, where's the telegraph office in this station? I want to wire to Murray, to ask him to keep me posted up during today if any news comes in about the yacht."

When Mr. Lindsey was in the telegraph office, I bought that morning's *Dundee Advertiser*, more to fill up a few spare moments than from any particular desire to get the news, for I was not a great newspaper reader. I had scarcely opened it when I saw my own name. And there I stood, in the middle of the bustling railway station, enjoying the sensation of reading my own obituary notice.

"Our Berwick-on-Tweed correspondent, telegraphing late last night, says:— Considerable anxiety is being felt in the town respecting the fate of Sir Gilbert Carstairs, Bart., of Hathercleugh House, and Mr. Hugh Moneylaws, who are feared to have suffered a disaster at sea. At noon yesterday, Sir Gilbert, accompanied by Mr. Moneylaws, went out in the former's yacht (a small vessel of light weight) for a sail which, according to certain fishermen who were about when the yacht left, was to be one of a few hours only. The yacht had not returned last night, nor has it been seen or heard of since its departure. Various Berwick fishing craft have been out well off the coast during today, but no tidings of the missing gentlemen have come to hand. Nothing has been heard of, or from, Sir Gilbert at Hathercleugh up to nine o'clock this evening, and the only ray of hope lies in the fact that Mr. Moneylaws' mother left the town hurriedly this afternoon—possibly having received some news of her son. It is believed here, however, that the light vessel was capsized in a sudden squall, and that both occupants have lost their lives. Sir Gilbert Carstairs, who was the seventh baronet, had only recently come to the neighbourhood on succeeding to the title and estates. Mr. Moneylaws, who was senior clerk to Mr. Lindsey, solicitor, of Berwick, was a very promising young man of great ability, and had recently been much before the public eye as a witness in connection with the mysterious murders of John Phillips and Abel Crone, which are still attracting so much attention."

I shoved the newspaper into Mr. Lindsey's hand as he came out of the telegraph office. He read the paragraph in silence, smiling as he read.

"Aye!" he said at last, "you have to leave home to get the home news. Well—they're welcome to be thinking that for the present. I've just wired Murray that I'll be here till at any rate this evening, and that he's to telegraph at once if there's tidings of that yacht or of Carstairs. Meanwhile, well go and see this Mr. Smeaton."

Mr. Smeaton was expecting us—he, too, was reading about me in the *Advertiser* when we entered, and he made some joking remark about it only being great men that were sometimes treated to death-notices before they were dead. And then he turned to Mr. Lindsey, who I noticed had been taking close stock of him.

"I've been thinking out things since Mr. Moneylaws was in here last night," he remarked. "Bringing my mind to bear, do you see, on certain points that I hadn't thought of before. And maybe there's something more than appears at first sight in yon man John Phillips having my name and address on him."

"Aye?" asked Mr. Lindsey, quietly. "How, now?"

"Well," replied Mr. Smeaton, "there may be something in it, and there may be nothing—just nothing at all. But it's the fact that my father hailed from Tweedside—and from some place not so far from Berwick."

CHAPTER XXIII

FAMILY HISTORY

I was watching Mr. Lindsey pretty closely, being desirous of seeing how he took to Mr. Gavin Smeaton, and what he made of him, and I saw him prick his ears at this announcement; clearly, it seemed to suggest something of interest to him.

"Aye?" he exclaimed. "Your father hailed from Berwick, or thereabouts? You don't know exactly from where, Mr. Smeaton?"

"No, I don't," replied Smeaton, promptly. "The truth is, strange as it may seem, Mr. Lindsey, I know precious little about my father, and what I do know is mostly from hearsay. I've no recollection of having ever seen him. And—more wondrous still, you'll say—I don't know whether he's alive or dead!"

Here, indeed, was something that bordered on the mysterious; and Mr. Lindsey and myself, who had been dealing in that commodity to some considerable degree of late, exchanged glances. And Smeaton saw us look at each other, and he smiled and went on.

"I was thinking all this out last night," he said, "and it came to me—I wonder if that man, John Phillips, who had, as I hear, my name and address in his pocket, could have been some man who was coming to see me on my father's behalf, or— it's an odd thing to fancy, and, considering what's happened him, not a pleasant one!—could have been my father himself?"

There was silence amongst us for a moment. This was a new vista down which we were looking, and it was full of thick shadow. As for me, I began to recollect things. According to the evidence which Chisholm had got from the British Linen Bank at Peebles, John Phillips had certainly come from Panama. Just as certainly he had made for Tweedside. And—with equal certainty—nobody at all had come forward to claim him, to assert kinship with him, though there had been the widest publicity given to the circumstances of his murder. In Gilverthwaite's instance, his sister had quickly turned up—to see what there was for her. Phillips had been just as freely mentioned in the newspapers as Gilverthwaite; but no one had made inquiries after him, though there was a tidy sum of money of his in the Peebles bank for his next-of-kin to claim. Who was he, then?

Mr. Lindsey was evidently deep in thought, or, I should perhaps say, in surmise. And he seemed to arrive where I did—at a question; which was, of course, just that which Smeaton had suggested.

"I might answer that better if I knew what you could tell me about your father,

Mr. Smeaton," he said. "And—about yourself."

"I'll tell you all I can, with pleasure," answered Smeaton. "To tell you the truth, I never attached much importance to this matter, in spite of my name and address being found on Phillips, until Mr. Moneylaws there came in last night—and then, after what he told me, I did begin to think pretty deeply over it, and I'm coming to the opinion that there's a lot more in all this than appears on the surface."

"You can affirm that with confidence!" remarked Mr. Lindsey, drily. "There is!"

"Well—about my father," continued Smeaton. "All I know is this—and I got it from hearsay: His name—the name given to me, anyway—was Martin Smeaton. He hailed from somewhere about Berwick. Whether it was on the English side or the Scottish side of the Tweed I don't know. But he went to America as a young man, with a young wife, and they were in New Orleans when I was born. And when I was born, my mother died. So I never saw her."

"Do you know her maiden name?" asked Mr. Lindsey.

"No more than that her Christian name was Mary," replied Smeaton. "You'll find out as I go on that it's very little I do know of anything—definitely. Well, when my mother died, my father evidently left New Orleans and went off travelling. I've made out that he must have been a regular rolling stone at all times—a man that couldn't rest long in one place. But he didn't take me with him. There was a Scotsman and his wife in New Orleans that my father had forgathered with—some people of the name of Watson,—and he left me with them, and in their care in New Orleans I remained till I was ten years old. From my recollection he evidently paid them well for looking after me—there was never, at any time, any need of money on my account. And of course, never having known any other, I came to look on the Watsons as father and mother. When I was ten years old they returned to Scotland—here to Dundee, and I came with them. I have a letter or two that my father wrote at that time giving instructions as to what was to be done with me. I was to have the best education—as much as I liked and was capable of—and, though I didn't then, and don't now, know all the details, it's evident he furnished Watson with plenty of funds on my behalf. We came here to Dundee, and I was put to the High School, and there I stopped till I was eighteen, and then I had two years at University College. Now, the odd thing was that all that time, though I knew that regular and handsome remittances came to the Watsons on my behalf from my father, he never expressed any wishes, or made any suggestions, as to what I should do with myself. But I was all for commercial life; and when I left college, I went into an office here in the town and began to study the ins and outs of foreign trade. Then, when I was just twenty-one, my father sent me a considerable sum—two thousand pounds, as a matter of fact—saying it was for me to start business with. And, do you know, Mr. Lindsey, from that day—now ten years ago—to this, I've never heard a word of him."

Mr. Lindsey was always an attentive man in a business interview, but I had never seen him listen to anybody so closely as he listened to Mr. Smeaton. And after his usual fashion, he at once began to ask questions.

"Those Watsons, now," he said. "They're living?"

"No," replied Smeaton. "Both dead—a few years ago."

"That's a pity," remarked Mr. Lindsey. "But you'll have recollections of what they told you about your father from their own remembrance of him?"

"They'd little to tell," said Smeaton. "I made out they knew very little indeed of him, except that he was a tall, fine-looking fellow, evidently of a superior class and education. Of my mother they knew less."

"You'll have letters of your father's?" suggested Mr. Lindsey.

"Just a few mere scraps—he was never a man who did more than write down what he wanted doing, and as briefly as possible," replied Smeaton. "In fact," he added, with a laugh, "his letters to me were what you might call odd. When the money came that I mentioned just now, he wrote me the shortest note—I can repeat every word of it: 'I've sent Watson two thousand pounds for you,' he wrote. 'You can start yourself in business with it, as I hear you're inclined that way, and some day I'll come over and see how you're getting along.' That was all!"

"And you've never heard of or from him since?" exclaimed Mr. Lindsey. "That's a strange thing, now. But—where was he then? Where did he send the money from?"

"New York," replied Smeaton. "The other letters I have from him are from places in both North and South America. It always seemed to me and the Watsons that he was never in any place for long—always going about."

"I should like to see those letters, Mr. Smeaton," said Mr. Lindsey. "Especially the last one."

"They're at my house," answered Smeaton. "I'll bring them down here this afternoon, and show them to you if you'll call in. But now—do you think this man Phillips may have been my father?"

"Well," replied Mr. Lindsey, reflectively, "it's an odd thing that Phillips, whoever he was, drew five hundred pounds in cash out of the British Linen Bank at Peebles, and carried it straight away to Tweedside—where you believe your father came from. It looks as if Phillips had meant to do something with that cash—to give it to somebody, you know."

"I read the description of Phillips in the newspapers," remarked Smeaton. "But, of course, it conveyed nothing to me."

"You've no photograph of your father?" asked Mr. Lindsey.

"No—none—never had," answered Smeaton. "Nor any papers of his—except those bits of letters."

Mr. Lindsey sat in silence for a time, tapping the point of his stick on the floor and staring at the carpet.

"I wish we knew what that man Gilverthwaite was wanting at Berwick and in the district!" he said at last.

"But isn't that evident?" suggested Smeaton. "He was looking in the parish registers. I've a good mind to have a search made in those quarters for particulars of my father."

Mr. Lindsey gave him a sharp look.

"Aye!" he said, in a rather sly fashion. "But—you don't know if your father's real name was Smeaton!"

Both Smeaton and myself started at that—it was a new idea. And I saw that it struck Smeaton with great force.

"True!" he replied, after a pause. "I don't! It might have been. And in that case—how could one find out what it was?"

Mr. Lindsey got up, shaking his head.

"A big job!" he answered. "A stiff job! You'd have to work back a long way. But—it could be done. What time can I look in this afternoon, Mr. Smeaton, to get a glance at those letters?"

"Three o'clock," replied Smeaton. He walked to the door of his office with us, and he gave me a smile. "You're none the worse for your adventure, I see," he remarked. "Well, what about this man Carstairs—what news of him?"

"We'll maybe be able to tell you some later in the day," replied Mr. Lindsey. "There'll be lots of news about him, one way or another, before we're through with all this."

We went out into the street then, and at his request I took Mr. Lindsey to the docks, to see the friendly skipper, who was greatly delighted to tell the story of my rescue. We stopped on his ship talking with him for a good part of the morning, and it was well past noon when we went back to the hotel for lunch. And the first thing we saw there was a telegram for Mr. Lindsey. He tore the envelope open as we stood in the hall, and I made no apology for looking over his shoulder and reading the message with him.

"Just heard by wire from Largo police that small yacht answering description of Carstairs' has been brought in there by fishermen who found it early this morning in Largo Bay, empty."

We looked at each other. And Mr. Lindsey suddenly laughed.

"Empty!" he exclaimed. "Aye!—but that doesn't prove that the man's dead!"

CHAPTER XXIV

THE SUIT OF CLOTHES

Mr. Lindsey made no further remark until we were half through our lunch — and it was not to me that he then spoke, but to a waiter who was just at his elbow.

"There's three things you can get me," he said. "Our bill — a railway guide — a map of Scotland. Bring the map first."

The man went away, and Mr. Lindsey bent across the table.

"Largo is in Fife," said he. "We'll go there. I'm going to see that yacht with my own eyes, and hear with my own ears what the man who found it has got to say. For, as I remarked just now, my lad, the mere fact that the yacht was found empty doesn't prove that Carstairs has been drowned! And we'll just settle up here, and go round and see Smeaton to get a look at those letters, and then we'll take train to Largo and make a bit of inquiry."

Mr. Smeaton had the letters spread out on his desk when we went in, and Mr. Lindsey looked them over. There were not more than half a dozen altogether, and they were mere scraps, as he had said — usually a few lines on half-sheets of paper. Mr. Lindsey appeared to take no great notice of any of them but the last — the one that Smeaton had quoted to us in the morning. But over that he bent for some time, examining it closely, in silence.

"I wish you'd lend me this for a day or two," he said at last. "I'll take the greatest care of it; it shan't go out of my own personal possession, and I'll return it by registered post. The fact is, Mr. Smeaton, I want to compare that writing with some other writing."

"Certainly," agreed Smeaton, handing the letter over. "I'll do anything I can to help. I'm beginning, you know, Mr. Lindsey, to fear I'm mixed up in this. You'll keep me informed?"

"I can give you some information now," answered Mr. Lindsey, pulling out the telegram. "There's more mystery, do you see? And Moneylaws and I are off to Largo now — we'll take it on our way home. For by this and that, I'm going to know what's become of Sir Gilbert Carstairs!"

We presently left Mr. Gavin Smeaton, with a promise to keep him posted up, and a promise on his part that he'd come to Berwick, if that seemed necessary; and then we set out on our journey. It was not such an easy business to get quickly to Largo, and the afternoon was wearing well into evening when we reached it, and found the police official who had wired to Berwick. There was not much that he could tell us, of his own knowledge. The yacht, he said, was now lying in the harbour at Lower Largo, where it had been brought in by a fisherman named Andrew Robertson, to whom he offered to take us. Him we found at a little inn, near the harbour—a taciturn, somewhat sour-faced fellow who showed no great desire to talk, and would probably have given us scant information if we had not been accompanied by the police official, though he brightened up when Mr. Lindsey hinted at the possibility of reward.

"When did you come across this yacht?" asked Mr. Lindsey.

"Between eight and nine o'clock this morning," replied Robertson.

"And where?"

"About seven miles out—a bit outside the bay."

"Empty?" demanded Mr. Lindsey, looking keenly at the man. "Not a soul in her?"

"Not a soul!" answered Robertson. "Neither alive nor dead!"

"Were her sails set at all?" asked Mr. Lindsey.

"They were not. She was just drifting—anywhere," replied the man. "And I put a line to her and brought her in."

"Any other craft than yours about at the time?" inquired Mr. Lindsey.

"Not within a few miles," said Robertson.

We went off to the yacht then. She had been towed into a quiet corner of the harbour, and an old fellow who was keeping guard over her assured us that nobody but the police had been aboard her since Robertson brought her in. We, of course, went aboard, Mr. Lindsey, after being assured by me that this really was Sir Gilbert Carstairs' yacht, remarking that he didn't know we could do much good by doing so. But I speedily made a discovery of singular and significant importance. Small as she was, the yacht possessed a cabin—there was no great amount of head-room in it, it's true, and a tall man could not stand upright in it, but it was spacious for a craft of that size, and amply furnished with shelving and lockers. And on these lockers lay the clothes—a Norfolk suit of grey tweed—in which Sir Gilbert Carstairs had set out with me from Berwick.

I let out a fine exclamation when I saw that, and the other three turned and stared at me.

"Mr. Lindsey!" said I, "look here! Those are the clothes he was wearing when I saw the last of him. And there's the shirt he had on, too, and the shoes. Wherever he is, and whatever happened to him, he made a complete change of linen and clothing before he quitted the yacht! That's a plain fact, Mr. Lindsey!"

A fact it was—and one that made me think, however it affected the others. It disposed, for instance, of any notion or theory of suicide. A man doesn't change his clothes if he's going to drown himself. And it looked as if this had been part of some premeditated plan: at the very least of it, it was a curious thing.

"You're sure of that?" inquired Mr. Lindsey, eyeing the things that had been thrown aside.

"Dead sure of it!" said I. "I couldn't be mistaken."

"Did he bring a portmanteau or anything aboard with him, then?" asked he.

"He didn't; but he could have kept clothes and linen and the like in these lockers," I pointed out, beginning to lift the lids. "See here!—here's brushes and combs and the like. I tell you before ever he left this yacht, or fell out of it, or whatever's happened him, he'd changed everything from his toe to his top—there's the very cap he was wearing."

They all looked at each other, and Mr. Lindsey's gaze finally fastened itself on Andrew Robertson.

"I suppose you don't know anything about this, my friend?" he asked.

"What should I know?" answered Robertson, a bit surlily. "The yacht's just as I found it—not a thing's been touched."

There was the luncheon basket lying on the cabin table—just as I had last seen it, except that Carstairs had evidently finished the provisions which he and I had left. And I think the same thought occurred to Mr. Lindsey and myself at the same moment—how long had he stopped on board that yacht after his cruel abandoning of me? For forty-eight hours had elapsed since that episode, and in forty-eight hours a man may do a great deal in the way of making himself scarce—which now seemed to me to be precisely what Sir Gilbert Carstairs had done, though in what particular fashion, and exactly why, it was beyond either of us to surmise.

"I suppose no one has heard anything of this yacht having been seen drifting about yesterday, or during last night?" asked Mr. Lindsey, putting his question to both men. "No talk of it hereabouts?"

But neither the police nor Andrew Robertson had heard a murmur of that nature, and there was evidently nothing to be got out of them more than we had already got. Nor had the police heard of any stranger being seen about there—though, as the man who was with us observed, there was no great likelihood of anybody noticing a stranger, for Largo was nowadays a somewhat popular seaside resort, and down there on the beach there were many strangers, it being summer, and holiday time, so that a strange man more or less would pass unobserved.

"Supposing a man landed about the coast, here," asked Mr. Lindsey—"I'm just putting a case to you—and didn't go into the town, but walked along the beach—where would he strike a railway station, now?"

The police official replied that there were railway stations to the right and left of the bay—a man could easily make Edinburgh in one direction, and St. Andrews in the other; and then, not unnaturally, he was wanting to know if Mr. Lindsey was suggesting that Sir Gilbert Carstairs had sailed his yacht ashore, left it, and that it had drifted out to sea again?

"I'm not suggesting anything," answered Mr. Lindsey. "I'm only speculating on possibilities. And that's about as idle work as standing here talking. What will be practical will be to arrange about this yacht being locked up in some boat-house, and we'd best see to that at once."

We made arrangements with the owner of a boat-house to pull the yacht in there, and to keep her under lock and key, and, after settling matters with the police to have an eye on her, and see that her contents were untouched until further instructions reached them from Berwick, we went off to continue our journey. But we had stayed so long in Largo that when we got to Edinburgh the last train for Berwick had gone, and we were obliged to turn into an hotel for the night. Naturally, all our talk was of what had just transpired—the events of the last two days, said Mr. Lindsey, only made these mysteries deeper than they were before, and why Sir Gilbert Carstairs should have abandoned his yacht, as he doubtless had, was a still further addition to the growing problem.

"And I'm not certain, my lad, that I believe yon man Robertson's tale," he remarked, as we were discussing matters from every imaginable point of view just before going to bed. "He may have brought the yacht in, but we don't know that he didn't bring Carstairs aboard her. Why was that change of clothes made? Probably because he knew that he'd be described as wearing certain things, and he wanted to come ashore in other things. For aught we know, he came safely ashore, boarded a train somewhere in the neighbourhood, or at Largo itself—why not?— and went off, likely here, to Edinburgh—where he'd mingle with a few thousand of folk, unnoticed."

"Then—in that case, you think he's—what, Mr. Lindsey?" I asked. "Do you mean he's running away?"

"Between you and me, that's not far from what I do think," he replied. "And I think I know what he's running away from, too! But we'll hear a lot more before many hours are over, or I'm mistaken."

We were in Berwick at an early hour next morning, and we went straight to the police station and into the superintendent's office. Chisholm was with Mr. Murray when we walked in, and both men turned to us with eagerness.

"Here's more mystery about this affair, Mr. Lindsey!" exclaimed Murray. "It's enough to make a man's wits go wool-gathering. There's no news of Sir Gilbert, and Lady Carstairs has been missing since twelve o'clock noon yesterday!"

CHAPTER XXV
THE SECOND DISAPPEARANCE

Mr. Lindsey was always one of the coolest of hands at receiving news of a startling nature, and now, instead of breaking out into exclamations, he just nodded his head, and dropped into the nearest chair.

"Aye?" he remarked quietly. "So her ladyship's disappeared, too, has she? And when did you get to hear that, now?"

"Half an hour ago," replied Murray. "The butler at Hathercleugh House has just been in—driven over in a hurry—to tell us. What do you make of it at all?"

"Before I answer that, I want to know what's been happening here while I've been away," replied Mr. Lindsey. "What's happened within your own province—officially, I mean?"

"Not much," answered Murray. "There began to be talk evening before last, amongst the fishermen, about Sir Gilbert's yacht. He'd been seen, of course, to go out with Moneylaws there, two days ago, at noon. And—there is Moneylaws! Doesn't he know anything? Where's Sir Gilbert, Moneylaws?"

"He'll tell all that—when I tell him to," said Mr. Lindsey, with a glance at me. "Go on with your story, first."

The superintendent shook his head, as if all these things were beyond his comprehension.

"Oh, well!" he continued. "I tell you there was talk—you know how they gossip down yonder on the beach. It was said the yacht had never come in, and, though many of them had been out, they'd never set eyes on her, and rumours of her soon began to spread. So I sent Chisholm there out to Hathercleugh to make some inquiry—tell Mr. Lindsey what you heard," he went on, turning to the sergeant. "Not much, I think."

"Next to nothing," replied Chisholm. "I saw Lady Carstairs. She laughed at me. She said Sir Gilbert was not likely to come to harm—he'd been sailing yachts, big and little, for many a year, and he'd no doubt gone further on this occasion than he'd first intended. I pointed out that he'd Mr. Moneylaws with him, and that he'd been due at his business early that morning. She laughed again at that, and said she'd no doubt Sir Gilbert and Mr. Moneylaws had settled that matter between them, and that, as she'd no anxieties, she was sure Berwick folk needn't have any. And so I came away."

"And we heard no more until we got your wire yesterday from Dundee, Mr. Lindsey," said Murray; "and that was followed not so very long after by one from the police at Largo, which I reported to you."

"Now, here's an important question," put in Mr. Lindsey, a bit hurriedly, as if something had just struck him. "Did you communicate the news from Largo to Hathercleugh?"

"We did, at once," answered Murray. "I telephoned immediately to Lady Carstairs—I spoke to her over the wire myself, telling her what the Largo police reported."

"What time would that be?" asked Mr. Lindsey, sharply.

"Half-past eleven," replied Murray.

"Then, according to what you tell me, she left Hathercleugh soon after you telephoned to her?" said Mr. Lindsey.

"According to what the butler told us this morning," answered Murray, "Lady Carstairs went out on her bicycle at exactly noon yesterday—and she's never been seen or heard of since."

"She left no message at the house?" asked Mr. Lindsey.

"None! And," added the superintendent, significantly, "she didn't mention to the butler that I'd just telephoned to her. It's a queer business, this, I'm thinking, Mr. Lindsey. But—what's your own news?—and what's Moneylaws got to tell about Sir Gilbert?"

Mr. Lindsey took no notice of the last question. He sat in silence for a while, evidently thinking. And in the end he pointed to some telegram forms that lay on the superintendent's desk.

"There's one thing must be done at once, Murray," he said; "and I'll take the responsibility of doing it myself. We must communicate with the Carstairs family solicitors."

"I'd have done it, as soon as the butler brought me the news about Lady Carstairs," remarked Murray, "but I don't know who they are."

"I do!" answered Mr. Lindsey. "Holmshaw and Portlethorpe of Newcastle. Here," he went on, passing a telegram form to me. "Write out this message: 'Sir Gilbert and Lady Carstairs are both missing from Hathercleugh under strange circumstances please send some authorized person here at once.' Sign that with my name, Hugh—and take it to the post-office, and come back here."

When I got back, Mr. Lindsey had evidently told Murray and Chisholm all about my adventures with Sir Gilbert, and the two men regarded me with a new interest as if I had suddenly become a person of the first importance. And the superintendent at once fell upon me for my reticence.

"You made a bad mistake, young man, in keeping back what you ought to have told at the inquest on Phillips!" he said, reprovingly. "Indeed, you ought to have told it before that—you should have told us."

"Aye!—if I'd only known as much as that," began Chisholm, "I'd have—"

"You'd probably have done just what he did!" broke in Mr. Lindsey—"held your tongue till you knew more!—so let that pass—the lad did what he thought was for the best. You never suspected Sir Gilbert of any share in these affairs, either of you—so come, now!"

"Why, as to that, Mr. Lindsey," remarked Murray, who looked somewhat nettled by this last passage, "you didn't suspect him yourself—or, if you did, you kept it uncommonly quiet!"

"Does Mr. Lindsey suspect him now?" asked Chisholm, a bit maliciously. "For if he does, maybe he'll give us a hand."

Mr. Lindsey looked at both of them in a way that he had of looking at people of whose abilities he had no very great idea—but there was some indulgence in the look on this occasion.

"Well, now that things have come to this pass," he said, "and after Sir Gilbert's deliberate attempt to get rid of Moneylaws—to murder him, in fact—I don't mind telling you the truth. I do suspect Sir Gilbert of the murder of Crone—and that's why I produced that ice-ax in court the other day. And—when he saw that ice-ax, he knew that I suspected him, and that's why he took Moneylaws out with him, intending to rid himself of a man that could give evidence against him. If I'd known that Moneylaws was going with him, I'd have likely charged Sir Gilbert there and then!—anyway, I wouldn't have let Moneylaws go."

"Aye!—you know something, then?" exclaimed Murray. "You're in possession of some evidence that we know nothing about?"

"I know this—and I'll make you a present of it, now," answered Mr. Lindsey. "As you're aware, I'm a bit of a mountaineer—you know that I've spent a good many of my holidays in Switzerland, climbing. Consequently, I know what alpenstocks and ice-axes are. And when I came to reflect on the circumstances of Crone's murder, I remember that not so long since, happening to be out along the riverside, I chanced across Sir Gilbert Carstairs using a very late type of ice-ax as a walking-stick—as he well could do, and might have picked up in his hall as some men'll pick up a golf-stick to go walking with, and I've done that myself, hundred of times. And I knew that I had an ice-ax of that very pattern at home—and so I just shoved it under the doctor's nose in court, and asked him if that hole in Crone's head couldn't have been made by the spike of it. Why? Because I knew that Carstairs would be present in court, and I wanted to see if he would catch what I was after!"

"And—you think he did?" asked the superintendent, eagerly.

"I kept the corner of an eye on him," answered Mr. Lindsey, knowingly. "He saw what I was after! He's a clever fellow, that—but he took the mask off his face for the thousandth part of a second. I saw!"

The two listeners were so amazed by this that they sat in silence for a while, staring at Mr. Lindsey with open-mouthed amazement.

"It's a dark, dark business!" sighed Murray at last. "What's the true meaning of it, do you think, Mr. Lindsey?"

"Some secret that's being gradually got at," replied Mr. Lindsey, promptly. "That's what it is. And there's nothing to do, just now, but wait until somebody comes from Holmshaw and Portlethorpe's. Holmshaw is an old man—probably Portlethorpe himself will come along. He may know something—they've been family solicitors to the Carstairs lot for many a year. But it's my impression that Sir Gilbert Carstairs is away!—and that his wife's after him. And if you want to be doing something, try to find out where she went on her bicycle yesterday—likely, she rode to some station in the neighbourhood, and then took train."

Mr. Lindsey and I then went to the office, and we had not been there long when a telegram arrived from Newcastle. Mr. Portlethorpe himself was coming on to Berwick immediately. And in the middle of the afternoon he arrived—a middle-aged, somewhat nervous-mannered man, whom I had seen two or three times when we had business at the Assizes, and whom Mr. Lindsey evidently knew pretty well, judging by their familiar manner of greeting each other.

"What's all this, Lindsey?" asked Mr. Portlethorpe, as soon as he walked in, and without any preliminaries. "Your wire says Sir Gilbert and Lady Carstairs have disappeared. Does that mean—"

"Did you read your newspaper yesterday?" interrupted Mr. Lindsey, who knew that what we had read in the *Dundee Advertiser* had also appeared in the *Newcastle Daily Chronicle*. "Evidently not, Portlethorpe, or you'd have known, in part at any rate, what my wire meant. But I'll tell you in a hundred words—and then I'll ask you a couple of questions before we go any further."

He gave Mr. Portlethorpe an epitomized account of the situation, and Mr. Portlethorpe listened attentively to the end. And without making any comment he said three words:

"Well—your questions?"

"The first," answered Mr. Lindsey, "is this—How long is it since you saw or heard from Sir Gilbert Carstairs?"

"A week—by letter," replied Mr. Portlethorpe.

"The second," continued Mr. Lindsey, "is much more important—much! What, Portlethorpe, do you know of Sir Gilbert Carstairs?"

Mr. Portlethorpe hesitated a moment. Then he replied, frankly and with evident candour.

"To tell you the truth, Lindsey," he said, "beyond knowing that he is Sir Gilbert Carstairs—nothing!"

CHAPTER XXVI

MRS. RALSTON OF CRAIG

Mr. Lindsey made no remark on this answer, and for a minute or two he and Mr. Portlethorpe sat looking at each other. Then Mr. Portlethorpe bent forward a little, his hands on his knees, and gave Mr. Lindsey a sort of quizzical but earnest glance.

"Now, why do you ask that last question?" he said quietly. "You've some object?"

"It's like this," answered Mr. Lindsey. "Here's a man comes into these parts to take up a title and estates, who certainly had been out of them for thirty years. His recent conduct is something more than suspicious—no one can deny that he left my clerk there to drown, without possibility of help! That's intended murder! And so I ask, What do you, his solicitor, know of him—his character, his doings during the thirty years he was away? And you answer—nothing!"

"Just so!" assented Mr. Portlethorpe. "And nobody does hereabouts. Except that he is Sir Gilbert Carstairs, nobody in these parts knows anything about him—how should they? We, I suppose, know more than anybody—and we know just a few bare facts."

"I think you'll have to let me know what these bare facts are," remarked Mr. Lindsey. "And Moneylaws, too. Moneylaws has a definite charge to bring against this man—and he'll bring it, if I've anything to do with it! He shall press it!—if he can find Carstairs. And I think you'd better tell us what you know, Portlethorpe. Things have got to come out."

"I've no objection to telling you and Mr. Moneylaws what we know," answered Mr. Portlethorpe. "After all, it is, in a way, common knowledge—to some people, at any rate. And to begin with, you are probably aware that the recent history of this Carstairs family is a queer one. You know that old Sir Alexander had two sons and one daughter—the daughter being very much younger than her brothers. When the two sons, Michael and Gilbert, were about from twenty-one to twenty-three, both quarrelled with their father, and cleared out of this neighbourhood altogether; it's always believed that Sir Alexander gave Michael a fair lot of money to go and do for himself, each hating the other's society, and that Michael went off to America. As to Gilbert, he got money at that time, too, and went south, and was understood to be first a medical student and then a doctor, in London and abroad. There is no doubt at all that both sons did get money—considerable amounts,—because from the time they went away, no allowance was ever paid to them, nor did Sir Alexander ever have any relations with them. What the cause of the quarrel was, nobody knows; but the quarrel itself, and the ensuing separation, were final—father and sons never resumed relations. And when the daughter, now Mrs. Ralston of Craig, near here, grew up and married, old Sir Alexander pursued a similar money policy towards her—he presented her with thirty thousand pounds the day she was married, and told her she'd never have another penny from him. I tell you, he was a queer man."

"Queer lot altogether!" muttered Mr. Lindsey. "And interesting!"

"Oh, it's interesting enough!" agreed Mr. Portlethorpe, with a chuckle. "Deeply so. Well, that's how things were until about a year before old Sir Alexander died—which, as you know, is fourteen months since. As I say, about six years before his death, formal notice came of the death of Michael Carstairs, who, of course, was next in succession to the title. It came from a solicitor in Havana, where Michael had died—there were all the formal proofs. He had died unmarried and intestate, and his estate amounted to about a thousand pounds. Sir Alexander put the affair in our hands; and of course, as he was next-of-kin to his eldest son, what there was came to him. And we then pointed out to him that now that Mr. Michael Carstairs was dead, Mr. Gilbert came next—he would get the title, in any case— and we earnestly pressed Sir Alexander to make a will. And he was always going to, and he never did—and he died intestate, as you know. And at that, of course, Sir Gilbert Carstairs came forward, and—"

"A moment," interrupted Mr. Lindsey. "Did anybody know where he was at the time of his father's death?"

"Nobody hereabouts, at any rate," replied Mr. Portlethorpe. "Neither his father, nor his sister, nor ourselves had heard of him for many a long year. But he called on us within twenty-four hours of his father's death."

"With proof, of course, that he was the man he represented himself to be?" asked Mr. Lindsey.

"Oh, of course—full proof!" answered Mr. Portlethorpe. "Papers, letters, all that sort of thing—all in order. He had been living in London for a year or two at that time; but, according to his own account, he had gone pretty well all over the world during the thirty years' absence. He'd been a ship's surgeon—he'd been attached to the medical staff of more than one foreign army, and had seen service— he'd been on one or two voyages of discovery—he'd lived in every continent—in fact, he'd had a very adventurous life, and lately he'd married a rich American heiress."

"Oh, Lady Carstairs is an American, is she?" remarked Mr. Lindsey.

"Just so—haven't you met her?" asked Mr. Portlethorpe.

"Never set eyes on her that I know of," replied Mr. Lindsey. "But go on."

"Well, of course, there was no doubt of Sir Gilbert's identity," continued Mr. Portlethorpe; "and as there was also no doubt that Sir Alexander had died intestate, we at once began to put matters right. Sir Gilbert, of course, came into the whole of the real estate, and he and Mrs. Ralston shared the personalty—which, by-the-by, was considerable: they both got nearly a hundred thousand each, in cash. And—there you are!"

"That all?" asked Mr. Lindsey.

Mr. Portlethorpe hesitated a moment—then he glanced at me.

"Moneylaws is safe at a secret," said Mr. Lindsey. "If it is a secret."

"Well, then," answered Mr. Portlethorpe, "it's not quite all. There is a circumstance which has—I can't exactly say bothered—but has somewhat disturbed me. Sir Gilbert Carstairs has now been in possession of his estates for a little over a year, and during that time he has sold nearly every yard of them except Hathercleugh!"

Mr. Lindsey whistled. It was the first symptom of astonishment that he had manifested, and I glanced quickly at him and saw a look of indescribable intelligence and almost undeniable cunning cross his face. But it went as swiftly as it came, and he merely nodded, as if in surprise.

"Aye!" he exclaimed. "Quick work, Portlethorpe."

"Oh, he gave good reasons!" answered Mr. Portlethorpe. "He said, from the first, that he meant to do it—he wanted, and his wife wanted too, to get rid of these small and detached Northern properties, and buy a really fine one in the South of England, keeping Hathercleugh as a sort of holiday seat. He'd no intention of selling that, at any time. But—there's the fact!—he's sold pretty nearly everything else."

"I never heard of these sales of land," remarked Mr. Lindsey.

"Oh, they've all been sold by private treaty," replied Mr. Portlethorpe. "The Carstairs property was in parcels, here and there—the last two baronets before this one had bought considerably in other parts. It was all valuable—there was no difficulty in selling to adjacent owners."

"Then, if he's been selling to that extent, Sir Gilbert must have large sums of money at command—unless he's bought that new estate you're talking of," said Mr. Lindsey.

"He has not bought anything—that I know of," answered Mr. Portlethorpe. "And he must have a considerable—a very large—sum of money at his bankers'. All of which," he continued, looking keenly at Mr. Lindsey, "makes me absolutely amazed to hear what you've just told me. It's very serious, this charge you're implying against him, Lindsey! Why should he want to take men's lives in this fashion! A man of his position, his great wealth—"

"Portlethorpe!" broke in Mr. Lindsey, "didn't you tell me just now that this man, according to his own account, has lived a most adventurous life, in all parts of the world? What more likely than that in the course of such a life he made acquaintance with queer characters, and—possibly—did some queer things himself? Isn't it a significant thing that, within a year of his coming into the title and estates, two highly mysterious individuals turn up here, and that all this foul play ensues? It's impossible, now, to doubt that Gilverthwaite and Phillips came into these parts because this man was already here! If you've read all the stuff that's been in the papers, and add to it just what we've told you about this last adventure with the yacht, you can't doubt it, either."

"It's very, very strange—all of it," agreed Mr. Portlethorpe. "Have you no theory, Lindsey?"

"I've a sort of one," answered Mr. Lindsey. "I think Gilverthwaite and Phillips probably were in possession of some secret about Sir Gilbert Carstairs, and that Crone may have somehow got an inkling of it. Now, as we know, Gilverthwaite died, suddenly—and it's possible that Carstairs killed both Phillips and Crone, as he certainly meant to kill this lad. And what does it all look like?"

Before Mr. Portlethorpe could reply to that last question, and while he was shaking his head over it, one of our junior clerks brought in Mrs. Ralston of Craig, at the mention of whose name Mr. Lindsey immediately bustled forward. She was a shrewd, clever-looking woman, well under middle age, who had been a widow for the last four or five years, and was celebrated in our parts for being a very managing and interfering sort of body who chiefly occupied herself with works of charity and philanthropy and was prominent on committees and boards. And she looked over the two solicitors as if they were candidates for examination, and she the examiner.

"I have been to the police, to find out what all this talk is about Sir Gilbert Carstairs," she began at once. "They tell me you know more than they do, Mr. Lindsey. Well, what have you to say? And what have you to say, Mr. Portlethorpe? You ought to know more than anybody. What does it all amount to!"

Mr. Portlethorpe, whose face had become very dismal at the sight of Mrs. Ralston, turned, as if seeking help, to Mr. Lindsey. He was obviously taken aback by Mrs. Ralston's questions, and a little afraid of her; but Mr. Lindsey was never afraid of anybody, and he at once turned on his visitor.

"Before we answer your questions, Mrs. Ralston," he said, "there's one I'll take leave to ask you. When Sir Gilbert came back at your father's death, did you recognize him?"

Mrs. Ralston tossed her head with obvious impatience.

"Now, what ridiculous nonsense, Mr. Lindsey!" she exclaimed. "How on earth do you suppose that I could recognize a man whom I hadn't seen since I was a child of seven—and certainly not for at least thirty years? Of course I didn't!—impossible!"

CHAPTER XXVII

THE BANK BALANCE

It was now Mr. Portlethorpe and I who looked at each other—with a mutual questioning. What was Mr. Lindsey hinting, suggesting? And Mr. Portlethorpe suddenly turned on him with a direct inquiry.

"What is it you are after, Lindsey?" he asked. "There's something in your mind."

"A lot," answered Mr. Lindsey. "And before I let it out, I think we'd better fully inform Mrs. Ralston of everything that's happened, and of how things stand, up to and including this moment. This is the position, Mrs. Ralston, and the facts"—and he went on to give his caller a brief but complete summary of all that he and Mr. Portlethorpe had just talked over. "You now see how matters are," he concluded, at the end of his epitome, during his delivery of which the lady had gradually grown more and more portentous of countenance. "Now,—what do you say?"

Mrs. Ralston spoke sharply and decisively.

"Precisely what I have felt inclined to say more than once of late!" she answered. "I'm beginning to suspect that the man who calls himself Sir Gilbert Carstairs is not Sir Gilbert Carstairs at all! He's an impostor!"

In spite of my subordinate position as a privileged but inferior member of the conference, I could not help letting out a hasty exclamation of astonishment at that. I was thoroughly and genuinely astounded—such a notion as that had never once occurred to me. An impostor!—not the real man? The idea was amazing—and Mr. Portlethorpe found it amazing, too, and he seconded my exclamation with another, and emphasized it with an incredulous laugh.

"My dear madam!" he said deprecatingly. "Really! That's impossible!"

But Mr. Lindsey, calmer than ever, nodded his head confidently.

"I'm absolutely of Mrs. Ralston's opinion," he declared. "What she suggests I believe to be true. An impostor!"

Mr. Portlethorpe flushed and began to look very uneasy.

"Really!" he repeated. "Really, Lindsey!—you forget that I examined into the whole thing! I saw all the papers—letters, documents—Oh, the suggestion is—you'll pardon me, Mrs. Ralston—ridiculous! No man could have been in possession of those documents unless he'd been the real man—the absolute Simon Pure! Why, my dear lady, he produced letters written by yourself, when you were a little girl—and—and all sorts of little private matters. It's impossible that there has been any imposture—a—a reflection on me!"

"Cleverer men than you have been taken in, Portlethorpe," remarked Mr. Lindsey. "And the matters you speak of might have been stolen. But let Mrs. Ralston give us her reasons for suspecting this man—she has some strong ones, I'll be bound."

Mr. Portlethorpe showed signs of irritation, but Mrs. Ralston promptly took up Mr. Lindsey's challenge.

"Sufficiently strong to have made me very uneasy of late, at any rate," she answered. She turned to Mr. Portlethorpe. "You remember," she went on, "that my first meeting with this man, when he came to claim the title and estates, was at your office in Newcastle, a few days after he first presented himself to you. He said then that he had not yet been down to Hathercleugh; but I have since found out that he had—or, rather, that he had been in the neighbourhood, incognito. That's a suspicious circumstance, Mr. Portlethorpe."

"Excuse me, ma'am—I don't see it," retorted Mr. Portlethorpe. "I don't see it at all."

"I do, then!" said Mrs. Ralston. "Suspicious, because I, his sister, and only living relation, was close by. Why didn't he come straight to me? He was here—he took a quiet look around before he let any one know who he was. That's one thing I have against him—whatever you say, it was very suspicious conduct; and he lied about it, in saying he had not been here, when he certainly had been here! But that's far from all. The real Gilbert Carstairs, Mr. Lindsey, as Mr. Portlethorpe knows, lived at Hathercleugh House until he was twenty-two years old. He was always at Hathercleugh, except when he was at Edinburgh University studying medicine. He knew the whole of the district thoroughly. But, as I have found out for myself, this man does not know the district! I have discovered, on visiting him—though I have not gone there much, as I don't like either him or his wife—that this is a strange country to him. He knows next to nothing—though he has done his best to learn—of its features, its history, its people. Is it likely that a man who had lived on the Border until he was two-and-twenty could forget all about it, simply because he was away from it for thirty years? Although I was only seven or eight when my brother Gilbert left home, I was then a very sharp child, and I remember that he knew every mile of the country round Hathercleugh. But—this man doesn't."

Mr. Portlethorpe muttered something about it being very possible for a man to forget a tremendous lot in thirty years, but Mrs. Ralston and Mr. Lindsey shook their heads at his dissent from their opinion. As for me, I was thinking of the undoubted fact that the supposed Sir Gilbert Carstairs had been obliged in my presence to use a map in order to find his exact whereabouts when he was, literally, within two miles of his own house.

"Another thing," continued Mrs. Ralston: "in my few visits to Hathercleugh since he came, I have found out that while he is very well posted up in certain details of our family history, he is unaccountably ignorant of others with which he ought to have been perfectly familiar. I found out, too, that he is exceedingly clever in avoiding subjects in which his ignorance might be detected. But, clever as he is, he has more than once given me grounds for suspicion. And I tell you plainly, Mr. Portlethorpe, that since he has been selling property to the extent you report, you ought, at this juncture, and as things are, to find out how money matters stand. He must have realized vast amounts in cash! Where is it!"

"At his bankers'—in Newcastle, my dear madam!" replied Mr. Portlethorpe. "Where else should it be? He has not yet made the purchase he contemplated, so of course the necessary funds are waiting until he does. I cannot but think that you and Mr. Lindsey are mistaken, and that there will be some proper and adequate explanation of all this, and—"

"Portlethorpe!" exclaimed Mr. Lindsey, "that's no good. Things have gone too far. Whether this man's Sir Gilbert Carstairs or an impostor, he did his best to murder my clerk, and we suspect him of the murder of Crone, and he's going to be brought to justice—that's flat! And your duty at present is to fall in with us to this extent—you must adopt Mrs. Ralston's suggestion, and ascertain how money matters stand. As Mrs. Ralston rightly says, by the sale of these properties a vast amount of ready money must have been accumulated, and at this man's disposal, Portlethorpe!—we must know if it's true!"

"How can I tell you that?" demanded Mr. Portlethorpe, who was growing more and more nervous and peevish. "I've nothing to do with Sir Gilbert Carstairs' private banking account. I can't go and ask, point blank, of his bankers how much money he has in their hands!"

"Then I will!" exclaimed Mr. Lindsey. "I know where he banks in Newcastle, and I know the manager. I shall go this very night to the manager's private house, and tell him exactly everything that's transpired—I shall tell him Mrs. Ralston's and my own suspicions, and I shall ask him where the money is. Do you understand that?"

"The proper course to adopt!" said Mrs. Ralston. "The one thing to do. It must be done!"

"Oh, very well—then in that case I suppose I'd better go with you," said Mr. Portlethorpe. "Of course, it's no use going to the bank—they'll be closed; but we can, as you say, go privately to the manager. And we shall be placed in a very unenviable position if Sir Gilbert Carstairs turns up with a perfectly good explanation of all this mystery."

Mr. Lindsey pointed a finger at me.

"He can't explain that!" he exclaimed. "He left that lad to drown! Is that attempted murder, or isn't it? I tell you, I'll have that man in the dock—never mind who he is! Hugh, pass me the railway guide."

It was presently settled that Mr. Portlethorpe and Mr. Lindsey should go off to Newcastle by the next train to see the bank manager. Mr. Lindsey insisted that I should go with them—he would have no hole-and-corner work, he said, and I should tell my own story to the man we were going to see, so that he would know some of the ground of our suspicion. Mrs. Ralston supported that; and when Mr. Portlethorpe remarked that we were going too fast, and were working up all the elements of a fine scandal, she tartly remarked that if more care had been taken at the beginning, all this would not have happened.

We found the bank manager at his private house, outside Newcastle, that evening. He knew both my companions personally, and he listened with great attention to all that Mr. Lindsey, as spokesman, had to tell; he also heard my story of the yacht affair. He was an astute, elderly man, evidently quick at sizing things up, and I knew by the way he turned to Mr. Portlethorpe and by the glance he gave him, after hearing everything, that his conclusions were those of Mr. Lindsey and Mrs. Ralston.

"I'm afraid there's something wrong, Portlethorpe," he remarked quietly. "The truth is, I've had suspicions myself lately."

"Good God! you don't mean it!" exclaimed Mr. Portlethorpe. "How, then?"

"Since Sir Gilbert began selling property," continued the bank manager, "very large sums have been paid in to his credit at our bank, where, previous to that, he already had a very considerable balance. But at the present moment we hold very little—that is, comparatively little—money of his."

"What?" said Mr. Portlethorpe. "What? You don't mean that?"

"During the past three or four months," said the bank manager, "Sir Gilbert has regularly drawn very large cheques in favour of a Mr. John Paley. They have been presented to us through the Scottish-American Bank at Edinburgh. And," he added, with a significant look at Mr. Lindsey, "I think you'd better go to Edinburgh—and find out who Mr. John Paley is."

Mr. Portlethorpe got up, looking very white and frightened.

"How much of all that money is there left in your hands?" he asked, hoarsely.

"Not more than a couple of thousand," answered the bank manager with promptitude.

"Then he's paid out—in the way you state—what?" demanded Mr.Portlethorpe.

"Quite two hundred thousand pounds! And," concluded our informant, with another knowing look, "now that I'm in possession of the facts you've just put before me, I should advise you to go and find out if Sir Gilbert Carstairs and John Paley are not one and the same person!"

CHAPTER XXVIII

THE HATHERCLEUGH BUTLER

The three of us went away from the bank manager's house struggling with the various moods peculiar to our individual characters—Mr. Portlethorpe, being naturally a nervous man, given to despondency, was greatly upset, and manifested his emotions in sundry ejaculations of a dark nature; I, being young, was full of amazement at the news just given us and of the excitement of hunting down the man we knew as Sir Gilbert Carstairs. But I am not sure that Mr. Lindsey struggled much with anything—he was cool and phlegmatic as usual, and immediately began to think of practical measures.

"Look here, Portlethorpe," he said, as soon as we were in the motor car which we had chartered from Newcastle station, "we've got to get going in this matter at once—straight away! We must be in Edinburgh as early as possible in the morning. Be guided by me—come straight back to Berwick, stop the night with me at my house, and we'll be on our way to Edinburgh by the very first train—we can get there early, by the time the banks are open. There's another reason why I want you to come—I've some documents that I wish you to see—documents that may have a very important bearing on this affair. There's one in my pocket-book now, and you'll be astonished when you hear how it came into my possession. But it's not one-half so astonishing as another that I've got at my house."

I remembered then that we had been so busily engaged since our return from the North that morning that we had had no time to go into the matter of the letter which Mr. Gavin Smeaton had entrusted to Mr. Lindsey—here, again, was going to be more work of the ferreting-out sort. But Mr. Portlethorpe, it was clear, had no taste for mysteries, and no great desire to forsake his own bed, even for Mr. Lindsey's hospitality, and it needed insistence before he consented to go back to Berwick with us. Go back, however, he did; and before midnight we were in our own town again, and passing the deserted streets towards Mr. Lindsey's home, I going with the others because Mr. Lindsey insisted that it was now too late for me to go home, and I should be nearer the station if I slept at his place. And just before we got to the house, which was a quiet villa standing in its own grounds, a little north of the top end of the town, a man who was sauntering ahead of us, suddenly turned and came up to Mr. Lindsey, and in the light of a street lamp I recognized in him the Hathercleugh butler.

Mr. Lindsey recognized the man, too—so also did Mr. Portlethorpe; and they both came to a dead halt, staring. And both rapped out the same inquiry, in identical words:

"Some news?"

I looked as eagerly at the butler as they did. He had been sour enough and pompous enough in his manner and attitude to me that night of my call on his master, and it surprised me now to see how polite and suave and—in a fashion— insinuating he was in his behaviour to the two solicitors. He was a big, fleshy, strongly-built fellow, with a rather flabby, deeply-lined face and a pallid complexion, rendered all the paler by his black overcoat and top hat; and as he stood there, rubbing his hands, glancing from Mr. Lindsey to Mr. Portlethorpe, and speaking in soft, oily, suggestive accents, I felt that I disliked him even more than when he had addressed me in such supercilious accents at the doors of Hathercleugh.

"Well—er—not precisely news, gentlemen," he replied. "The fact is, I wanted to see you privately, Mr. Lindsey, sir—but, of course, I've no objections to speaking before Mr. Portlethorpe, as he's Sir Gilbert's solicitor. Perhaps I can come in with you, Mr. Lindsey?—the truth is, I've been waiting about, sir—they said you'd gone to Newcastle, and might be coming back by this last train. And—it's—possibly—of importance."

"Come in," said Mr. Lindsey. He let us all into his house with his latch-key, and led us to his study, where he closed the door. "Now," he went on, turning to the butler. "What is it? You can speak freely—we are all three—Mr. Portlethorpe, Mr. Moneylaws, and myself—pretty well acquainted with all that is going on, by this time. And—I'm perhaps not far wrong when I suggest that you know something?"

The butler, who had taken the chair which Mr. Lindsey had pointed out, rubbed his hands, and looked at us with an undeniable expression of cunning and slyness.

"Well, sir!" he said in a low, suggesting tone of voice. "A man in my position naturally gets to know things—whether he wants to or not, sometimes. I have had ideas, gentlemen, for some time."

"That something was wrong?" asked Mr. Portlethorpe.

"Approaching to something of that nature, sir," replied the butler. "Of course, you will bear in mind that I am, as it were, a stranger—I have only been in Sir Gilbert's Carstairs' employ nine months. But—I have eyes. And ears. And the long and short of it is, gentlemen, I believe Sir Gilbert—and Lady Carstairs—have gone!"

"Absolutely gone?" exclaimed Mr. Portlethorpe. "Good gracious, Hollins!— you don't mean that!"

"I shall be much surprised if it is not found to be the case, sir," answered Hollins, whose name I now heard for the first time. "And—incidentally, as it were—I may mention that I think it will be discovered that a good deal has gone with them!"

"What—property?" demanded Mr. Portlethorpe. "Impossible!—they couldn't carry property away—going as they seem to have done—or are said to have done!"

Hollins coughed behind one of his big, fat hands, and glanced knowingly at Mr. Lindsey, who was listening silently but with deep attention.

"I'm not so sure about that, sir," he said. "You're aware that there were certain small matters at Hathercleugh of what we may term the heirloom nature, though whether they were heirlooms or not I can't say—the miniature of himself set in diamonds, given by George the Third to the second baronet; the necklace, also diamonds, which belonged to a Queen of Spain; the small picture, priceless, given to the fifth baronet by a Czar of Russia; and similar things, Mr. Portlethorpe. And, gentlemen, the family jewels!—all of which had been reset. They've got all those!"

"You mean to say—of your own knowledge—they're not at Hathercleugh?" suddenly inquired Mr. Lindsey.

"I mean to say they positively are not, sir," replied the butler. "They were kept in a certain safe in a small room used by Lady Carstairs as her boudoir. Her lady-ship left very hastily and secretly yesterday, as I understand the police have told you, and, in her haste, she forgot to lock up that safe—which she had no doubt un-locked before her departure. That safe, sir, is empty—of those things, at any rate."

"God bless my soul!" exclaimed Mr. Portlethorpe, greatly agitated. "This is really terrible!"

"Could she carry those things—all of them—on her bicycle—by which I hear she left?" asked Mr. Lindsey.

"Easily, sir," replied Hollins. "She had a small luggage-carrier on her bicy-cle—it would hold all those things. They were not bulky, of course."

"You've no idea where she went on that bicycle?" inquired Mr. Lindsey.

Hollins smiled cunningly, and drew his chair a little nearer to us.

"I hadn't—when I went to Mr. Murray, at the police-station, this morning," he answered. "But—I've an idea, now. That's precisely why I came in to see you, Mr. Lindsey."

He put his hand inside his overcoat and produced a pocket-book, from which he presently drew out a scrap of paper.

"After I'd seen Mr. Murray this morning," he continued, "I went back to Ha-thercleugh, and took it upon myself to have a look round. I didn't find anything of a remarkably suspicious nature until this afternoon, pretty late, when I made the discovery about the safe in the boudoir—that all the articles I'd mentioned had disappeared. Then I began to examine a waste-paper basket in the boudoir—I'd personally seen Lady Carstairs tear up some letters which she received yesterday morning by the first post, and throw the scraps into that basket, which hadn't been emptied since. And I found this, gentlemen—and you can, perhaps, draw some conclusion from it—I've had no difficulty in drawing one myself."

He laid on the table a torn scrap of paper, over which all three of us at once bent. There was no more on it than the terminations of lines—but the wording was certainly suggestive:—

".... at once, quietly .... best time would be before lunch .... at Kelso .... usual place in Glasgow."

Mr. Portlethorpe started at sight of the handwriting.

"That's Sir Gilbert's!" he exclaimed. "No doubt of that. What are we to understand by it, Lindsey?"

"What do you make of this?" asked Mr. Lindsey, turning to Hollins. "You say you've drawn a deduction?"

"I make this out, sir," answered the butler, quietly. "Yesterday morning there were only four letters for Lady Carstairs. Two were from London—in the handwriting of ladies. One was a tradesman's letter—from Newcastle. The fourth was in a registered envelope—and the address was typewritten—and the post-mark Edinburgh. I'm convinced, Mr. Lindsey, that the registered one contained—that! A letter, you understand, from Sir Gilbert—I found other scraps of it, but so small that it's impossible to piece them together, though I have them here. And I conclude that he gave Lady Carstairs orders to cycle to Kelso—an easy ride for her,—and to take the train to Glasgow, where he'd meet her. Glasgow, sir, is a highly convenient city, I believe, for people who wish to disappear. And—I should suggest that Glasgow should be communicated with."

"Have you ever known Sir Gilbert Carstairs visit Glasgow recently?" asked Mr. Lindsey, who had listened attentively to all this.

"He was there three weeks ago," replied Hollins.

"And—Edinburgh?" suggested Mr. Lindsey.

"He went regularly to Edinburgh—at one time—twice a week," said the butler. And then, Mr. Lindsey not making any further remark, he glanced at him and at Mr. Portlethorpe. "Of course, gentlemen," he continued, "this is all between ourselves. I feel it my duty, you know."

Mr. Lindsey answered that we all understood the situation, and presently he let the man out, after a whispered sentence or two between them in the hall. Then he came back to us, and without a word as to what had just transpired, drew the Smeaton letter from his pocket.

CHAPTER XXIX
ALL IN ORDER

So that we might have it to ourselves, we had returned from Newcastle to Berwick in a first-class compartment, and in its privacy Mr. Lindsey had told Mr. Portlethorpe the whole of the Smeaton story. Mr. Portlethorpe had listened—so it seemed to me—with a good deal of irritation and impatience; he was clearly one of those people who do not like interference with what they regard as an established order of things, and it evidently irked him to have any questions raised as to the Carstairs affairs—which, of course, he himself had done much to settle when Sir Gilbert succeeded to the title. In his opinion, the whole thing was cut, dried, and done with, and he was still impatient and restive when Mr. Lindsey laid before him the letter which Mr. Gavin Smeaton had lent us, and invited him to look carefully at the handwriting. He made no proper response to that invitation; what he did was to give a peevish glance at the letter, and then push it aside, with an equally peevish exclamation.

"What of it?" he said. "It conveys nothing to me!"

"Take your time, Portlethorpe," remonstrated Mr. Lindsey, who was unlocking a drawer in his desk. "It'll perhaps convey something to you when you compare that writing with a certain signature which I shall now show you. This," he continued, as he produced Gilverthwaite's will, and laid it before his visitor, "is the will of the man whose coming to Berwick ushered in all these mysteries. Now, then—do you see who was one of the witnesses to the will? Look, man!"

Mr. Portlethorpe looked—and was startled out of his peevishness.

"God bless me!" he exclaimed. "Michael Carstairs!"

"Just that," said Mr. Lindsey. "Now then, compare Michael Carstairs' handwriting with the handwriting of that letter. Come here, Hugh!—you, too, have a look. And—there's no need for any very close or careful looking, either!—no need for expert calligraphic evidence, or for the use of microscopes. I'll stake all I'm worth that that signature and that letter are the work of the same hand!"

Now that I saw the Smeaton letter and the signature of the first witness to Gilverthwaite's will, side by side, I had no hesitation in thinking as Mr. Lindsey did. It was an exceptionally curious, not to say eccentric, handwriting—some of the letters were oddly formed, other letters were indicated rather than formed at all. It seemed impossible that two different individuals could write in that style; it was rather the style developed for himself by a man who scorned all conventional matters, and was as self-distinct in his penmanship as he probably was in his life and thoughts. Anyway, there was an undeniable, an extraordinary similarity, and even Mr. Portlethorpe had to admit that it was—undoubtedly—there. He threw off his impatience and irritability, and became interested—and grave.

"That's very strange, and uncommonly important, Lindsey!" he said. "I—yes, I am certainly inclined to agree with you. Now, what do you make of it?"

"If you want to know my precise idea," replied Mr. Lindsey, "it's just this— Michael Carstairs and Martin Smeaton are one and the same man—or, I should say, were! That's about it, Portlethorpe."

"Then in that case—that young fellow at Dundee is Michael Carstairs' son?" exclaimed Mr. Portlethorpe.

"And, in my opinion, that's not far off the truth," said Mr. Lindsey. "You've hit it!"

"But—Michael Carstairs was never married!" declared Mr. Portlethorpe.

Mr. Lindsey picked up Gilverthwaite's will and the Smeaton letter, and carefully locked them away in his drawer.

"I'm not so sure about that," he remarked, drily. "Michael Carstairs was very evidently a queer man who did a lot of things in a peculiar fashion of his own, and—"

"The solicitor who sent us formal proof of his death, from Havana, previous to Sir Alexander's death, said distinctly that Michael had never been married," interrupted Mr. Portlethorpe. "And surely he would know!"

"And I say just as surely that from all I've heard of Michael Carstairs there'd be a lot of things that no solicitor would know, even if he sat at Michael's dying bed!" retorted Mr. Lindsey. "But we'll see. And talking of beds, it's time I was showing you to yours, and that we were all between the sheets, for it's one o'clock in the morning, and we'll have to be stirring again at six sharp. And I'll tell you what we'll do, Portlethorpe, to save time—we'll just take a mere cup of coffee and a mouthful of bread here, and we'll breakfast in Edinburgh—we'll be there by eight-thirty. So now come to your beds."

He marshalled us upstairs—he and Mr. Portlethorpe had already taken their night-caps while they talked,—and when he had bestowed the senior visitor in his room, he came to me in mine, carrying an alarm clock which he set down at my bed-head.

"Hugh, my man!" he said, "you'll have to stir yourself an hour before Mr. Portlethorpe and me. I've set that implement for five o'clock. Get yourself up when it rings, and make yourself ready and go round to Murray at the police-station—rouse him out of his bed. Tell him what we heard from that man Hollins tonight, and bid him communicate with the Glasgow police to look out for Sir Gilbert Carstairs. Tell him, too, that we're going on to Edinburgh, and why, and that, if need be, I'll ring him up from the Station Hotel during the morning with any news we have, and I'll ask for his at the same time. Insist on his getting in touch with Glasgow—it's there, without doubt, that Lady Carstairs went off, and where Sir Gilbert would meet her; let him start inquiries about the shipping offices and the like. And that's all—and get your bit of sleep."

I had Murray out of his bed before half-past five that morning, and I laid it on him heavily about the Glasgow affair, which, as we came to know later, was the biggest mistake we made, and one that involved us in no end of sore trouble; and at a quarter-past six Mr. Lindsey and Mr. Portlethorpe and I were drinking our coffee and blinking at each other over the rims of the cups. But Mr. Lindsey was sharp enough of his wits even at that hour, and before we set off from Berwick he wrote out a telegram to Mr. Gavin Smeaton, asking him to meet us in Edinburgh during the day, so that Mr. Portlethorpe might make his acquaintance. This telegram he left with his housekeeper—to be dispatched as soon as the post-office was open. And then we were off, and by half-past eight were at breakfast in the Waverley Station; and as the last stroke of ten was sounding from the Edinburgh clocks we were walking into the premises of the Scottish-American Bank.

The manager, who presently received us in his private rooms, looked at Mr. Lindsey and Mr. Portlethorpe with evident surprise—it may have been that there was mystery in their countenances. I know that I, on my part, felt as if a purblind man might have seen that I was clothed about with mystery from the crown of my head to the sole of my foot! And he appeared still more surprised when Mr. Lindsey, briefly, but fully, explained why we had called upon him.

"Of course, I've read the newspapers about your strange doings at Berwick," he observed, when Mr. Lindsey—aided by some remarks from Mr. Portlethorpe—had come to the end of his explanation. "And I gather that you now want to know what we, here, know of Sir Gilbert Carstairs and Mr. John Paley. I can reply to that in a sentence—nothing that is to their discredit! They are two thoroughly estimable and trustworthy gentlemen, so far as we are aware."

"Then there *is* a Mr. John Paley?" demanded Mr. Lindsey, who was obviously surprised.

The manager, evidently, was also surprised—by the signs of Mr. Lindsey's surprise.

"Mr. John Paley is a stockbroker in this city," he replied. "Quite well known! The fact is, we—that is, I—introduced Sir Gilbert Carstairs to him. Perhaps," he continued, glancing from one gentleman to the other, "I had better tell you all the facts. They're very simple, and quite of an ordinary nature. Sir Gilbert Carstairs came in here, introducing himself, some months ago. He told me that he was intending to sell off a good deal of the Carstairs property, and that he wanted to reinvest his proceeds in the very best American securities. I gathered that he had spent a lot of time in America, that he preferred America to England, and, in short, that he had a decided intention of going back to the States, keeping Hathercleugh as a place to come to occasionally. He asked me if I could recommend him a broker here in Edinburgh who was thoroughly well acquainted with the very best class of American investments, and I at once recommended Mr. John Paley. And—that's all I know, gentlemen."

"Except," remarked Mr. Lindsey, "that you know that considerable transactions have taken place between Mr. Paley and Sir Gilbert Carstairs. We know that, from what we heard last night in Newcastle."

"Precisely!—then you know as much as I can tell you," replied the manager. "But I have no objection to saying that large sums of money, coming from Sir Gilbert Carstairs, have certainly been passed through Mr. Paley's banking account here, and I suppose Mr. Paley has made the investments which Sir Gilbert desired—in fact, I know he has. And—I should suggest you call on Mr. Paley himself."

We went away upon that, and it seemed to me that Mr. Lindsey was somewhat taken aback. And we were no sooner clear of the bank than Mr. Portlethorpe, a little triumphantly, a little maliciously, turned on him.

"There! what did I say?" he exclaimed. "Everything is in order, you see, Lindsey! I confess I'm surprised to hear about those American investments; but, after all, Sir Gilbert has a right to do what he likes with his own. I told you we were running our heads against the wall—personally, I don't see what use there is in seeing this Mr. Paley. We're only interfering with other people's business. As I say, Sir Gilbert can make what disposal he pleases of his own property."

"And what I say, Portlethorpe," retorted Mr. Lindsey, "is that I'm going to be convinced that it is his own property! I'm going to see Paley whether you do or not—and you'll be a fool if you don't come."

Mr. Portlethorpe protested—but he accompanied us. And we were very soon in Mr. John Paley's office—a quiet, self-possessed sort of man who showed no surprise at our appearance; indeed, he at once remarked that the bank manager had just telephoned that we were on the way, and why.

"Then I'll ask you a question at once," said Mr. Lindsey. "And I'm sure you'll be good enough to answer it. When did you last see Sir Gilbert Carstairs?"

Mr. Paley immediately turned to a diary which lay on his desk, and gave one glance at it. "Three days ago," he answered promptly. "Wednesday—eleven o'clock."

CHAPTER XXX

THE CARSTAIRS MOTTO

Mr. Lindsey reflected a moment after getting that precise answer, and he glanced at me as if trying to recollect something.

"That would be the very morning after the affair of the yacht?" he asked of me.

But before I could speak, Mr. Paley took the words out of my mouth.

"Quite right." he said quietly. "I knew nothing of it at the time, of course, but I have read a good deal in the newspapers since. It was the morning after Sir Gilbert left Berwick in his yacht."

"Did he mention anything about the yacht to you?" inquired Mr. Lindsey.

"Not a word! I took it that he had come in to see me in the ordinary way," replied the stockbroker. "He wasn't here ten minutes. I had no idea whatever that anything had happened."

"Before we go any further," said Mr. Lindsey, "may I ask you to tell us what he came for? You know that Mr. Portlethorpe is his solicitor?—I am asking the question on his behalf as well as my own."

"I don't know why I shouldn't tell you," answered Mr. Paley. "He came on perfectly legitimate business. It was to call for some scrip which I held—scrip of his own, of course."

"Which he took away with him?" suggested Mr. Lindsey.

"Naturally!" replied the stockbroker. "That was what he came for."

"Did he give you any hint as to where he was going?" asked Mr. Lindsey. "Did he, for instance, happen to mention that he was leaving home for a time?"

"Not at all," answered Mr. Paley. "He spoke of nothing but the business that had brought him. As I said just now, he wasn't here ten minutes."

It was evident to me that Mr. Lindsey was still more taken aback. What we had learned during the last half-hour seemed to surprise him. And Mr. Portlethorpe, who was sharp enough of observation, saw this, and made haste to step into the arena.

"Mr. Lindsey," he said, "has been much upset by the apparently extraordinary circumstances of Sir Gilbert Carstairs' disappearance—and so, I may say, has Sir Gilbert's sister, Mrs. Ralston. I have pointed out that Sir Gilbert himself may have—probably has—a quite proper explanation of his movements. Wait a minute, Lindsey!" he went on, as Mr. Lindsey showed signs of restiveness. "It's my turn, I think." He looked at Mr. Paley again. "Your transactions with Sir Gilbert have been quite in order, all through, I suppose—and quite ordinary?"

"Quite in order, and quite ordinary," answered the stockbroker readily. "He was sent to me by the manager of the Scottish-American Bank, who knows that I do a considerable business in first-class American securities and investments. Sir Gilbert told me that he was disposing of a great deal of his property in England and wished to re-invest the proceeds in American stock. He gave me to understand that he wished to spend most of his time over there in future, as neither he nor his wife cared about Hathercleugh, though they meant to keep it up as the family estate and headquarters. He placed considerable sums of money in my hands from time to time, and I invested them in accordance with his instructions, handing him the securities as each transaction was concluded. And—that's really all I know."

Mr. Lindsey got in his word before Mr. Portlethorpe could speak again.

"There are just two questions I should like to ask—to which nobody can take exception, I think," he said. "One is—I gather that you've invested all the money which Sir Gilbert placed in your hands?"

"Yes—about all," replied Mr. Paley. "I have a balance—a small balance."

"And the other is this," continued Mr. Lindsey: "I suppose all these American securities which he now has are of such a nature that they could be turned into cash at any time, on any market?"

"That is so—certainly," assented Mr. Paley. "Yes, certainly so."

"Then that's enough for me!" exclaimed Mr. Lindsey, rising and beckoning me to follow. "Much obliged to you, sir."

Without further ceremony he stumped out into the street, with me at his heels, to be followed a few minutes later by Mr. Portlethorpe. And thereupon began a warm altercation between them which continued until all three of us were stowed away in a quiet corner of the smoking-room in the hotel at which it had been arranged Mr. Gavin Smeaton was to seek us on his arrival—and there it was renewed with equal vigour; at least, with equal vigour on Mr. Lindsey's part. As for me, I sat before the two disputants, my hands in my pockets, listening, as if I were judge and jury all in one, to what each had to urge.

They were, of course, at absolutely opposite poles of thought. One man was approaching the matter from one standpoint; the other from one diametrically opposed to it. Mr. Portlethorpe was all for minimizing things, Mr. Lindsey all for taking the maximum attitude. Mr. Portlethorpe said that even if we had not come to Edinburgh on a fool's errand—which appeared to be his secret and private notion—we had at any rate got the information which Mr. Lindsey wanted, and had far better go home now and attend to our proper business, which, he added, was not to pry and peep into other folks' affairs. He was convinced that Sir Gilbert Carstairs was Sir Gilbert Carstairs, and that Mrs. Ralston's and Mr. Lindsey's suspicions were all wrong. He failed to see any connection between Sir Gilbert and the Berwick mysteries and murders; it was ridiculous to suppose it. As for the yacht incident, he admitted it looked at least strange; but, he added, with a half-apologetic glance at me, he would like to hear Sir Gilbert's version of that affair before he himself made up his mind about it.

"If we can lay hands on him, you'll be hearing his version from the dock!" retorted Mr. Lindsey. "Your natural love of letting things go smoothly, Portlethorpe, is leading you into strange courses! Man alive!—take a look at the whole thing from a dispassionate attitude! Since the fellow got hold of the Hathercleugh property, he's sold everything, practically, but Hathercleugh itself; he's lost no time in converting the proceeds—a couple of hundred thousand pounds!—into foreign securities, which, says yon man Paley, are convertible into cash at any moment in any market! Something occurs—we don't know what, yet—to make him insecure in his position; without doubt, it's mixed up with Phillips and Gilverthwaite, and no doubt, afterwards, with Crone. This lad here accidentally knows something which might be fatal—Carstairs tries, having, as I believe, murdered Crone, to drown Moneylaws! And what then? It's every evident that, after leaving Moneylaws, he ran his yacht in somewhere on the Scottish coast, and turned her adrift; or, which is more likely, fell in with that fisher-fellow Robertson at Largo, and bribed him to tell a cock-and-bull tale about the whole thing—made his way to Edinburgh next morning, and possessed himself of the rest of his securities, after which, he clears out, to be joined somewhere by his wife, who, if what Hollins told us last night is true—and it no doubt is,—carried certain valuables off with her! What does it look like but that he's an impostor, who's just made all he can out of the property while he'd the chance, and is now away to enjoy his ill-gotten gains? That's what I'm saying, Portlethorpe—and I insist on my common-sense view of it!"

"And I say it's just as common-sense to insist, as I do, that it's all capable of proper and reasonable explanation!" retorted Mr. Portlethorpe. "You're a good hand at drawing deductions, Lindsey, but you're bad in your premises! You start off by asking me to take something for granted, and I'm not fond of mental gymnastics. If you'd be strictly logical—"

They went on arguing like that, one against the other, for a good hour, and it seemed to me that the talk they were having would have gone on for ever, indefinitely, if, on the stroke of noon, Mr. Gavin Smeaton had not walked in on us. At sight of him they stopped, and presently they were deep in the matter of the similarity of the handwritings, Mr. Lindsey having brought the letter and the will with him. Deep, at any rate, Mr. Lindsey and Mr. Portlethorpe were; as for Mr. Gavin Smeaton, he appeared to be utterly amazed at the suggestion which Mr. Lindsey threw out to him—that the father of whom he knew so little was, in reality, Michael Carstairs.

"Do you know what it is you're suggesting, Lindsey?" demanded Mr. Portlethorpe, suddenly. "You've got the idea into your head now that this young man's father, whom he's always heard of as one Martin Smeaton, was in strict truth the late Michael Carstairs, elder son of the late Sir Alexander—in fact, being the wilful and headstrong man that you are, you're already positive of it?"

"I am so!" declared Mr. Lindsey. "That's a fact, Portlethorpe."

"Then what follows?" asked Mr. Portlethorpe. "If Mr. Smeaton there is the true and lawful son of the late Michael Carstairs, his name is not Smeaton at all, but Carstairs, and he's the true holder of the baronetcy, and, as his grandfather died intestate, the legal owner of the property! D'you follow that?"

"I should be a fool if I didn't!" retorted Mr. Lindsey. "I've been thinking of it for thirty-six hours."

"Well—it'll have to be proved," muttered Mr. Portlethorpe. He had been staring hard at Mr. Gavin Smeaton ever since he came in, and suddenly he let out a frank exclamation. "There's no denying you've a strong Carstairs look on you!" said he. "Bless and save me!—this is the strangest affair!"

Smeaton put his hand into his pocket, and drew out a little package which he began to unwrap.

"I wonder if this has anything to do with it," he said. "I remembered, thinking things over last night, that I had something which, so the Watsons used to tell me, was round my neck when I first came to them. It's a bit of gold ornament, with a motto on it. I've had it carefully locked away for many a long year!"

He took out of his package a heart-shaped pendant, with a much-worn gold chain attached to it, and turned it over to show an engraved inscription on the reverse side.

"There's the motto," he said. "You see—*Who Will, Shall*. Whose is it?"

"God bless us!" exclaimed Mr. Portlethorpe. "The Carstairs motto! Aye!—their motto for many a hundred years! Lindsey, this is an extraordinary thing!—I'm inclined to think you may have some right in your notions. We must—"

But before Mr. Portlethorpe could say what they must do, there was a diversion in our proceedings which took all interest in them clean away from me, and made me forget whatever mystery there was about Carstairs, Smeaton, or anybody else. A page lad came along with a telegram in his hand asking was there any gentleman there of the name of Moneylaws? I took the envelope from him in a whirl of wonder, and tore it open, feeling an unaccountable sense of coming trouble. And in another minute the room was spinning round me; but the wording of the telegram was clear enough:

"Come home first train Maisie Dunlop been unaccountably missing since last evening and no trace of her. Murray."

I flung the bit of paper on the table before the other three, and, feeling like my head was on fire, was out of the room and the hotel, and in the street and racing into the station, before one of them could find a word to put on his tongue.

CHAPTER XXXI
NO TRACE

That telegram had swept all the doings of the morning clear away from me. Little I cared about the Carstairs affairs and all the mystery that was wrapping round them in comparison with the news which Murray had sent along in that peculiarly distressing fashion! I would cheerfully have given all I ever hoped to be worth if he had only added more news; but he had just said enough to make me feel as if I should go mad unless I could get home there and then. I had not seen Maisie since she and my mother had left Mr. Lindsey and me at Dundee—I had been so fully engaged since then, what with the police, and Mrs. Ralston, and Mr. Portlethorpe, and the hurried journeys, first to Newcastle and then to Edinburgh, that I had never had a minute to run down and see how things were going on. What, of course, drove me into an agony of apprehension was Murray's use of that one word "unaccountably." Why should Maisie be "unaccountably" missing? What had happened to take her out of her father's house?—where had she gone, that no trace of her could be got?—what had led to this utterly startling development?—what—

But it was no use speculating on these things—the need was for action. And I had seized on the first porter I met, and was asking him for the next train to Berwick, when Mr. Gavin Smeaton gripped my arm.

"There's a train in ten minutes, Moneylaws," said he quietly. "Come away to it—I'll go with you—we're all going. Mr. Lindsey thinks we'll do as much there as here, now."

Looking round I saw the two solicitors hurrying in our direction, Mr. Lindsey carrying Murray's telegram in his hand. He pulled me aside as we all walked towards the train.

"What do you make of this, Hugh?" he asked. "Can you account for any reason why the girl should be missing?"

"I haven't an idea," said I. "But if it's anything to do with all the rest of this business, Mr. Lindsey, let somebody look out! I'll have no mercy on anybody that's interfered with her—and what else can it be? I wish I'd never left the town!"

"Aye, well, we'll soon be back in it," he said, consolingly. "And we'll hope to find better news. I wish Murray had said more; it's a mistake to frighten folk in that way—he's said just too much and just too little."

It was a fast express that we caught for Berwick, and we were not long in covering the distance, but it seemed like ages to me, and the rest of them failed to get a word out of my lips during the whole time. And my heart was in my mouth when, as we ran into Berwick station, I saw Chisholm and Andrew Dunlop on the platform waiting us. Folk that have had bad news are always in a state of fearing to receive worse, and I dreaded what they might have come to the station to tell us. And Mr. Lindsey saw how I was feeling, and he was on the two of them with an instant question.

"Do you know any more about the girl than was in Murray's wire?" he demanded. "If so, what? The lad here's mad for news!"

Chisholm shook his head, and Andrew Dunlop looked searchingly at me.

"We know nothing more," he answered. "You don't know anything yourself, my lad?" he went on, staring at me still harder.

"I, Mr. Dunlop!" I exclaimed. "What do you think, now, asking me a question like yon! What should I know?"

"How should I know that?" said he. "You dragged your mother and my lass all the way to Dundee for nothing — so far as I could learn; and —"

"He'd good reason," interrupted Mr. Lindsey. "He did quite right. Now what is this about your daughter, Mr. Dunlop? Just let's have the plain tale of it, and then we'll know where we are."

I had already seen that Andrew Dunlop was not over well pleased with me — and now I saw why. He was a terrible hand at economy, saving every penny he could lay hands on, and as nothing particular seemed to have come of it, and — so far as he could see — there had been no great reason for it, he was sore at my sending for his daughter to Dundee, and all the sorer because — though I, of course, was utterly innocent of it — Maisie had gone off on that journey without as much as a by-your-leave to him. And he was not over ready or over civil to Mr. Lindsey.

"Aye, well!" said he. "There's strange doings afoot, and it's not my will that my lass should be at all mixed up in them, Mr. Lindsey! All this running up and down, hither and thither, on business that doesn't concern —"

Mr. Lindsey had the shortest of tempers on occasion, and I saw that he was already impatient. He suddenly turned away with a growl and collared Chisholm.

"You're a fool, Dunlop," he exclaimed over his shoulder; "it's your tongue that wants to go running! Now then, sergeant! — what is all this about Miss Dunlop? Come on!"

My future father-in-law drew off in high displeasure, but Chisholm hurriedly explained matters.

"He's in a huffy state, Mr. Lindsey," he said, nodding at Andrew's retreating figure. "Until you came in, he was under the firm belief that you and Mr. Hugh had got the young lady away again on some of this mystery business — he wouldn't have it any other way. And truth to tell, I was wondering if you had, myself! But since you haven't, it's here — and I hope nothing's befallen the poor young thing, for —"

"For God's sake, man, get it out!" said I. "We've had preface enough—come to your tale!"

"I'm only explaining to you, Mr. Hugh," he answered, calmly. "And I understand your impatience. It's like this, d'ye see?—Andrew Dunlop yonder has a sister that's married to a man, a sheep-farmer, whose place is near Coldsmouth Hill, between Mindrum and Kirk Yetholm—"

"I know!" I said. "You mean Mrs. Heselton. Well, man?"

"Mrs. Heselton, of course," said he. "You're right there. And last night—about seven or so in the evening—a telegram came to the Dunlops saying Mrs. Heselton was taken very ill, and would Miss Dunlop go over? And away she went there and then, on her bicycle, and alone—and she never reached the place!"

"How do you know that?" demanded Mr. Lindsey.

"Because," answered Chisholm, "about nine o'clock this morning in comes one of the Heselton lads to Dunlop to tell him his mother had died during the night; and then, of course, they asked did Miss Dunlop get there in time, and the lad said they'd never set eyes on her. And—that's all there is to tell, Mr. Lindsey."

I was for starting off, with, I think, the idea of instantly mounting my bicycle and setting out for Heselton's farm, when Mr. Lindsey seized my elbow.

"Take your time, lad," said he. "Let's think what we're doing. Now then, how far is it to this place where the girl was going?"

"Seventeen miles," said I, promptly.

"You know it?" he asked. "And the road?"

"I've been there with her—many a time, Mr. Lindsey," I answered. "I know every inch of the road."

"Now then!" he said, "get the best motor car there is in the town, and be off! Make inquiries all the way along; it'll be a queer thing if you can't trace something—it would be broad daylight all the time she'd be on her journey. Make a thorough search and full inquiry—she must have been seen." He turned to Mr. Smeaton, who had stood near, listening. "Go with him!" he said. "It'll be a good turn to do him—he wants company."

Mr. Smeaton and I hurried outside the station—a car or two stood in the yard, and we picked out the best. As we got in, Chisholm came up to us.

"You'd better have a word or two with our men along the road, Mr. Hugh," said he. "There's not many between here and the part you're going to, but you'd do no harm to give them an idea of what it is you're after, and tell them to keep their eyes open—and their ears, for that matter."

"Aye, we'll do that, Chisholm," I answered. "And do you keep eyes and ears open here in Berwick! I'll give ten pounds, and cash in his hand, to the first man that gives me news; and you can let that be known as much as you like, and at once—whether Andrew Dunlop thinks it's throwing money away or not!"

And then we were off; and maybe that he might draw me away from over much apprehension, Mr. Smeaton began to ask me about the road which Maisie would take to get to the Heseltons' farm—the road which we, of course, were taking ourselves. And I explained to him that it was just the ordinary high-road that ran between Berwick and Kelso that Maisie would follow, until she came to Cornhill, where she would turn south by way of Mindrum Mill, where—if that fact had anything to do with her disappearance—she would come into a wildish stretch of country at the northern edge of the Cheviots.

"There'll be places—villages and the like—all along, I expect?" he asked.

"It's a lonely road, Mr. Smeaton," I answered. "I know it well—what places there are, are more off than on it, but there's no stretch of it that's out of what you might term human reach. And how anybody could happen aught along it of a summer's evening is beyond me!—unless indeed we're going back to the old kidnapping times. And if you knew Maisie Dunlop, you'd know that she's the sort that would put up a fight if she was interfered with! I'm wondering if this has aught to do with all yon Carstairs affair? There's been such blackness about that, and such villainy, that I wish I'd never heard the name!"

"Aye!" he answered. "I understand you. But—it's coming to an end. And in queer ways—queer ways, indeed!"

I made no reply to him—and I was sick of the Carstairs matters; it seemed to me I had been eating and drinking and living and sleeping with murder and fraud till I was choked with the thought of them. Let me only find Maisie, said I to myself, and I would wash my hands of any further to-do with the whole vile business.

But we were not to find Maisie during the long hours of that weary afternoon and the evening that followed it. Mr. Lindsey had bade me keep the car and spare no expense, and we journeyed hither and thither all round the district, seeking news and getting none. She had been seen just once, at East Ord, just outside Berwick, by a man that was working in his cottage garden by the roadside—no other tidings could we get. We searched all along the road that runs by the side of Bowmont Water, between Mindrum and the Yetholms, devoting ourselves particularly to that stretch as being the loneliest, and without result. And as the twilight came on, and both of us were dead weary, we turned homeward, myself feeling much more desperate than even I did when I was swimming for my very life in the North Sea.

"And I'm pretty well sure of what it is, now, Mr. Smeaton!" I exclaimed as we gave up the search for that time. "There's been foul play! And I'll have all the police in Northumberland on this business, or—"

"Aye!" he said, "it's a police matter, this, without doubt, Moneylaws. We'd best get back to Berwick, and insist on Murray setting his men thoroughly to work."

We went first to Mr. Lindsey's when we got back, his house being on our way. And at sight of us he hurried out and had us in his study. There was a gentleman with him there—Mr. Ridley, the clergyman who had given evidence about Gilverthwaite at the opening of the inquest on Phillips.

CHAPTER XXXII

THE LINK

I knew by one glance at Mr. Lindsey's face that he had news for us; but there was only one sort of news I was wanting at that moment, and I was just as quick to see that, whatever news he had, it was not for me. And as soon as I heard him say that nothing had been heard of Maisie Dunlop during our absence, I was for going away, meaning to start inquiries of my own in the town, there and then, dead-beat though I was. But before I could reach the door he had a hand on me.

"You'll just come in, my lad, and sit you down to a hot supper that's waiting you and Mr. Smeaton there," he said, in that masterful way he had which took no denial from anybody. "You can do no more good just now—I've made every arrangement possible with the police, and they're scouring the countryside. So into that chair with you, and eat and drink—you'll be all the better for it. Mr. Smeaton," he went on, as he had us both to the supper-table and began to help us to food, "here's news for you—for such news as it is affects you, I'm thinking, more than any man that it has to do with. Mr. Ridley here has found out something relating to Michael Carstairs that'll change the whole course of events!—especially if we prove, as I've no doubt we shall, that Michael Carstairs was no other than your father, whom you knew as Martin Smeaton."

Smeaton turned in his chair and looked at Mr. Ridley, who—he and Mr. Lindsey having taken their supper before we got in—was sitting in a corner by the fire, eyeing the stranger from Dundee with evident and curious interest.

"I've heard of you, sir," said he. "You gave some evidence at the inquest on Phillips about Gilverthwaite's searching of your registers, I think?"

"Aye; and it's a fortunate thing—and shows how one thing leads to another—that Gilverthwaite did go to Mr. Ridley!" explained Mr. Lindsey. "It set Mr. Ridley on a track, and he's been following it up, and—to cut matters short—he's found particulars of the marriage of Michael Carstairs, who was said to have died unmarried. And I wish Portlethorpe hadn't gone home to Newcastle before Mr. Ridley came to me with the news."

Tired as I was, and utterly heart-sick about Maisie, I pricked up my ears at that. For at intervals Mr. Lindsey and I had discussed the probabilities of this affair, and I knew that there was a strong likelihood of its being found out that the mysterious Martin Smeaton was no other than the Michael Carstairs who had left Hathercleugh for good as a young man. And if it were established that he was married, and that Gavin Smeaton was his lawful son, why, then—but Mr. Ridley was speaking, and I broke off my own speculations to listen to him.

"You've scarcely got me to thank for this, Mr. Smeaton," he said. "There was naturally a good deal of talk in the neighbourhood after that inquest on Phillips—people began wondering what that man Gilverthwaite wanted to find in the parish registers, of which, I now know, he examined a good many, on both sides the Tweed. And in the ordinary course of things—and if some one had made a definite search with a definite object—what has been found now could have been found at once. But I'll tell you how it was. Up to some thirty years ago there was an old parish church away in the loneliest part of the Cheviots which had served a village that gradually went out of existence—though it's still got a name, Walholm, there's but a house or two in it now; and as there was next to no congregation, and the church itself was becoming ruinous, the old parish was abolished, and merged in the neighbouring parish of Felside, whose rector, my friend Mr. Longfield, has the old Walholm registers in his possession. When he read of the Phillips inquest, and what I'd said then, he thought of those registers and turned them up, out of a chest where they'd lain for thirty years anyway; and he at once found the entry of the marriage of one Michael Carstairs with a Mary Smeaton, which was by licence, and performed by the last vicar of Walholm—it was, as a matter of fact, the very last marriage which ever took place in the old church. And I should say," concluded Mr. Ridley, "that it was what one would call a secret wedding—secret, at any rate, in so far as this: as it was by licence, and as the old church was a most lonely and isolated place, far away from anywhere, even then there'd be no one to know of it beyond the officiating clergyman and the witnesses, who could, of course, be asked to hold their tongues about the matter, as they probably were. But there's the copy of the entry in the old register."

Smeaton and I looked eagerly over the slip of paper which Mr. Ridley handed across. And he, to whom it meant such a vast deal, asked but one question:

"I wonder if I can find out anything about Mary Smeaton!"

"Mr. Longfield has already made some quiet inquiries amongst two or three old people of the neighbourhood on that point," remarked Mr. Ridley. "The two witnesses to the marriage are both dead—years ago. But there are folk living in the neighbourhood who remember Mary Smeaton. The facts are these: she was a very handsome young woman, not a native of the district, who came in service to one of the farms on the Cheviots, and who, by a comparison of dates, left her place somewhat suddenly very soon after that marriage."

Smeaton turned to Mr. Lindsey in the same quiet fashion.

"What do you make of all this?" he asked.

"Plain as a pikestaff," answered Mr. Lindsey in his most confident manner. "Michael Carstairs fell in love with this girl and married her, quietly—as Mr. Ridley says, seeing that the marriage was by licence, it's probable, nay, certain, that nobody but the parson and the witnesses ever knew anything about it. I take it that immediately after the marriage Michael Carstairs and his wife went off to America, and that he, for reasons of his own, dropped his own proper patronymic and adopted hers. And," he ended, slapping his knee, "I've no doubt that you're the child of that marriage, that your real name is Gavin Carstairs, and that you're the successor to the baronetcy, and—the real owner of Hathercleugh,—as I shall have pleasure in proving."

"We shall see," said Smeaton, quietly as ever. "But—there's a good deal to do before we get to that, Mr. Lindsey! The present holder, or claimant, for example? What of him?"

"I've insisted on the police setting every bit of available machinery to work in an effort to lay hands on him," replied Mr. Lindsey. "Murray not only communicated all that Hollins told us last night to the Glasgow police this morning, first thing, but he's sent a man over there with the fullest news; he's wired the London authorities, and he's asked for special detective help. He's got a couple of detectives from Newcastle—all's being done that can be done. And for you too, Hugh, my lad!" he added, turning suddenly to me. "Whatever the police are doing in the other direction, they're doing in yours. For, ugly as it may sound and seem, there's nothing like facing facts, and I'm afraid, I'm very much afraid, that this disappearance of Maisie Dunlop is all of a piece with the rest of the villainy that's been going on—I am indeed!"

I pushed my plate away at that, and got on my feet. I had been dreading as much myself, all day, but I had never dared put it into words.

"You mean, Mr. Lindsey, that she's somehow got into the hands of—what?—who?" I asked him.

"Something and somebody that's at the bottom of all this!" he answered, shaking his head. "I'm afraid, lad, I'm afraid!"

I went away from all of them then, and nobody made any attempt to stop me, that time—maybe they saw in my face that it was useless. I left the house, and went—unconsciously, I think—away through the town to my mother's, driving my nails into the palms of my hands, and cursing Sir Gilbert Carstairs—if that was the devil's name!—between my teeth. And from cursing him, I fell to cursing myself, that I hadn't told at once of my seeing him at those crossroads on the night I went the errand for Gilverthwaite.

It had been late when Smeaton and I had got to Mr. Lindsey's, and the night was now fallen on the town—a black, sultry night, with great clouds overhead that threatened a thunderstorm. Our house was in a badly-lighted part of the street, and it was gloomy enough about it as I drew near, debating in myself what further I could do—sleep I knew I should not until I had news of Maisie. And in the middle of my speculations a man came out of the corner of a narrow lane that ran from the angle of our house, and touched me on the elbow. There was a shaft of light just there from a neighbour's window; in it I recognized the man as a fellow named Scott that did odd gardening jobs here and there in the neighbourhood.

"Wisht, Mr. Hugh!" said he, drawing me into the shadows of the lane; "I've been waiting your coming; there's a word I have for you—between ourselves."

"Well?" said I.

"I hear you're promising ten pounds—cash on the spot—to the man that can give you some news of your young lady?" he went on eagerly. "Is it right, now?"

"Can you?" I asked. "For if you can, you'll soon see that it's right."

"You'd be reasonable about it?" he urged, again taking the liberty to grip my arm. "If I couldn't just exactly give what you'd call exact and definite news, you'd consider it the same thing if I made a suggestion, wouldn't you, now, Mr. Hugh?—a suggestion that would lead to something?"

"Aye, would I!" I exclaimed. "And if you've got any suggestions, Scott, out with them, and don't beat about! Tell me anything that'll lead to discovery, and you'll see your ten pound quickly."

"Well," he answered, "I have to be certain, for I'm a poor man, as you know, with a young family, and it would be a poor thing for me to hint at aught that would take the bread out of their mouths—and my own. And I have the chance of a fine, regular job now at Hathercleugh yonder, and I wouldn't like to be putting it in peril."

"It's Hathercleugh you're talking of, then?" I asked him eagerly. "For God's sake, man, out with it! What is it you can tell me?"

"Not a word to a soul of what I say, then, at any time, present or future, Mr. Hugh?" he urged.

"Oh, man, not a word!" I cried impatiently. "I'll never let on that I had speech of you in the matter!"

"Well, then," he whispered, getting himself still closer: "mind you, I can't say anything for certain—it's only a hint I'm giving you; but if I were in your shoes, I'd take a quiet look round yon old part of Hathercleugh House—I would so! It's never used, as you'll know—nobody ever goes near it; but, Mr. Hugh, whoever and however it is, there's somebody in it now!"

"The old part!" I exclaimed. "The Tower part?"

"Aye, surely!" he answered. "If you could get quietly to it—"

I gave his arm a grip that might have told him volumes.

"I'll see you privately tomorrow, Scott," I said. "And if your news is any good—man! there'll be your ten pound in your hand as soon as I set eyes on you!"

And therewith I darted away from him and headlong into our house doorway.

CHAPTER XXXIII

THE OLD TOWER

My mother was at her knitting, in her easy-chair, in her own particular corner of the living-room when I rushed in, and though she started at the sight of me, she went on knitting as methodically as if all the world was regular as her own stitches.

"So you've come to your own roof at last, my man!" she said, with a touch of the sharpness that she could put into her tongue on occasion. "There's them would say you'd forgotten the way to it, judging by experience—why did you not let me know you were not coming home last night, and you in the town, as I hear from other folks?"

"Oh, mother!" I exclaimed. "How can you ask such questions when you know how things are!—it was midnight when Mr. Lindsey and I got in from Newcastle, and he would make me stop with him—and we were away again to Edinburgh first thing in the morning."

"Aye, well, if Mr. Lindsey likes to spend his money flying about the country, he's welcome!" she retorted. "But I'll be thankful when you settle down to peaceful ways again. Where are you going now?" she demanded. "There's a warm supper for you in the oven!"

"I've had my supper at Mr. Lindsey's, mother," I said, as I dragged my bicycle out of the back-place. "I've just got to go out, whether I will or no, and I don't know when I'll be in, either—do you think I can sleep in my bed when I don't know where Maisie is?"

"You'll not do much good, Hugh, where the police have failed," she answered. "There's yon man Chisholm been here during the evening, and he tells me they haven't come across a trace of her, so far."

"Chisholm's been here, then?" I exclaimed. "For no more than that?"

"Aye, for no more than that," she replied. "And then this very noon there was that Irishwoman that kept house for Crone, asking at the door for you."

"What, Nance Maguire!" I said. "What did she want?"

"You!" retorted my mother. "Nice sort of people we have coming to our door in these times! Police, and murderers, and Irish—"

"Did she say why she wanted me?" I interrupted her.

"I gave her no chance," said my mother. "Do you think I was going to hold talk with a creature like that at my steps?"

"I'd hold talk with the devil himself, mother, if I could get some news of Maisie!" I flung back at her as I made off. "You're as bad as Andrew Dunlop!"

There was the house door between her and me before she could reply to that, and the next instant I had my bicycle on the road and my leg over the saddle, and was hesitating before I put my foot to the pedal. What did Nance Maguire want of me? Had she any news of Maisie? It was odd that she should come down—had I better not ride up the town and see her? But I reflected that if she had any news—which was highly improbable—she would give it to the police; and so anxious was I to test what Scott had hinted at, that I swung on to my machine without further delay or reflection and went off towards Hathercleugh.

And as I crossed the old bridge, in the opening murmur of a coming storm, I had an illumination which came as suddenly as the first flash of lightning that followed just afterwards. It had been a matter of astonishment to me all day long that nobody, with the exception of the one man at East Ord, had noticed Maisie as she went along the road between Berwick and Mindrum on the previous evening—now I remembered, blaming myself for not having remembered it before, that there was a short cut, over a certain right-of-way, through the grounds of Hathercleugh House, which would save her a good three miles in her journey. She would naturally be anxious to get to her aunt as quickly as possible; she would think of the nearest way—she would take it. And now I began to understand the whole thing: Maisie had gone into the grounds of Hathercleugh, and—she had never left them!

The realization made me sick with fear. The idea of my girl being trapped by such a villain as I firmly believed the man whom we knew as Sir Gilbert Carstairs to be was enough to shake every nerve in my body; but to think that she had been in his power for twenty-four hours, alone, defenceless, brought on me a faintness that was almost beyond sustaining. I felt physically and mentally ill—weak. And yet, God knows! there never was so much as a thought of defeat in me. What I felt was that I must get there, and make some effort that would bring the suspense to an end for both of us. I was beginning to see how things might be—passing through those grounds she might have chanced on something, or somebody, or Sir Gilbert himself, who, naturally, would not let anybody escape him that could tell anything of his whereabouts. But if he was at Hathercleugh, what of the tale which Hollins had told us the night before?—nay, that very morning, for it was after midnight when he sat there in Mr. Lindsey's parlour. And, suddenly, another idea flashed across me—Was that tale true, or was the man telling us a pack of lies, all for some end? Against that last notion there was, of course, the torn scrap of letter to be set; but—but supposing that was all part of a plot, meant to deceive us while these villains—taking Hollins to be in at the other man's game—got clear away in some totally different direction? If it was, then it had been successful, for we had taken the bait, and all attention was being directed on Glasgow, and none elsewhere, and—as far as I knew—certainly none at Hathercleugh itself, whither nobody expected Sir Gilbert to come back.

But these were all speculations—the main thing was to get to Hathercleugh, acting on the hint I had just got from Scott, and to take a look round the old part of the big house, as far as I could. There was no difficulty about getting there—although I had small acquaintance with the house and grounds, never having been in them till the night of my visit to Sir Gilbert Carstairs. I knew the surroundings well enough to know how to get in amongst the shrubberies and coppices—I could have got in there unobserved in the daytime, and it was now black night. I had taken care to extinguish my lamp as soon as I got clear of the Border Bridge, and now, riding along in the darkness, I was secure from the observation of any possible enemy. And before I got to the actual boundaries of Hathercleugh, I was off the bicycle, and had hidden it in the undergrowth at the roadside; and instead of going into the grounds by the right-of-way which I was convinced Maisie must have taken, I climbed a fence and went forward through a spinny of young pine in the direction of the house. Presently I had a fine bit of chance guidance to it—as I parted the last of the feathery branches through which I had quietly made my way, and came out on the edge of the open park, a vivid flash of lightning showed me the great building standing on its plateau right before me, a quarter of a mile off, its turrets and gables vividly illuminated in the glare. And when that glare passed, as quickly as it had come, and the heavy blackness fell again, there was a gleam of light, coming from some window or other, and I made for that, going swiftly and silently over the intervening space, not without a fear that if anybody should chance to be on the watch another lightning flash might reveal my advancing figure.

But there had been no more lightning by the time I reached the plateau on which Hathercleugh was built; then, however, came a flash that was more blinding than the last, followed by an immediate crash of thunder right overhead. In that flash I saw that I was now close to the exact spot I wanted—the ancient part of the house. I saw, too, that between where I stood and the actual walls there was no cover of shrubbery or coppice or spinny—there was nothing but a closely cropped lawn to cross. And in the darkness I crossed it, there and then, hastening forward with outstretched hands which presently came against the masonry. In the same moment came the rain in torrents. In the same moment, too, came something else that damped my spirits more than any rains, however fierce and heavy, could damp my skin—the sense of my own utter helplessness. There I was—having acted on impulse—at the foot of a mass of grey stone which had once been impregnable, and was still formidable! I neither knew how to get in, nor how to look in, if that had been possible; and I now saw that in coming at all I ought to have come accompanied by a squad of police with authority to search the whole place, from end to end and top to bottom. And I reflected, with a grim sense of the irony of it, that to do that would have been a fine long job for a dozen men—what, then, was it that I had undertaken single-handed?

It was at this moment, as I clung against the wall, sheltering myself as well as I could from the pouring rain, that I heard through its steady beating an equally steady throb as of some sort of machine. It was a very subdued, scarcely apparent sound, but it was there—it was unmistakable. And suddenly—though in those days we were only just becoming familiar with them—I knew what it was—the engine of some sort of automobile; but not in action; the sound came from the boilers or condensers, or whatever the things were called which they used in the steam-driven cars. And it was near by—near at my right hand, farther along the line of the wall beneath which I was cowering. There was something to set all my curiosity aflame!—what should an automobile be doing there, at that hour—for it was now nearing well on to midnight—and in such close proximity to a half-ruinous place like that? And now, caring no more for the rain than if it had been a springtide shower, I slowly began to creep along the wall in the direction of the sound.

And here you will understand the situation of things better, if I say that the habitable part of Hathercleugh was a long way from the old part to which I had come. The entire mass of building, old and new, was of vast extent, and the old was separated from the new by a broken and utterly ruinous wing, long since covered over with ivy. As for the old itself, there was a great square tower at one corner of it, with walls extending from its two angles; it was along one of these walls that I was now creeping. And presently—the sound of the gentle throbbing growing slightly louder as I made my way along—I came to the tower, and to the deep-set gateway in it, and I knew at once that in that gateway there was an automobile drawn up, all ready for being driven out and away.

Feeling quietly for the corner of the gateway, I looked round, cautiously, lest a headlight on the car should betray my presence. But there was no headlight, and there was no sound beyond the steady throb of the steam and the ceaseless pouring of the rain behind me. And then, as I looked, came a third flash of lightning, and the entire scene was lighted up for me—the deep-set gateway with its groined and arched roof, the grim walls at each side, the dark massive masonry beyond it, and there, within the shelter, a small, brand-new car, evidently of fine and powerful make, which even my inexperienced eyes knew to be ready for departure from that place at any moment. And I saw something more during that flash—a half-open door in the wall to the left of the car, and the first steps of a winding stair.

As the darkness fell again, blacker than ever, and the thunder crashed out above the old tower, I stole along the wall to that door, intending to listen if aught were stirring within, or on the stairs, or in the rooms above. And I had just got my fingers on the rounded pillar of the doorway, and the thunder was just dying to a grumble, when a hand seized the back of my neck as in a vice, and something hard, and round, and cold pressed itself insistingly into my right temple. It was all done in the half of a second; but I knew, just as clearly as if I could see it, that a man of no ordinary strength had gripped me by the neck with one hand, and was holding a revolver to my head with the other.

CHAPTER XXXIV

THE BARGAIN

It may be that when one is placed in such a predicament as that in which I then found myself, one's wits are suddenly sharpened, and a new sense is given to one. Whether that is so or not, I was as certain as if I actually saw him that my assailant was the butler, Hollins. And I should have been infinitely surprised if any other voice than his had spoken—as he did speak when the last grumble of the thunder died out in a sulky, reluctant murmur.

"In at that door, and straight up the stairs, Moneylaws!" he commanded. "And quick, if you don't want your brains scattering. Lively, now!"

He trailed the muzzle of the revolver round from my temple to the back of my head as he spoke, pressing it into my hair in its course in a fashion that was anything but reassuring. I have often thought since of how I expected the thing to go off at any second, and how I was—for it's a fact—more curious than frightened about it. But the sense of self-preservation was on me, self-assertive enough, and I obliged him, stumbling in at the door under the pressure of his strong arm and of the revolver, and beginning to boggle at the first steps—old and much worn ones, which were deeply hollowed in the middle. He shoved me forward.

"Up you go," he said, "straight ahead! Put your arms up and out—in front of you till you feel a door—push it open."

He kept one hand on the scruff of my neck—too tightly for comfort—and with the other pressed the revolver into the cavity just above it, and in this fashion we went up. And even in that predicament I must have had my wits about me, for I counted two-and-twenty steps. Then came the door—a heavy, iron-studded piece of strong oak, and it was slightly open, and as I pushed it wider in the darkness, a musty, close smell came from whatever was within.

"No steps," said he, "straight on! Now then, halt—and keep halting! If you move one finger, Moneylaws, out fly your brains! No great loss to the community, my lad—but I've some use for them yet."

He took his hand away from my neck, but the revolver was still pressed into my hair, and the pressure never relaxed. And suddenly I heard a snap behind me, and the place in which we stood was lighted up—feebly, but enough to show me a cell-like sort of room, stone-walled, of course, and destitute of everything in the furnishing way but a bit of a cranky old table and a couple of three-legged stools on either side of it. With the released hand he had snapped the catch of an electric pocket-lamp, and in its blue glare he drew the revolver away from my head, and stepping aside, but always covering me with his weapon, motioned me to the further stool. I obeyed him mechanically, and he pulled the table a little towards him, sat down on the other stool, and, resting his elbow on the table ledge, poked the revolver within a few inches of my nose.

"Now, we'll talk for a few minutes, Moneylaws," he said quietly, "Storm or no storm, I'm bound to be away on my business, and I'd have been off now if it hadn't been for your cursed peeping and prying. But I don't want to kill you, unless I'm obliged to, so you'll just serve your own interests best if you answer a question or two and tell no lies. Are there more of you outside or about?"

"Not to my knowledge!" said I.

"You came alone?" he asked.

"Absolutely alone," I replied.

"And why?" he demanded.

"To see if I could get any news of Miss Dunlop," I answered.

"Why should you think to find Miss Dunlop here—in this old ruin?" he argued; and I could see he was genuinely curious. "Come now—straight talk, Moneylaws!—and it'll be all the better for you."

"She's missing since last night," I replied. "It came to me that she likely took a short cut across these grounds, and that in doing so she fell in with Sir Gilbert—or with you—and was kept, lest she should let out what she'd seen. That's the plain truth, Mr. Hollins."

He was keeping his eyes on me just as steadily as he kept the revolver, and I saw from the look in them that he believed me.

"Aye!" he said. "I see you can draw conclusions, if it comes to it. But—did you keep that idea of yours strictly to yourself, now?"

"Absolutely!" I repeated.

"You didn't mention it to a soul?" he asked searchingly.

"Not to a soul!" said I. "There isn't man, woman, or child knowsI'm here."

I thought he might have dropped the muzzle of the revolver at that, but he still kept it in a line with my nose and made no sign of relaxing his vigilance. But, as he was silent for the moment, I let out a question at him.

"It'll do you no harm to tell me the truth, Mr. Hollins," I said. "Do you know anything about Miss Dunlop? Is she safe? You've maybe had a young lady yourself one time or another—you'll understand what I'm feeling about it?"

He nodded solemnly at that and in quite a friendly way.

"Aye!" he answered. "I understand your feelings well enough, Moneylaws—and I'm a man of sentiment, so I'll tell you at once that the lass is safe enough, and there's not as much harm come to her as you could put on a sixpence—so there! But—I'm not sure yet that you're safe yourself," he went on, still eyeing me consideringly. "I'm a soft-hearted man, Moneylaws—or else you wouldn't have your brains in their place at this present minute!"

"There's a mighty lot of chance of my harming you, anyway!" said I, with a laugh that surprised myself. "Not so much as a penknife on me, and you with that thing at my head."

"Aye!—but you've got a tongue in that head," said he. "And you might be using it! But come, now—I'm loth to harm you, and you'd best tell me a bit more. What's the police doing?"

"What police do you mean?" I inquired.

"Here, there, everywhere, anywhere!" he exclaimed. "No quibbles, now!—you'll have had plenty of information."

"They're acting on yours," I retorted. "Searching about Glasgow for Sir Gilbert and Lady Carstairs—you put us on to that, Mr. Hollins."

"I had to," he answered. "Aye, I put Lindsey on to it, to be sure—and he took it all in like it was gospel, and so did all of you! It gained time, do you see, Money-laws—it had to be done."

"Then—they aren't in Glasgow?" I asked.

He shook his big head solemnly at that, and something like a smile came about the corners of his lips.

"They're not in Glasgow, nor near it," he answered readily, "but where all the police in England—and in Scotland, too, for that matter—'ll find it hard to get speech with them. Out of hand, Moneylaws!—out of hand, d'ye see—for the police!"

He gave a sort of chuckle when he said this, and it emboldened me to come to grips with him—as far as words went.

"Then what harm can I do you, Mr. Hollins?" I asked. "You're not in any danger that I know of."

He looked at me as if wondering whether I wasn't trying a joke on him, and after staring a while he shook his head.

"I'm leaving this part—finally," he answered. "That's Sir Gilbert's brand-new car that's all ready for me down the stairs; and as I say, whether it's storm or no storm, I must be away. And there's just two things I can do, Moneylaws—I can lay you out on the floor here, with your brains running over your face, or I can—trust to your honour!"

We looked at each other for a full minute in silence—our eyes meeting in the queer, bluish light of the electric pocket-lamp which he had set on the table before us. Between us, too, was that revolver—always pointing at me out of its one black eye.

"If it's all the same to you, Mr. Hollins," said I at length, "I'd prefer you to trust to my honour. Whatever quality my brains may have, I'd rather they were used than misused in the way you're suggesting! If it's just this—that you want me to hold my tongue—"

"I'll make a bargain with you," he broke in on me. "You'd be fine and glad to see your sweetheart, Moneylaws, and assure yourself that she's come to no harm, and is safe and well?"

"Aye! I would that!" I exclaimed. "Give me the chance, Mr. Hollins!"

"Then give me your word that whatever happens, whatever comes, you'll not mention to the police that you've seen me tonight, and that whenever you're questioned you'll know nothing about me!" he said eagerly. "Twelve hours' start—aye, six!—means safety to me, Moneylaws. Will you keep silence?"

"Where's Miss Dunlop?" asked I.

"You can be with her in three minutes," he answered, "if you'll give me your word—and you're a truthful lad, I think—that you'll both bide where you are till morning, and that after that you'll keep your tongue quiet. Will you do that?"

"She's close by?" I demanded.

"Over our heads," he said calmly. "And you've only to say the word—"

"It's said, Mr. Hollins!" I exclaimed. "Go your ways! I'll never breathe a syllable of it to a soul! Neither in six, nor twelve, nor a thousand hours!—your secret's safe enough with me—so long as you keep your word about her—and just now!"

He drew his free hand off the table, still watching me, and still keeping up the revolver, and from a drawer in the table between us pulled out a key and pushed it over.

"There's a door behind you in yon corner," he said. "And you'll find a lantern at its foot—you've matches on you, no doubt. And beyond the door there's another stair that leads up to the turret, and you'll find her there—and safe—and so—go your ways, now, Moneylaws, and I'll go mine!"

He dropped the revolver into a side pocket of his waterproof coat as he spoke, and, pointing me to the door in the corner, turned to that by which he had entered. And as he turned he snapped off the light of his electric lamp, while I myself, having fumbled for a box of matches, struck one and looked around me for this lantern he had mentioned. In its spluttering light I saw his big figure round the corner—then, just as I made for the lantern, the match went out and all was darkness again. As I felt for another match, I heard him pounding the stair—and suddenly there was a sort of scuffle and he cried out loudly once, and there was the sound of a fall, and then of lighter steps hurrying away, and then a heavy, rattling groan. And with my heart in my mouth and fingers trembling so that I could scarcely hold the match, I made shift to light the candle in the lantern, and went fearfully after him. There, in an angle of the stairway, he was lying, with the blood running in dark streams from a gap in his throat; while his hands, which he had instinctively put up to it, were feebly dropping away and relaxing on his broad chest. And as I put the lantern closer to him he looked up at me in a queer, puzzled fashion, and died before my very eyes.

CHAPTER XXXV

THE SWAG

I shrank back against the mouldy wall of that old stairway shivering as if I had been suddenly stricken with the ague. I had trembled in every limb before ever I heard the sound of the sudden scuffle, and from a variety of reasons—the relief of having Hollins's revolver withdrawn from my nose; the knowledge that Maisie was close by; the gradual wearing-down of my nerves during a whole day of heart-sickening suspense,—but now the trembling had deepened into utter shaking: I heard my own teeth chattering, and my heart going like a pump, as I stood there, staring at the man's face, over which a grey pallor was quickly spreading itself. And though I knew that he was as dead as ever a man can be, I called to him, and the sound of my own voice frightened me.

"Mr. Hollins!" I cried. "Mr. Hollins!"

And then I was frightened still more, for, as if in answer to my summons, but, of course, because of some muscular contraction following on death, the dead lips slightly parted, and they looked as if they were grinning at me. At that I lost what nerve I had left, and let out a cry, and turned to run back into the room where we had talked. But as I turned there were sounds at the foot of the stair, and the flash of a bull's-eye lamp, and I heard Chisholm's voice down in the gateway below.

"Hullo, up there!" he was demanding. "Is there anybody above?"

It seemed as if I was bursting my chest when I got an answer out to him.

"Oh, man!" I shouted, "come up! There's me here—and there's murder!"

I heard him exclaim in a dismayed and surprised fashion, and mutter some words to somebody that was evidently with him, and then there was heavy tramping below, and presently Chisholm's face appeared round the corner; and as he held his bull's-eye before him, its light fell full on Hollins, and he jumped back a step or two.

"Mercy on us!" he let out. "What's all this? The man's lying dead!"

"Dead enough, Chisholm!" said I, gradually getting the better of my fright. "And murdered, too! But who murdered him, God knows—I don't! He trapped me in here, not ten minutes ago, and had me at the end of a revolver, and we came to terms, and he left me—and he was no sooner down the stairs here than I heard a bit of a scuffle, and him fall and groan, and I ran out to find—that! And somebody was off and away—have you seen nobody outside there?"

"You can't see an inch before your eyes—the night's that black," he answered, bending over the dead man. "We've only just come—round from the house. But whatever were you doing here, yourself?"

"I came to see if I could find any trace of Miss Dunlop in this old part," I answered, "and he told me—just before this happened—she's in the tower above, and safe. And I'll go up there now, Chisholm; for if she's heard aught of all this—"

There was another policeman with him, and they stepped past the body and followed me into the little room and looked round curiously. I left them whispering, and opened the door that Hollins had pointed out. There was a stair there, as he had said, set deep in the thick wall, and I went a long way up it before I came to another door, in which there was a key set in the lock. And in a moment I had it turned, and there was Maisie, and I had her in my arms and was flooding her with questions and holding the light to her face to see if she was safe, all at once.

"You've come to no harm?—you're all right?—you've not been frightened out of your senses?—how did it all come about?" I rapped out at her. "Oh, Maisie, I've been seeking for you all day long, and—"

And then, being utterly overwrought, I was giving out, and I suddenly felt a queer giddiness coming over me; and if it had not been for her, I should have fallen and maybe fainted, and she saw it, and got me to a couch from which she had started when I turned the key, and was holding a glass of water to my lips that she snatched up from a table, and encouraging me, who should have been consoling her—all within the minute of my setting eyes on her, and me so weak, as it seemed, that I could only cling on to her hand, making sure that I had really got her.

"There, there, it's all right, Hugh!" she murmured, patting my arm as if I had been some child that had just started awake from a bad dream. "There's no harm come to me at all, barring the weary waiting in this black hole of a place!—I've had food and drink and a light, as you see—they promised me I should have no harm when they locked me in. But oh, it's seemed like it was ages since then!"

"They? Who?" I demanded. "Who locked you in?"

"Sir Gilbert and that butler of his—Hollins," she answered. "I took the short cut through the grounds here last night, and I ran upon the two of them at the corner of the ruins, and they stopped me, and wouldn't let me go, and locked me up here, promising I'd be let out later on."

"Sir Gilbert!" I exclaimed. "You're sure it was Sir Gilbert?"

"Of course I'm sure!" she replied. "Who else? And I made out they were afraid of my letting out that I'd seen them—it was Sir Gilbert himself said they could run no risks."

"You've seen him since?" I asked. "He's been in here?"

"No—not since last night," she answered. "And Hollins not since this morning when he brought me some food—I've not wanted for that," she went on, with a laugh, pointing to things that had been set on the table. "And he said, then, that about midnight, tonight, I'd hear the key turned, and after that I was free to go, but

I'd have to make my way home on foot, for he wasn't wanting me to be in Berwick again too soon."

"Aye!" I said, shaking my head. "I'm beginning to see through some of it! But, Maisie, you'll be a good girl, and just do what I tell you?—and that's to stay where you are until I fetch you down. For there's more dreadfulness below—where Sir Gilbert may be, Heaven knows, but Hollins is lying murdered on the stair; and if I didn't see him murdered, I saw him take his last breath!"

She, too, shook a bit at that, and she gripped me tighter.

"You're not by yourself, Hugh?" she asked anxiously. "You're in no danger?"

But just then Chisholm called up the stair of the turret, asking was Miss Dunlop safe, and I bade Maisie speak to him.

"That's good news!" said he. "But will you tell Mr. Hugh to come down to us?—and you'd best stop where you are yourself, Miss Dunlop—there's no very pleasant sight down this way. Have you no idea at all who did this?" he asked, as I went down to him. "You were with him?"

"Man alive, I've no more idea than you have!" I exclaimed. "He was making off somewhere in yon car that's below—he threatened me with the loss of my life if I didn't agree to let him get away in peace, and he was going down the stairs to the car when it happened. But I'll tell you this: Miss Dunlop says Sir Gilbert was here last night!—and it was he and Hollins imprisoned her above there—frightened she'd let out on them if she got away."

"Then the Glasgow tale was all lies?" he exclaimed. "It came from this man, too, that's lying dead—it's been a put-up thing, d'ye think, Mr. Hugh?"

"It's all part of a put-up thing, Chisholm," said I. "Hadn't we better get the man in here, and see what's on him? And what made you come here yourselves?—and are there any more of you about?"

"We came asking some information at the house," he answered, "and we were passing round here, under the wall, on our way to the road, when we heard that car throbbing, and then saw your bit of a light. And that's a good idea of yours, and we'll bring him into this place and see if there's aught to give us a clue. Slip down," he went on, turning to the other man, "and bring the headlights off the car, so that we can see what we're doing. Do you think this is some of Sir Gilbert's work, Mr. Hugh?" he whispered when we were alone. "If he was about here, and this Hollins was in some of his secrets—?"

"Oh, don't ask me!" I exclaimed. "It seems like there was nothing but murder on every hand of us! And whoever did this can't be far away—only the night's that black, and there's so many holes and corners hereabouts that it would be like searching a rabbit-warren—you'll have to get help from the town."

"Aye, to be sure!" he agreed. "But we'll take a view of things ourselves, first. There may be effects on him that'll suggest something."

We carried the body into the room when the policeman came up with the lamps from the car, and stretched it out on the table at which Hollins and I had sat not so long before; though that time, indeed, now seemed to me to belong to some other life! And Chisholm made a hasty examination of what there was in the man's pockets, and there was little that had any significance, except that in a purse which he carried in an inner pocket of his waistcoat there was a considerable sum of money in notes and gold.

The other policeman, who held one of the lamps over the table while Chisholm was making this search, waited silently until it was over, and then he nodded his head at the stair.

"There's some boxes, or cases, down in yon car," he remarked. "All fastened up and labelled—it might be worth while to take a look into them, sergeant. What's more, there's tools lying in the car that looks like they'd been used to fasten them up."

"We'll have them up here, then," said Chisholm. "Stop you here, Mr. Hugh, while we fetch them—and don't let your young lady come down while that's lying here. You might cover him up," he went on, with a significant nod. "It's an ill sight for even a man's eyes, that!"

There were some old, moth-eaten hangings about the walls here and there, and I took one down and laid it over Hollins, wondering while I did this office for him what strange secret it was that he had carried away into death, and why that queer and puzzled expression had crossed his face in death's very moment. And that done, I ran up to Maisie again, bidding her be patient awhile, and we talked quietly a bit until Chisholm called me down to look at the boxes. There were four of them—stout, new-made wooden cases, clamped with iron at the corners, and securely screwed down; and when the policemen invited me to feel the weight, I was put in mind, in a lesser degree, of Gilverthwaite's oak-chest.

"What do you think's like to be in there, now, Mr. Hugh?" asked Chisholm. "Do you know what I think? There's various heavy metals in the world—aye, and isn't gold one of the heaviest?—it'll not be lead that's in here! And look you at that!"

He pointed to some neatly addressed labels tacked strongly to each lid—the writing done in firm, bold, print-like characters:

John Harrison, passenger, by S.S. Aerolite. Newcastle to Hamburg.

I was looking from one label to the other and finding them all alike, when we heard voices at the foot of the stair, and from out of them came Superintendent Murray's, demanding loudly who was above.

CHAPTER XXXVI

GOLD

There was quite a company of men came up the stair with Murray, crowding, all of them, into the room, with eyes full of astonishment at what they saw: Mr. Lindsey and Mr. Gavin Smeaton, and a policeman or two, and—what was of more interest to me—a couple of strangers. But looking at these more closely, I saw that I had seen one of them before—an elderly man, whom I recognized as having been present in court when Carter was brought up before the magistrates; a quiet, noticing sort of man whom I remembered as appearing to take great and intelligent interest in the proceedings. And he and the other man now with him seemed to take just as keen an interest in what Chisholm and I had to tell; but while Murray was full of questions to both of us, they asked none. Only—during that questioning—the man whom I had never seen before quietly lifted the hanging which I had spread over Hollins's dead body, and took a searching look at his face.

Mr. Lindsey drew me aside and pointed at the elderly man whom I remembered seeing in the police court.

"You see yon gentleman?" he whispered. "That's a Mr. Elphinstone, that was formerly steward to old Sir Alexander Carstairs. He's retired—a good many years, now, and lives the other side of Alnwick, in a place of his own. But this affair's fetched him into the light again—to some purpose!"

"I saw him in the court when Carter was before the bench, Mr. Lindsey," I remarked.

"Aye!—and I wish he'd told me that day what he could have told!" exclaimed Mr. Lindsey under his breath. "But he's a cautious, a very cautious man, and he preferred to work quietly, and it wasn't until very late tonight that he came to Murray and sent for me—an hour, it was, after you'd gone home. The other man with him is a London detective. Man! there's nice revelations come out!—and pretty much on the lines I was suspecting. We'd have been up here an hour ago if it hadn't been for yon storm. And—but now that the storm's over, Hugh, we must get Maisie Dunlop out of this; come up, now, and show me where she is—that first, and the rest after."

We left the others still grouped around the dead man and the boxes which had been brought up from the car, and I took Mr. Lindsey up the stairs to the room in the turret which had served Maisie for a prison all that weary time. And after a word or two with her about her sore adventures, Mr. Lindsey told her she must be away, and he would get Murray to send one of the policemen with her to see her safe home—I myself being still wanted down below. But at that Maisie began to show signs of distinct dislike and disapproval.

"I'll not go a yard, Mr. Lindsey," she declared, "unless you'll give me your word that you'll not let Hugh out of your sight again till all this is settled and done with! Twice within this last few days the lad's been within an inch of his life, and they say the third time pays for all—and how do I know there mightn't be a third time in his case? And I'd rather stay by him, and we'll take our chances together—"

"Now, now!" broke in Mr. Lindsey, patting her arm. "There's a good half-dozen of us with him now, and we'll take good care no harm comes to him or any of us; so be a good lass and get you home to Andrew—and tell him all about it, for the worthy man's got a bee in his bonnet that we've been in some way responsible for your absence, my girl. You're sure you never set eyes on Sir Gilbert again after he and Hollins stopped you?" he asked suddenly, as we went down the stair. "Nor heard his voice down here—or anywhere?"

"I never saw him again, nor heard him," answered Maisie. "And till Hugh came just now, I'd never seen Hollins himself since morning and—Oh!"

She had caught sight of the still figure stretched out in the lower room, and she shrank to me as we hurried her past it and down to the gateway below. Thither Murray followed us, and after a bit more questioning he put her in a car in which he and some of the others had come up, and sent one of his men off with her; but before this Maisie pulled me away into the darkness and gripped me tight by the arm.

"You'll promise me, Hugh, before ever I go, that you'll not run yourself into any more dangers?" she asked earnestly. "We've been through enough of that, and I'm just more than satisfied with it, and it's like as if there was something lurking about—"

She began to shiver as she looked into the black night about us—and it was indeed, although in summer time, as black a night as ever I saw—and her hand got a tighter grip on mine.

"How do you know yon bad man isn't still about?" she whispered. "It was he killed Hollins, of course!—and if he wanted to kill you yon time in the yacht, he'll want again!"

"It's small chance he'll get, then, now!" I said. "There's no fear of that, Maisie—amongst all yon lot of men above. Away you go, now, and get to your bed, and as sure as sure I'll be home to eat my breakfast with you. It's my opinion all this is at an end."

"Not while yon man's alive!" she answered. "And I'd have far rather stayed with you—till it's daylight, anyway."

However, she let me put her into the car; and when I had charged the policeman who went with her not to take his eyes off her until she was safe in Andrew Dunlop's house, they went off, and Mr. Lindsey and I turned up the stair again. Murray had preceded us, and under his superintendence Chisholm was beginning to open the screwed-up boxes. The rest of us stood round while this job was going on, waiting in silence. It was no easy or quick job, for the screws had been fastened in after a thoroughly workmanlike fashion, and when he got the first lid off we saw that the boxes themselves had been evidently specially made for this purpose. They were of some very strong, well-seasoned wood, and they were lined, first with zinc, and then with thick felt. And—as we were soon aware—they were filled to the brim with gold. There it lay—roll upon roll, all carefully packed—gold! It shone red and fiery in the light of our lamps, and it seemed to me that in every gleam of it I saw devils' eyes, full of malice, and mockery, and murder.

But there was one box, lighter than the rest, in which, instead of gold, we found the valuable things of which Hollins had told Mr. Lindsey and Mr. Portlethorpe and myself when he came to us on his lying mission, only the previous midnight. There they all were—the presents that had been given to various of the Carstairs baronets by royal donors—carefully packed and bestowed. And at sight of them, Mr. Lindsey looked significantly at me, and then at Murray.

"He was a wily and a clever man, this fellow that's lying behind us," he muttered. "He pulled our hair over our eyes to some purpose with his tale of Lady Carstairs and her bicycle—but I'm forgetting," he broke off, and drew me aside. "There's another thing come out since you left me and Smeaton tonight," he whispered. "The police have found out something for themselves—I'll give them that credit. That was all lies—lies, nothing but lies!—that Hollins told us,—all done to throw us off the scent. You remember the tale of the registered letter from Edinburgh?—the police found out last evening from the post folks that there never was any registered letter. You remember Hollins said Lady Carstairs went off on her bicycle? The police have found out she never went off on any bicycle—she wasn't there to go off. She was away early that morning; she took a train south from Beal station before breakfast—at least, a veiled woman answering her description did,—and she's safe hidden in London, or elsewhere, by now, my lad!"

"But him—the man—Sir Gilbert, or whoever he is?" I whispered. "What of him, Mr. Lindsey?"

"Aye, just so!" he said. "I'm gradually piecing it together, as we go on. It would seem to me that he made his way to Edinburgh after getting rid of you, as he thought and hoped—probably got there the very next morning, through the help of yon fisherman at Largo, Robertson, who, of course, told us and the police a pack of lies!—and when he'd got the last of these securities from Paley, he worked back here, secretly, and with the help of Hollins, and has no doubt kept quiet in this old tower until they could get away with that gold! Of course, Hollins has been in at all this—but now—who's killed Hollins? And where's the chief party—the other man?"

"What?" I exclaimed. "You don't think he killed Hollins, then?"

"I should be a fool if I did, my lad," he answered. "Bethink yourself!—when all was cut and dried for their getting off, do you think he'd stick a knife in his confederate's throat? No!—I can see their plan, and it was a good one. Hollins would have run those cases down to Newcastle in a couple of hours; there'd have been no suspicion about them, and no questions which he couldn't answer—he'd have gone across to Hamburg with them himself. As for the man we know as Sir Gilbert, you'll be hearing something presently from Mr. Elphinstone yonder; but my impression is, as Maisie never saw or heard of him during the night and day, that he got away after his wife last night—and with those securities on him!"

"Then—who killed Hollins?" I said in sheer amazement. "Are there others in at all this?"

"You may well ask that, lad," he responded, shaking his head. "Indeed, though we're nearing it, I think we're not quite at the end of the lane, and there'll be a queer turning or two in it, yet, before we get out. But here's Murray come to an end of the present business."

Murray had finished his inspection of the cases and was helping Chisholm to replace the lids. He, Chisholm, and the detective were exchanging whispered remarks over this job; Mr. Elphinstone and Mr. Gavin Smeaton were talking together in low voices near the door. Presently Murray turned to us.

"We can do no more here, now, Mr. Lindsey," he said, "and I'm going to lock this place up until daylight and leave a man in the gateway below, on guard. But as to the next step—you haven't the least idea in your head, Moneylaws, about Hollins's assailant?" he went on, turning to me. "You heard and saw—nothing?"

"I've told you what I heard, Mr. Murray," I answered. "As to seeing anything, how could I? The thing happened on the stair there, and I was in this corner unlocking the inner door."

"It's as big a mystery as all the rest of it!" he muttered. "And it's just convincing me there's more behind all this than we think for. And one thing's certain—we can't search these grounds or the neighbourhood until the light comes. But we can go round to the house."

He marched us all out at that, and himself locked up the room, leaving the dead man with the chests of gold; and having stationed a constable in the gateway of the old tower, he led us off in a body to the habited part of the house. There were lights there in plenty, and a couple of policemen at the door, and behind them a whole troop of servants in the hall, half dressed, and open-mouthed with fright and curiosity.

CHAPTER XXXVII

THE DARK POOL

As I went into that house with the rest of them, I had two sudden impressions. One was that here at my side, in the person of Mr. Gavin Smeaton, was, in all probability, its real owner, the real holder of the ancient title, who was coming to his lawful rights in this strange fashion. The other was of the contrast between my own coming at that moment and the visit which I had paid there, only a few evenings previously, when Hollins had regarded me with some disfavour and the usurper had been so friendly. Now Hollins was lying dead in the old ruin, and the other man was a fugitive—and where was he?

Murray had brought us there to do something towards settling that point, and he began his work at once by assembling every Jack and Jill in the house and, with the help of the London detective, subjecting them to a searching examination as to the recent doings of their master and mistress and the butler. But Mr. Lindsey motioned Mr. Elphinstone, and Mr. Gavin Smeaton, and myself into a side-room and shut the door on us.

"We can leave the police to do their own work," he remarked, motioning us to be seated at a convenient table. "My impression is that they'll find little out from the servants. And while that's afoot, I'd like to have that promised story of yours, Mr. Elphinstone—I only got an idea of it, you know, when you and Murray came to my house. And these two would like to hear it—one of them, at any rate, is more interested in this affair than you'd think or than he knew of himself until recently."

Now that we were in a properly lighted room, I took a more careful look at the former steward of Hathercleugh. He was a well-preserved, shrewd-looking man of between sixty and seventy: quiet and observant, the sort of man that you could see would think a lot without saying much. He smiled a little as he put his hands together on the table and glanced at our expectant faces—it was just the smile of a man who knows what he is talking about.

"Aye, well, Mr. Lindsey," he responded, "maybe there's not so much mystery in this affair as there seems to be once you've got at an idea. I'll tell you how I got at mine and what's come of it. Of course, you'll not know, for I think you didn't come to Berwick yourself until after I'd left the neighbourhood—but I was connected with the Hathercleugh estate from the time I was a lad until fifteen years ago, when I gave up the steward's job and went to live on a bit of property of my own, near Alnwick. Of course, I knew the two sons—Michael and Gilbert; and I remember well enough when, owing to perpetual quarrelling with their father, he gave them both a good lot of money and they went their several ways. And after that, neither ever came back that I heard of, nor did I ever come across either, except on one occasion—to which I'll refer in due course. In time, as I've just said, I retired; in time, too, Sir Alexander died, and I heard that, Mr. Michael being dead in the West Indies, Sir Gilbert had come into the title and estates. I did think, once or twice, of coming over to see him; but the older a man gets, the fonder he is of his own fireside—and I didn't come here, nor did I ever hear much of him; he certainly made no attempt to see me. And so we come to the beginning of what we'll call the present crisis. That beginning came with the man who turned up in Berwick this spring."

"You mean Gilverthwaite?" asked Mr. Lindsey.

"Aye—but I didn't know him by that name!" assented Mr. Elphinstone, with a sly smile. "I didn't know him by any name. What I know is this. It must have been about a week—certainly not more—before Gilverthwaite's death that he—I'm sure of his identity, because of his description—called on me at my house, and with a good deal of hinting and such-like told me that he was a private inquiry agent, and could I tell him something about the late Michael Carstairs?—and that, it turned out, was: Did I know if Michael was married before he left England, and if so, where, and to whom? Of course, I knew nothing about it, and as the man wouldn't give me the least information I packed him off pretty sharply. And the next thing I heard was of the murder of John Phillips. I didn't connect that with the visit of the mysterious man at first; but of course I read the account of the inquest, and Mr. Ridley's evidence, and then I began to see there was some strange business going on, though I couldn't even guess at what it could be. And I did nothing, and said nothing—there seemed nothing, then, that I could do or say, though I meant to come forward later—until I saw the affair of Crone in the newspapers, and I knew then that there was more in the matter than was on the surface. So, when I learnt that a man named Carter had been arrested on the charge of murdering Crone, I came to Berwick, and went to the court to hear what was said when Carter was put before the magistrates. I got a quiet seat in the court—and maybe you didn't see me."

"I did!" I exclaimed. "I remember you perfectly, Mr. Elphinstone."

"Aye!" he said with an amused smile. "You're the lad that's had his finger in the pie pretty deep—you're well out of it, my man! Well—there I was, and a man sitting by me that knew everybody, and before ever the case was called this man pointed out Sir Gilbert Carstairs coming in and being given a seat on the bench. And I knew that there was a fine to-do, and perhaps nobody but myself knowing of it, for the man pointed out to me was no Sir Gilbert Carstairs, nor any Carstairs at all—not he! But—I knew him!"

"You knew him!" exclaimed Mr. Lindsey. "Man!—that's the first direct bit of real illumination we've had! And—who is he, then, Mr. Elphinstone?"

"Take your time!" answered Mr. Elphinstone. "We'll have to go back a bit: you'll put the police court out of your mind a while. It's about—I forget rightly how long since, but it was just after I gave up the stewardship that I had occasion to go up to London on business of my own. And there, one morning, as I was sauntering down the lower end of Regent Street, I met Gilbert Carstairs, whom I'd never seen since he left home. He'd his arm in mine in a minute, and he would have me go with him to his rooms in Jermyn Street, close by—there was no denying him. I went, and found his rooms full of trunks, and cases, and the like—he and a friend of his, he said, were just off on a sort of hunting-exploration trip to some part of Central America; I don't know what they weren't going to do, but it was to be a big affair, and they were to come back loaded up with natural-history specimens and to make a pile of money out of the venture, too. And he was telling me all about it in his eager, excitable way when the other man came in, and I was introduced to him. And, gentlemen, that's the man I saw—under the name of Sir Gilbert Carstairs—on the bench at Berwick only the other day! He's changed, of course—more than I should have thought he would have done in fifteen years, for that's about the time since I saw him and Gilbert together there in Jermyn Street,—but I knew him as soon as I clapped eyes on him, and whatever doubt I had went as soon as I saw him lift his right hand to his moustache, for there are two fingers missing on that hand—the middle ones—and I remembered that fact about the man Gilbert Carstairs had introduced to me. I knew, I tell you, as I sat in that court, that the fellow there on the bench, listening, was an impostor!"

We were all bending forward across the table, listening eagerly—and there was a question in all our thoughts, which Mr. Lindsey put into words.

"The man's name?"

"It was given to me, in Jermyn Street that morning, as Meekin—Dr. Meekin," answered Mr. Elphinstone. "Gilbert Carstairs, as you're aware, was a medical man himself—he'd qualified, anyway—and this was a friend of his. But that was all I gathered then—they were both up to the eyes in their preparations, for they were off for Southampton that night, and I left them to it—and, of course, never heard of them again. But now to come back to the police court the other day: I tell you, I was—purposely—in a quiet corner, and there I kept till the case was over; but just when everybody was getting away, the man on the bench caught sight of me—"

"Ah!" exclaimed Mr. Lindsey, looking across at me. "Ah! that's another reason—that supplements the ice-ax one! Aye!—he caught sight of you, Mr. Elphinstone—"

"And," continued Mr. Elphinstone, "I saw a queer, puzzled look come into his face. He looked again—looked hard. I took no notice of his look, though I continued to watch him, and presently he turned away and went out. But I knew he had recognized me as a man he had seen somewhere. Now remember, when Gilbert Carstairs introduced me to this man, Gilbert did not mention any connection of mine with Hathercleugh—he merely spoke of me as an old friend; so Meekin, when he came into these parts, would have no idea of finding me here. But I saw he was afraid—badly afraid—because of his recognition and doubt about me. And the next question was—what was I to do? I'm not the man to do things in haste, and I could see this was a black, deep business, with maybe two murders in it. I went off and got my lunch—and thought. At the end of it, rather than go to the police, I went to your office, Mr. Lindsey. And your office was locked up, and you were all away for the day. And then an idea struck me: I have a relative—the man outside with Murray—who's a high-placed officer in the Criminal Investigation Department at New Scotland Yard—I would go to him. So—I went straight off to London by the very next South express. Why? To see if he could trace anything about this Meekin."

"Aye!" nodded Mr. Lindsey admiringly. "You were in the right of it, there—that was a good notion. And—you did?"

"Not since the Jermyn Street affair," answered Mr. Elphinstone. "We traced him in the medical register all right up to that point. His name is Francis Meekin—he's various medical letters to it. He was in one of the London hospitals with Gilbert Carstairs—he shared those rooms in Jermyn Street with Gilbert Carstairs. We found—easily—a man who'd been their valet, and who remembered their setting off on the hunting expedition. They never came back—to Jermyn Street, anyway. Nothing was ever heard or seen of them in their old haunts about that quarter from that time. And when we'd found all that out, we came straight down, last evening, to the police—and that's all, Mr. Lindsey. And, of course, the thing is plain to me—Gilbert probably died while in this man's company; this man possessed himself of his letters and papers and so on; and in time, hearing how things were, and when the chance came, he presented himself to the family solicitors as Gilbert Carstairs. Could anything be plainer?"

"Nothing!" exclaimed Mr. Lindsey. "It's a sure case—and simple when you see it in the light of your knowledge; a case of common personation. But I'm wondering what the connection between the Gilverthwaite and Phillips affair and this Meekin has been—if we could get at it?"

"Shall I give you my theory?" suggested Mr. Elphinstone. "Of course, I've read all there's been in the newspapers, and Murray told me a lot last night before we came to you, and you mentioned Mr. Ridley's discovery,—well, then, I've no doubt whatever that this young gentleman is Michael Carstairs' son, and therefore the real owner of the title and estates! And I'll tell you how I explain the whole thing. Michael Carstairs, as I remember him—and I saw plenty of him as a lad and a young man—was what you'd call violently radical in his ideas. He was a queer, eccentric, dour chap in some ways—kindly enough in others. He'd a most extraordinary objection to titles, for one thing; another, he thought that, given a chance, every man ought to make himself. Now, my opinion is that when he secretly married a girl who was much below him in station, he went off to America, intending to put his principles in practice. He evidently wanted his son to owe nothing to his birth; and though he certainly made ample and generous provision for him, and gave him a fine start, he wanted him to make his own life and fortune. That accounts for Mr. Gavin Smeaton's bringing-up. But now as regards the secret. Michael Carstairs was evidently a rolling stone who came up against some queer characters—Gilverthwaite was one, Phillips—whoever he may have been—another. It's very evident, from what I've heard from you, that the three men were associates at one time. And it may be—it's probably the case—that in some moment of confidence, Michael let out his secret to these two, and that when he was dead they decided to make more inquiries into it—possibly to blackmail the man who had stepped in, and whom they most likely believed to be the genuine Sir Gilbert Carstairs. Put it this way: once they'd found the documentary evidence they wanted, the particulars of Michael's marriage, and so on, what had they to do but go to Sir Gilbert—as they thought him to be—and put it to him that, if he didn't square them to keep silence, they'd reveal the truth to his nephew, whom, it's evident, they'd already got to know of as Mr. Gavin Smeaton. But as regards the actual murder of Phillips—ah, that's a mystery that, in my opinion, is not like to be solved! The probability is that a meeting had been arranged with Sir Gilbert—which means, of course, Meekin—that night, and that Phillips was killed by him. As to Crone—it's my opinion that Crone's murder came out of Crone's own greed and foolishness; he probably caught Meekin unawares, told what he knew, and paid the penalty."

"There's another possible theory about the Phillips murder," remarked Mr. Gavin Smeaton. "According to what you know, Mr. Elphinstone, this Meekin is a man who has travelled much abroad—so had Phillips. How do we know that when Meekin and Phillips met that night, Meekin wasn't recognized by Phillips as Meekin—and that Meekin accordingly had a double incentive to kill him?"

"Good!" exclaimed Mr. Lindsey. "Capital theory!—and probably the right one. But," he continued, rising and making for the door, "all the theories in the world won't help us to lay hands on Meekin, and I'm going to see if Murray has made out anything from his search and his questioning."

Murray had made out nothing. There was nothing whatever in the private rooms of the supposed Sir Gilbert Carstairs and his wife to suggest any clue to their whereabouts: the servants could tell nothing of their movements beyond what the police already knew. Sir Gilbert had never been seen by any of them since the morning on which he went into Berwick to hear the case against Carter: Lady Carstairs had not been seen since her departure from the house secretly, two mornings later. Not one of all the many servants, men or women, could tell anything of their master or mistress, nor of any suspicious doings on the part of Hollins during the past two days, except that he had been away from the house a good deal. Whatever share the butler had taken in these recent events, he had played his part skilfully.

So—as it seemed—there was nothing for it but to look further away, the impression of the police being that Meekin had escaped in one direction and his wife in another, and that it had been their plan that Hollins should foregather with them somewhere on the Continent; and presently we all left Hathercleugh House to go back to Berwick. As we crossed the threshold, Mr. Lindsey turned to Mr. Gavin Smeaton with a shrewd smile.

"The next time you step across here, sir, it'll be as Sir Gavin Carstairs!" he said. "And we'll hope that'll not long be delayed!"

"I'm afraid there's a good deal to do before you'll be seeing that, Mr. Lindsey," answered the prospective owner. "We're not out of the wood yet, you know."

We certainly were not out of the wood—so far as I was concerned, those last words might have been prophetic, as, a little later, I was inclined to think Maisie's had been before she went off in the car. The rest of them, Mr. Lindsey and his group, Murray and his, had driven up from Berwick in the first conveyances they could get at that time of night, and they now went off to where they had been waiting in a neighbouring shed. They wanted me to go with them—but I was anxious about my bicycle, a nearly new machine. I had stowed it away as securely as I could under some thick undergrowth on the edge of the woods, but the downpour of rain had been so heavy that I knew it must have soaked through the foliage, and that I should have a nice lot of rust to face, let alone a saturated saddle. So I went away across the park to where I had left it, and the others drove off to Berwick—and so both Mr. Lindsey and myself broke our solemn words to Maisie. For now I was alone—and I certainly did not anticipate more danger.

But not only danger, but the very threatening of death was on me as I went my way. We had stayed some time in Hathercleugh House, and the dawn had broken before we left. The morning came clear and bright after the storm, and the newly-risen sun—it was just four o'clock, and he was nicely above the horizon— was transforming the clustering raindrops on the firs and pines into glistening diamonds as I plunged into the thick of the woods. I had no other thought at that moment but of getting home and changing my clothes before going to Andrew Dunlop's to tell the news—when, as I crossed a narrow cut in the undergrowth, I saw, some distance away, a man's head slowly look out from the trees. I drew back on the instant, watching. Fortunately—or unfortunately—he was not looking in my direction, and did not catch even a momentary glance of me, and when he twisted his neck in my direction I saw that he was the man we had been talking of, and whom I now knew to be Dr. Meekin. And it flashed on me at once that he was hanging about for Hollins—all unconscious that Hollins was lying dead there in the old tower.

So—it was not he who had driven that murderous knife into Hollins's throat!

I watched him—myself securely hidden. He came out of his shelter, crossed the cut, went through the belt of wood which I had just passed, and looked out across the park to the house—all this I saw by cautiously edging through the trees and bushes behind me. He was a good forty yards away from me at that time, but I could see the strained, anxious expression on his face. Things had gone wrong— Hollins and the car had not met him where he had expected them—and he was trying to find out what had happened. And once he made a movement as if he would skirt the coppices and make for the tower, which lay right opposite, but with an open space between it and us—and then he as suddenly drew back, and began to go away among the trees.

I followed him, cautiously. I had always been a bit proud of what I called my woodcraft, having played much at Red Indians as a youngster, and I took care to walk lightly as I stalked him from one brake to another. He went on and on—a long way, right away from Hathercleugh, and in the direction of where Till meets Tweed. And at last he was out of the Hathercleugh grounds, and close to the Till, and in the end he took to a thin belt of trees that ran down the side of the Till, close by the place where Crone's body had been found, and almost opposite the very spot, on the other bank, where I had come across Phillips lying dead; and suddenly I saw what he was after. There, right ahead, was an old boat, tied up to the bank—he was making for it, intending doubtless to put himself across the two rivers, to get the north bank of the Tweed, and so to make for safety in other quarters.

It was there that things went wrong. I was following cautiously, from tree to tree, close to the river-bank, when my foot caught in a trail of ground bramble, and I went headlong into the brushwood. Before I was well on my feet, he had turned and was running back at me, his face white with rage and alarm, and a revolver in his hand. And when he saw who it was, he had the revolver at the full length of his arm, covering me.

"Go back!" he said, stopping and steadying himself.

"No!" said I.

"If you come a yard further, Moneylaws, I'll shoot you dead!" he declared. "I mean it! Go back!"

"I'm not coming a foot nearer," I retorted, keeping where I was. "But I'm not going back. And whenever you move forward, I'm following. I'm not losing sight of you again, Mr. Meekin!"

He fairly started at that—and then he began looking on all sides of me, as if to find out if I was accompanied. And all of a sudden he plumped me with a question.

"Where is Hollins?" he asked. "I'll be bound you know!"

"Dead!" I answered him. "Dead, Mr. Meekin! As dead as Phillips, or as Abel Crone. And the police are after you—all round—and you'd better fling that thing into the Till there and come with me. You'll not get away from me as easily now as you did yon time in your yacht."

It was then that he fired at me—from some twelve or fifteen yards' distance. And whether he meant to kill me, or only to cripple me, I don't know; but the bullet went through my left knee, at the lower edge of the knee-cap, and the next thing I knew I was sprawling on all-fours on the earth, and the next—and it was in the succeeding second, before even I felt a smart—I was staring up from that position to see the vengeance that fell on my would-be murderer in the very instant of his attempt on me. For as he fired and I fell, a woman sprang out of the bushes at his side, and a knife flashed, and then he too fell with a cry that was something between a groan and a scream—and I saw that his assailant was the Irishwoman Nance Maguire, and I knew at once who it was that had killed Hollins.

But she had not killed Meekin. He rose like a badly wounded thing—half rose, that is, as I have seen crippled animals rise, and he cried like a beast in a trap, fighting with his hands. And the woman struck again with the knife—and again he sank back, and again he rose, and … I shut my eyes, sick with horror, as she drove the knife into him for the third time.

But that was nothing to the horror to come. When I looked again, he was still writhing and crying, and fighting blindly for his life, and I cried out on her to leave him alone, for I saw that in a few minutes he would be dead. I even made an effort to crawl to them, that I might drag her away from him, but my knee gave at the movement and I fell back half-fainting. And taking no more notice of me than if I had been one of the stocks and stones close by, she suddenly gripped him, writhing as he was, by the throat, and drawing him over the bank as easily as if he had been a child in her grasp, she plunged knee-deep into the Till and held him down under the water until he was drowned.

There was a most extraordinary horror came over me as I lay there, powerless to move, propped up on my elbow, watching. The purposeful deliberation with which the woman finished her work; the dead silence about us, broken only by an occasional faint lapping of the river against its bank; the knowledge that this was a deed of revenge—all these things produced a mental state in me which was as near to the awful as ever I approached it. I could only lie and watch—fascinated. But it was over at last, and she let the body go, and stood watching for a moment as it floated into a dark pool beneath the alders; and then, shaking herself like a dog, she came up the bank and looked at me, in silence.

"That was—in revenge for Crone," I managed to get out.

"It was them killed Crone," she answered in a queer dry voice. "Let the pollis find this one where they found Crone! You're not greatly hurt yourself—and there's somebody at hand."

Then she suddenly turned and vanished amongst the trees, and, twisting myself round in the direction to which she had pointed, I saw a gamekeeper coming along. His gun was thrown carelessly in the crook of his arm, and he was whistling, gaily and unconcernedly.

I have a perpetual memento of that morning in my somewhat crippled knee. And once, two years ago, when I was on business in a certain English town, and in a quarter of it into which few but its own denizens penetrate, I met for one moment, at a slum corner, a great raw-boned Irishwoman who noticed my bit of a limp, and turned her eyes for an instant to give me a sharp look that won as sharp an answer. And there may have been mutual understanding and sympathy in the glance we thus exchanged—certainly, when it had passed between us, we continued on our separate ways, silent.

THE END

Lector House believes that a society develops through a two-fold approach of continuous learning and adaptation, which is derived from the study of classic literary works spread across the historic timeline of literature records. Therefore, we aim at reviving, repairing and redeveloping all those inaccessible or damaged but historically as well as culturally important literature across subjects so that the future generations may have an opportunity to study and learn from past works to embark upon a journey of creating a better future.

This book is a result of an effort made by Lector House towards making a contribution to the preservation and repair of original ancient works which might hold historical significance to the approach of continuous learning across subjects.

HAPPY READING & LEARNING!

LECTOR HOUSE LLP
E-MAIL: lectorpublishing@gmail.com

9 789353 364977

CPSIA information can be obtained
at www.ICGtesting.com
Printed in the USA
BVHW072233270519
549348BV00002B/228/P